Who gives this woman . . . ?

The seed of an idea that had been planted in my brain for who knows how long—maybe years—was taking root. We were in Napa. I looked over at Liv, at the smile slowly spreading across her face.

"What are you thinking?" I asked, suddenly nervous.

"I'm thinking what you're thinking. Let's go find him."

"I wasn't—" I began.

"You wanted to find him, let's find him. Maybe it will help you resolve some stuff."

I started to shake my head, but Liv held up her hand. "I know one thing. We aren't staying here eating grass and getting rubbed with Ayurvedic oil while your father is hanging out a few miles down the road."

"But we don't know that for sure. We don't know anything!" I protested.

"We're lawyers. All we do all day long is research. Emma, face it, we're going to San Francisco." She looked me straight in the eyes. "We're going to find your dad."

Cold Feet

AMY FITZHENRY

B

BERKLEY BOOKS, NEW YORK

BERKLEY

An imprint of Penguin Random House LLC
375 Hudson Street, New York, New York 10014

This book is an original publication of Penguin Random House LLC.

Library of Congress Cataloging-in-Publication Data

FitzHenry, Amy.
Cold feet / Amy FitzHenry. — Berkley trade paperback edition.
pages cm
ISBN 978-0-425-28111-6 (paperback)
1. Runaway women—Fiction.   2. Commitment (Psychology) —Fiction.
3. Families—Fiction.   4. Psychological fiction.   I. Title.
PS3606.I8846C65 2015
813'.6—dc23
2015011012

PUBLISHING HISTORY
Berkley trade paperback edition / September 2015

PRINTED IN THE UNITED STATES OF AMERICA

10 9 8 7 6 5 4 3 2 1

Cover design by Annette Fiore DeFex.
Interior text design by Kristin del Rosario.

Penguin
Random
House

For Natalie

PROLOGUE

I'm not a particularly nervous flier, but like most people, I'm scared of turbulence. As soon as it begins I'm ready for it to end, urgently praying I'm not that one-in-a-million statistic. That morning, however, when sharp pockets of wind caused my hour-long flight from San Francisco to Los Angeles to morph from uneventful to hairy, I glanced up from my airport-purchased paperback. I took note of the tattooed woman on my right, who was violently gripping our supposedly shared armrest and staring out the window in fear. The plane rocked and rolled.

As the seat belt light pinged repeatedly and the captain urged the flight attendants to take their seats, I closed my eyes, ready for the adrenaline rush of fear to kick in, the inner bargaining to be a better person and the flat-out begging with any higher power to get us out of this alive.

My inner monologue, however, was silent. Was I braver? Probably not. More composed? Unlikely. More rational and thus less fearful of statistically improbable events? Not a chance. Then I figured it out. Near-death experiences are only scary if you have something to lose. My wedding was off, my family nonexistent, and my best friend in the world never wanted to speak to me again. Plane crash, schplane crash. Who cared?

CHAPTER 1

One week earlier

I groped for the snooze button, but when I managed to reach my phone on the bedside table and bring it closer, I realized with a jolt that it wasn't my alarm at all. Sitting up and attempting to clear my throat in order to sound as awake as possible, I braced myself and pressed accept.

"Hi, Mom."

"Hello, Emma. Are you still in bed?"

"No. Well, kinda. I was asleep when you called but I'm basically up."

She didn't linger on the inconsistency.

"I'm calling about your wedding. I have a slight change but I hope it won't throw too much of a wrench in your plans."

"I'm sure it's fine. Did you want to switch to the vegetarian meal?" My mom, a lobbyist in Washington, becomes an herbivore every once in a while, usually when her anti-tobacco lobby makes a deal with a congressman to support his vegan outreach initiative in exchange for a cigarette packaging vote.

"Actually, it's about the rehearsal dinner."

"Oh, we're having pasta, so you'll be okay," I answered, still half-asleep.

"No, Emma," she said, clearly frustrated. "It's not about the food."

My mother, Caroline Moon, who most people call Caro, is one of those brilliant people who can't understand why everyone else isn't automatically keeping up with her hopscotching thoughts. I wanted to remind her that I was on West Coast time and still in bed, thus at an unfair disadvantage. I looked over at Sam, my fiancé, who was somehow managing to sleep through the passive aggression emanating through the airwaves.

"It's the scheduling of the rehearsal dinner on a Friday night," she said, as if referring to a peculiar Samoan wedding ritual, rather than what everyone in the world who was getting married on a Saturday did, ever. "I don't think I'll be able to make it."

I was silent, not sure how I was supposed to feel about this, although *like I'd been punched in the stomach* jumped to mind.

"I'll be at the wedding, of course," she added in a rush, with the first note of something like guilt creeping in. "Unfortunately, a congressional hearing was scheduled for Friday and I have to be there. I can fly out Friday evening, directly to Santa Barbara, and I'll get in around midnight. I'll be there for the whole day on Saturday."

Wow, you'll be there the *whole day* of my wedding, Mom? Let's not get carried away.

I pushed away the sarcastic responses that popped to mind. "Sure, well . . . okay. I understand. The rehearsal dinner is kind of a joke anyway, right? I mean, why do we need to practice eating dinner?" I sounded like a bad stand-up act from the '90s. I had the tendency to act awkward and unnatural around my mother, like a robot programmed with lame one-liners and pointless observations.

"Seriously, it's fine," I added.

"Great. I'm glad we cleared that up. I'll see you in a week." Caro hung up without passing Sam a hello or asking for a single detail on the wedding, which I gather is something the mother of the bride usually cares a bit about. In fact, our only substantial communications about the wedding specifics thus far were my phone call to ask her if the date worked, my formal invite, and her postcard RSVP, which she returned in the prestamped envelope, with a careful checkmark next to: *Yes, see you there!*

To be fair, I'd set the precedent. When we decided to have the wedding in California, I e-mailed her the details. When I picked my dress, she wasn't consulted. She had no idea whether or not we were writing our own vows (absolutely not). But honestly, getting her input at this point would have just been strange. I wasn't trying to be mean, but I wasn't going to be fake and pretend we were best friends either. For most of my life, my mother and I have behaved like two mothers in a playgroup who don't really like each other, but whose kids are friends—stilted, slightly uncomfortable, but for the most part polite.

"What's up with your mom?" Sam asked, coming to life.

"Oh, no big deal. She can't come to the rehearsal dinner. It's not a big deal."

Shoot. It's a universal truth that the second time you state something isn't a big deal, it automatically is.

"Oh no," he said, sitting up with concern. "Are you okay?"

"Sure." I pushed off the covers. "It's fine. But let's not talk about it right now. I should get going."

He looked concerned, but didn't press it. Sam's like that. He likes to let things sink in, to consider all the options, before he decides how to act. Whereas I enjoy jumping to conclusions, behaving impulsively, and making snap judgments. I like to think this is a result of our chosen professions. I'm a lawyer, which requires me to think fast on my feet and be ready to respond within seconds to any argument from opposing counsel. I try not to advertise the lawyer thing too much, since after meter maids they are the number one most hated group in America. This strategy works pretty well in Los Angeles. Since I'm not in the entertainment industry, no one really cares what my job is. People usually end up discovering my chosen career path when someone we know gets a DUI. A mutual friend will suggest, Why don't you ask Emma for advice; she's a lawyer. This is usually followed by a look of disgust, a few bad jokes, and thirty questions about the best place to hide drugs. The trunk, people, the trunk!

Sam, on the other hand, is a screenwriter. He spends days thoughtfully crafting the perfect dialogue for a scene, or pondering the best way to tie the end of a movie together. It's a job he loves, despite having struggled to sell a movie in the last couple of years and his constant frustration with the industry. But besides having normal job stress, he's one of the most stable, optimistic people I've ever met.

Sam was out of bed, heading toward the kitchen. "Get ready for work, but I'm cooking you breakfast, so save time to eat. I'm making breakfast for my almost wife."

Climbing into the shower, I considered his sweet words. I was an almost wife. He was an almost husband. I repeated these variations silently, attempting to wrap my head around them. I felt weird, weirder than normal, probably due to Caro's unexpected wake-up call. It's only a rehearsal dinner, I reminded myself. Her presence probably would have stressed me out anyway, wondering if she was having fun and making a futile attempt to connect over the bruschetta. But she was supposed to sit next to me, I thought involuntarily. She was supposed to represent the entirety of the Moons. Well, technically, I reminded myself, taking a deep breath and attempting to untwist the knot in my chest, this behavior was a *perfect* representation of the Moons.

If I could use one word to describe my family, it would be *absent*. My parents weren't that bad. They didn't withhold food or lock me in a closet. They just weren't there. My mother, emotionally, and my father, physically. In fact, I'd never even met the guy. All I knew about him was that his name was Hunter Moon, he was from San Francisco, and he'd left when I was a baby. Also, that he sounded like he could be a werewolf with that name.

My mom and I aren't close, so logically it shouldn't have mattered if she was there on Friday, but there's just something about your mom. Do you know the first thing Albert Einstein did in 1919, when his theory of relativity was proven? He wrote a postcard to his mom telling her about it. And I'm pretty sure she didn't respond, *Sounds nice, dear, but I'm too busy with work to deal with you right now.* But Caro wasn't rejecting my first space-time discovery. It was just a dinner, albeit a relatively important one. I halfheartedly congratulated myself on the pun.

Funnily enough, Sam, who should have been experiencing the traditional male commitment-phobe freak-out and making unfunny ball-and-chain jokes, seemed perfectly comfortable with our plan to be together for the rest of our lives. He never seemed to question it, whereas I worried endlessly how two people could possibly stay together forever and be happy.

Standing in the hot shower, already embarrassed about explaining my mother's absence to Sam's family on Friday, I realized how much more likely I was to fail at this marriage than Sam. I wasn't being hard on myself. It was a perfectly logical assumption based on one of my favorite things—the Law. Specifically, a very famous case from the 1920s in which plaintiff Mrs. Helen Palsgraf sued the Long Island Railroad. The case that introduced the American justice system to a concept vital to all lawsuits today: foreseeability.

You see, in 1924, Mrs. Palsgraf was waiting on a train platform in New York minding her own business, when out of nowhere, fireworks struck the tracks. This, understandably, caused a panic, and a few scales fell off the overhang of the platform, right on top of poor Mrs. P. Who carries fireworks on a train, you ask? Furthermore, who drops them? I don't know, some moron. That's not the point. The point is, when poor innocent Mrs. Palsgraf sued the railroad for her pain, suffering, and other damages, the court said, Sorry, you don't get a dime. Why? Because, the judges wrote, who could have predicted such an occurrence? Who could have known a bonehead with a box of fireworks would be boarding the train and they would accidentally go off? It wasn't even the Fourth of July.

In a much-quoted opinion, the New York Court of Appeals explained that Mrs. Palsgraf could not be compensated by the railroad, and that it wasn't their fault, because her injuries were not *foreseeable*, which established the rule that in order for a defendant to be held liable for damages, the plaintiff's injuries had to be somewhat predictable. Someone can only be held responsible for injuries that could have been foreseen and prevented. This was hugely important in the law because it placed a great limit on liability, and hugely important to my morning shower because I was beginning to realize how likely it was that I was about to drop a box of explosive pyrotechnics into my relationship.

Based on circumstances and history, it was completely foreseeable that I was going to fail at this marriage. I was a by-product of the two emotional car wrecks Caroline Moon and Hunter Moon. I was a marriage liability waiting to happen. After all I had the Moon gene, accompanied by characteristics that include a tendency to leave, an inability to maintain emotional connection, and a dash of self-destruction. Bailing on marriage, or screwing up to the point where Sam left me, was completely foreseeable. If I ruined this, I would have no one to blame but myself. And, of course, my parents for making me this way.

After pondering Sam and my future for what felt like hours, the water started to get chilly and I realized that a cold shower would not be a positive addition to my mood.

Getting out and reaching for the one fluffy guest towel I owned as a special treat to myself, I tried to shake off a lurking feeling of doom and reclassify the foreshadowing of marital failure as morning fog. After all, weren't thoughts like these normal the week before your wedding?

CHAPTER 2

In the kitchen the air smelled of coffee and eggs sizzled on the burner. I was momentarily cheered. Sam is an excellent cook of breakfast meals, but once it gets to be about noon, he's out. Presumably this has something to do with the first love of his life, bacon.

"Sugar?" Sam asked, stirring my embarrassing choice of two sugar cubes, along with a drop of milk, into a steaming mug. With his springy blond hair and startlingly blue eyes he constantly looks like he's auditioning for the role of a cherub. As always, when I looked directly into his eyes I was surprised at how cute he was. It was like unwrapping a present each time I saw him. I smoothed down my dark blond hair (I prefer this description to "dirty"), and tried to look like a sexy librarian rather than the nerd I felt like in my suit, or as I called it, my lawyer costume.

"Thanks, buddy." I went over to the stove where he was pushing the eggs around with a spatula and meticulously adding shakes of salt and pepper. I hugged him from behind, resting my head on his back. I didn't know what I was so worried about in the shower. I definitely wanted to be with Sam. Maybe the problem was that we didn't live together yet, so I wasn't used to the idea of joining our lives, and subsequently, I was still a little scared of the concept of marriage. Maybe once he moved himself and all of his stuff in, it would feel more real. I looked around my little house, imagining it getting even smaller.

After Venice Beach went from gang-ridden and grimy to artsy and hip—the most complete of coincidences to my residential status—it became incredibly difficult to find an affordable place to live in my neighborhood. I was lucky to find a tiny studio bungalow that I could afford, five blocks from the beach, on a tiny tree-lined street. Contrary to popular belief, just because I was a corporate lawyer didn't mean I had a whole lot of spare cash. Nope, that bitch Sallie Mae took care of that.

My little house was extremely compact, but beautifully made. It had built-in shelves, large French windows, and a gorgeous ceramic kitchen sink. But the outside was the real selling point. The gate to the house led you into a secret garden–esque front yard, stuffed with thick palm trees, thick succulents, and lush flowers. All of this vegetation provided a filter for the constant Los Angeles sunlight, which shone through the palm fronds and created a lovely pattern throughout my house every afternoon. It's a fact of life that all girls have been longing for a secret garden ever since they read the book. Finally, at the age of twenty-nine, I had one. Although in reality I had nothing to do with the sprawling vines or the delicately blooming flowers (my neighbors, landscape architects who loved to experiment on my yard, took care of that), I tried to keep the myth alive by smiling humbly when someone complimented my garden, and changing the subject when they asked me what kind of flowers I grew. Um, pink?

I loved it, but the place was pretty small. Because of this, when we got engaged, it seemed like a good idea to push back the move-in date. Frankly, I had no idea where to put Sam's stuff, and as an extremely tidy person—I can't concentrate all day if I don't make my bed in the morning—I wasn't about to throw it all in the corner willy-nilly. Besides, we spent almost every night together anyway. What was the difference?

Sam lived about a mile away, in a creaky dark-wooded beach house in Santa Monica, with an unmistakable shiplike vibe. At times, the sound of not-so-distant crashing waves could make you positively seasick. Or maybe that was just his cleaning habits. Sam was about as messy as I was clean. I'd actually seen him finish a bag of chips, drop it on the counter, and *walk away*. I was shocked, but at the same time, intrigued. When Sam has trash (at home at least, it's not like he littered or anything evil like that) he doesn't throw it away, he drops it and . . . leaves it. What must it be like to have such fascinatingly disgusting impulses? In order to avoid a full-blown panic attack, I tried not to think about what this inherent difference in personality meant for our future. It'll work itself out, I told myself. He'll get cleaner, or I'll loosen up. I can be chill, I assured myself, with the certain knowledge that this was a lie.

The big move was loosely scheduled for "right after" we returned from our honeymoon. The wedding was being held at a gorgeous, rambling Spanish hacienda I'd found in Santa Barbara, in what should be perfect Southern California September weather. The house was on a high bluff, one hundred years old, and steps from the beach, with a huge backyard framed by the ocean and the mountains. We would be married right at sunset, at what they called the "pink moment" when the fading sunlight creates a shade of pink in the air, which bounces off the mountains in the Ojai Valley to the east. I even drove up to Santa Barbara on a Saturday once, all by myself— since I was surprising Sam with that particular detail—to test it out. I found that standing with the ocean at your back, facing the pink hues in the distance, was truly magical.

The ceremony and the reception would both be held there, first, high on the bluff overlooking the mountain range in the distance, and then down to a party on the beach. The day after, we planned to leave for what Sam called the mystery honeymoon, which sounded like a prize on a game show but was really just because he was, supposedly, planning it alone.

That was the deal we'd made when we got engaged ten months earlier: I would plan the wedding, for the most part—I'd cleared the location and cocktail options with Sam—if he would organize the honeymoon. As I've mentioned, my mother isn't exactly a *Say Yes to the Dress* fan, so I was left to plan freely on my own, without going back and forth ten thousand times about the seating chart. It was kind of like when you're over at people's houses and they insist on loading the dishwasher alone. "It's easier that way," they claim. And of course it isn't, really, but it makes sense.

The question of when Sam was going to move in his stuff, and where we were going to put it all, was coming up with increasing frequency, and every time it did, it stressed me out more. I vocalized these thoughts over breakfast, hoping he would have some sort of magical solution.

"Well, have you ever thought about adding on to this house?" Sam suggested. "We could fit everything in here a lot better if we added another bedroom."

"Are you kidding? We can't even afford patio furniture. Do you have a secret pile of money I don't know about?" I tried to make a joke, despite the fact that Sam's suggestion gave me heart palpitations. He laughed lightly and went back to the paper.

Despite the fact that we'd experienced a recent major economic crisis and the movie industry was constantly in flux, which definitely hadn't helped Sam's career, or anyone in Hollywood's really, he didn't worry about money the same way I did. For me, money was a subject that was always, if not in the front of my mind, floating somewhere in the back. In the single-mother home I grew up in, we weren't exactly destitute, but—how should I put it?—cash challenged.

"Are you sure you don't want to talk about what happened with Caro?" Sam asked, noticing my anxiety or perhaps exercising some previously dormant psychic abilities. I made a mental note to cut down on dirty thoughts about Bradley Cooper. "You must be upset she isn't coming."

"Honestly, it's fine. I'm okay with it."

Sam reached out to cover my hand with his. I gave him my best imitation of a carefree smile, practically pulling a muscle in the attempt.

"Okay, so I care a little. But I'll have you, and your amazing family. Plus, Liv will be with me every step of the way."

"What time is she coming in tonight?" Sam stood and reached for the coffeepot, pouring us both fresh cups.

"Around six," I answered, feeling pure happiness for the first time all day.

That evening my best friend, Olivia, was flying into town from New York City to treat me to a toned-down version of a bachelorette party. A trip to a luxury spa in Napa Valley, from Saturday to Wednesday, when we would leisurely travel back from Northern California. Then on Thursday we would repack, double-check that I had my wedding dress, and get a good night's sleep before we all headed to Santa Barbara on Friday morning. Friday night was the (crazily scheduled, by Caro's standards) rehearsal dinner, and then, on Saturday, Sam and I would get married.

This was all part of the plan to keep the wedding simple, in the hope that it could be a drama-free affair. I dreaded turning into the kind of Bridezilla I'd seen my girlfriends become. Perfectly normal, well-adjusted women suddenly screaming about the length of their veil five minutes before walking down the aisle, or making you participate in a wedding talent show in place of a rehearsal dinner. Thanks to these women, I have learned both that there is a vast difference between shoulder- and chin-length and that brides do not appreciate Beat poetry read aloud the night before their nuptials, based on your junior-year spring break trip to Cabo. ("Seven tequila shots did she scarf / causing Katie later to barf." I thought it was pretty good myself.)

The obsession with weddings was a mystery to me. The first time I even pictured anything wedding-related was in college, when my roommate's sister got married and she left for the weekend to help her prepare. When she got back she described cake sampling over our standard Monday night dinner of curly fries at the dining hall.

"First, we tried red velvet," she explained dreamily, "then mocha butter cream, and we rounded it off with chocolate devil's food cake." I sighed in satisfaction and the idea of weddings took on a lovely buttery hue for about a year, until a friend from high school asked me to be her bridesmaid, and I had to drop a class in order to fit in all my assigned tasks.

The only person who really seemed to get it was Liv. Growing up, Liv was the only one of my friends who, when I questioned if I even *wanted* to get married someday, wouldn't look away in discomfort or murmur supportively that I would change my mind when I met the right guy. This, and the fact that it saved me from having to pick bridesmaids, was why I'd decided to make Liv my entire wedding party. She was my maid of honor, flower girl, and guest book officiate, all rolled into one.

"And what's the plan for tonight?" Sam asked, piling scrambled eggs on top of his bagel.

"Liv lands around six," I repeated, mentally viewing the schedule. "I'm going to sneak out of work early to stock up on snacks, then pick her up at LAX. Are you and Dante still meeting us for dinner?"

"Yep, can't wait. I'll remind him." Dante is Sam's oldest friend and one of his current roommates in the dirty ship house. Sam and Dante met in high school in London when both of their fathers were transferred there, from New York and Rome, respectively. Sam's family eventually moved back to the States, but the years he and Dante spent drinking pints and watching footie were enough to make them best mates for life.

Dante must be the person for whom the term *Italian Stallion* was invented, or at least a direct descendant of same. He's quite proud of his heritage and embraces it fully, especially when he's trying to get ass. Then it's all, *My family's villa in Tuscany* this, and *I'll make you homemade penne arrabbiata* that. If for some crazy reason she hates villas or she's gluten-free, he throws out a British accent, picked up from his high school years, in a last-ditch effort to close the deal. As Dante always says, if one aspect of your foreign background isn't helping you get laid, try another.

"Think Liv and Dante will finally hook up at the wedding?" Sam asked, creepily following my train of thought yet again. Put some pants on, Mr. Cooper!

"I wouldn't get your hopes up. We've been waiting for years. Most likely Liv will be dating three guys in New York, Dante will bring an underage girl to the rehearsal dinner, and we'll get arrested for serving alcohol to a minor."

"Well, I'm rooting for them," Sam said loyally.

I checked the clock and realized I had to leave in the next five minutes if I wanted to beat traffic on the freeway and make it to work on time. I grabbed my bag and hustled Sam out the door. I watched him glide down the street on his road bike, his typical vehicle of choice, before climbing in my L.A.-mandated black Prius.

Driving through the quiet, cool streets of Venice on a perfect September morning, I pictured Sam and me at breakfast. Him, reading about movie deals; me, obsessing about not obsessing about our marriage; both of us gossiping about our best friends' sex lives. We were the classic tableau of a normal couple in love, but I couldn't help but feel like an imposter. Caro's call, and the reminder that my failure at a long-term relationship was highly foreseeable, was still lurking in the back of my head. What was I doing with this guy for whom good things always happened, if for no other reason than because he intrinsically knew they would? And why in the world did he want to marry someone like me?

CHAPTER 3

Picking up Liv from LAX is one of my very favorite things to do. For one thing, I score major friend points by actually meeting her at the airport instead of making her take a cab, which is easy when you live in Venice, twenty minutes away. But mainly it's because it means my best friend is in town. I don't know how to explain it, but when Liv is around I feel like a more real version of myself. It's like everything I put on for other people is filtered out and I'm just me.

Liv and I met in high school in Arlington, Virginia, where we became instant best friends. We were both at peak stages in our awkward years and didn't even notice each other's braces and frizzy hair, probably because they matched. The popular crowd didn't know our names, the average kids were too busy trying to be cool, and the dorks had their own problems to worry about, so Liv and I didn't join any group. The only problem was we weren't sure which lunch table was ours. Instead we sat in the auditorium lobby by the gym every day with our turkey sandwiches. This area was commonly known as the aud-lob, although after we started sitting there, some of the mean girls starting referring to it as the *odd*-lob. I had to give it to them: It was clever.

Honestly, I didn't really care, because, as I discovered then, and continue to believe to this day, as long as you have one real friend, you're okay. Liv and I were perfectly happy to sit in the odd-lob day after day in our mom jeans, drinking regular Cokes and laughing until our stomachs hurt. Even after Liv discovered her incredible singing voice, grew size-C boobs, and learned how to scrunch her strawberry-blond hair, shot with natural strands of gold, into soft curls, and I remained in my awkward years (which lasted roughly from age twelve to twenty-five), our dynamic never changed.

After high school, Liv attended Rice in Texas and I went to the University of Virginia, mostly due to the fact that I could get in-state tuition and also because I harbored a strange affinity for Thomas Jefferson. There I halfheartedly joined a sorority and floated around various clubs and activities. College was fun, of course, but it wasn't the same without Liv. I never again found a friend with whom I could be so completely myself.

Then magically, it happened. Liv and I both applied to law school the fall of senior year of college, got into Berkeley and spent the next three blissful years as roommates, happily living in the East Bay. After law school, Liv got a job as a corporate attorney in the dreaded New York legal scene, and I headed to Los Angeles. I wasn't quite sure why, but I always felt like I belonged on the West Coast. After only three years at Berkeley, California already felt more like home than Virginia. When choosing where to live after law school, the Westside of Los Angeles seemed like the logical place to land. It felt to me like going somewhere new while also staying in the laid-back environment I'd come to know and love.

At the airport, I scanned the curb for Liv's gorgeous hair but saw only strangers, including a few cute guys milling around Arrivals. One guy had dark curly hair and the perfect amount of scruff. What if *he* was my destiny, I wondered, not Sam? What if he was the guy I was meant to be with, but I simply hadn't met him yet and in one week it would be too late?

This had been happening a lot lately, seeing interesting-looking guys or thinking about exes and wondering whether I was missing something by not being with them. I knew that I was being ridiculous. It wasn't so much about the idea of someone else, but more the concept of forever. Two people promising they would never leave each other. It made my stomach tighten up and my throat narrow. How in the world was that possible? I wondered. I'd certainly never witnessed it.

Of course, I felt extremely disloyal even considering any of this. If Sam was thinking this way, I would murder him. On the other hand, everyone is always talking about how scared guys are to get married and their inevitable last-minute doubts. Why shouldn't I be the same? More than anything, I wished I could talk to Sam about my fears, but I was pretty sure that was verging on *too* honest.

I noticed a rent-a-cop behind me, flashing his lights to get me to keep going. Emotional turmoil notwithstanding, I was about to be forced to wind once more through Terminals 1 to 7. Luckily, as I glanced at the curb one last time, I saw my best friend, with a wide smile on her pretty face, waving wildly next to her scary black travel bag, usually reserved for traveling to depositions. To prove her suitcase wrong, she wore a floral maxi dress and a wide brim fedora. Whenever Liv came to L.A., she pulled out her funkiest garb and told me she was trying to fit in with the Venice fashionistas crawling all over my quirky beach town. I did the same chameleon act whenever I went to New York, emerging from the taxi in my most citylike ensemble, inevitably involving black booties.

"Straight hair!" I cried, as she tossed her bag in the back.

"I know! I wanted to look good for our trip."

"But I love your hair curly," I commented, pulling out into traffic. As usual, Liv and I jumped right back into conversation as if we had never been apart. Which we hadn't really, considering we were virtually in constant contact, whether it be by phone, text, or Instagram comment chain.

"I know, Em, but you aren't really my target audience." Liv has a theory that there's a certain kind of guy who likes straight hair and a certain type who likes curly. Fans of straight hair are superficial, player types, who just want sex without breakfast, and curly-haired lovers are the sweeter, boyfriend types. Tonight, I supposed by her straightened locks, she was preaching to the one-night-stand congregation.

"Did you get your hair cut or a blow-out?"

This kind of pointless question was how we ended up sharing every inane detail of our lives with each other. For instance, I knew for a fact that Liv had gotten a mani-pedi the previous day and chosen Friar, Friar, Pants on Fire red for both her fingers and her toes. Meaningless to anyone else, but terribly important to me.

"A blow-out," Liv said, pulling on her seat belt and motioning for me to watch the road. I'm a terrible driver. Partly because of my "problem" with depth perception (I don't have any) and partly because I'd never really grasped the talent, inherent to most females, of multitasking. You know, having an orgasm while you mentally redecorate your bedroom and draft a work e-mail. I wasn't born with it, and as a result had to pay real attention to signaling before I merged.

"Okay, on to more important things. I want to hear the itinerary for the week."

Excitedly, I reminded her that we had dinner with Sam and Dante that night, our flight the next morning, a rental car reserved at SFO, and an on-call masseuse waiting for us to pull into Calistoga.

The Calistoga Ranch, the ridiculously amazing resort in Napa where we were staying, recommended by the coolest female partner at my law firm, promised to be the most relaxing five days of our lives. I didn't care much about mud wraps or massages, but Liv loves that kind of thing and the champagne brunches sounded right up my alley. I was determined to force myself to relax. I considered *forcing myself* to force myself to relax but got even more confused so I decided to leave it.

Talking the entire way home about everything and nothing, Liv and I pulled into my beach bungalow a half hour later. We dragged in her bags, overflowing with cute sundresses and soft tanks, and the bags of food I'd grabbed from my bodega. Without a word, we plopped onto my cozy couch and tore open my poor excuse for groceries: a box of rainforest crackers and a hunk of Jarlsberg. Liv took on the job of official cheese cutter and passed me thick wedges for the mini-sandwiches I was constructing as she filled me in on her boy drama.

With her tiny five-foot-four frame, bright blue eyes, thick strawberry-blond hair, and incredible ability to quote dialogue from Will Ferrell movies, Olivia Lucci is one of those beautiful, funny girls who make everything more fun. Not to mention that she's smart and nice to boot. There have been points in our friendship when I felt like her *pimp*, so many guys cornered me in bars to ask me to put in a good word. Despite this, Liv didn't have the best track record with dating suitable men. I'd only seen Liv in love once, with someone I considered the worst person possible. He would probably come up at some point in this trip, but probably not until we were firmly entrenched in Napa Valley, over a glass of Malbec (or four).

Since that hot mess, Liv had rarely had a steady boyfriend. She would get crushes and go on dates, but she hadn't fallen for anyone in years, much to the dismay of the collective male population.

When I asked her the current status and if there was anything I wasn't fully updated on, she paused thoughtfully.

"There's this one guy I haven't told you much about, the guy I met a couple weeks ago who works at Citi. Did I tell you he's really tall? Like, notably tall. Everywhere we go people ask him if he plays basketball, which is actually the most unoriginal thing ever to say to a tall person, even though I'm sure I've done it myself. Then when he says no, they suggest he should! As if a thirty-six-year-old banker really needs to start hitting the courts on Saturday mornings. But I don't know, I can't see myself with a finance guy long term."

"What about the public defender you met at the Berkeley reunion? He's probably more up your alley on social stratification issues."

"He turned out to be bipolar. Which I'm totally okay with, but he also hated brunch. Who hates brunch?" She had a point. "Okay, can we please talk about the wedding now?" Liv said, turning to me with an expectant smile.

"I have a piece of news on that front. Guess who canceled on the rehearsal dinner?" I was eager to get this piece of news out of the way.

"I really hope you're going to say Sam's brother, who their family thinks has been teaching English in Costa Rica, but has really been surfing for the past two years."

"Nope."

"Oh no." She paused. "Caroline?"

"You got it."

"I'm sorry, Em," Liv said, looking concerned.

"It's really okay. It's more annoying than anything else because I have to redo some stuff and explain it to Sam's parents. I honestly can't think of why I would really care that much, considering we haven't had a twenty-line conversation in about a decade."

"Because you want your mom to be at your rehearsal dinner."

"Not if she doesn't want to be there. She said it was a work thing. It's a good excuse. Probably even true."

"How did she sound? She was probably really upset that she has to miss it."

Liv has a much softer spot for my mom than I do, probably because my mother is funny in a dry, clinical way, she has what is considered a cool job, especially in D.C. where liberal political involvement is revered, and in high school she let Liv tell her parents she was at our house when she was really going to third base in Sean Garrett's basement. Caro, in turn, likes Liv because she finds her interesting and confident. She likes her as an equal, whereas it is my secret belief that my mother and I don't get along for the simple reason that she doesn't like my grown-up self very much.

Sure, when I was little I adored her and thought she was the prettiest woman in the world and all that. But things change. Of course, she's still beautiful, but everything else is different. Things first started to change when she finished grad school and started full time at the anti-tobacco lobby, right before I entered high school. It's such a cliché, but that was when she started to care more about her career than about being a mother. A lot more. The cynical side of me says she likes working for the lobby so much because it gives her enough credentials to feel smarter than the average do-gooder and enough integrity to feel superior to the Capitol Hill suits. She claims it's because her beloved father died of lung cancer, inspiring her to work her way through George-town, eventually obtaining her master's degree in political science. I've heard the story more times than I can count, and I do mean story. The truth is, she hated her dad, Mickey Rigazi, a lifetime member of the lesser-known AA, Alcoholic Assholes.

Caro Moon, née Rigazi, grew up in a family of northern Italian blonds, which made them one of the strangest families on a very homogenous block, or in their case the Marconi Plaza in South Philly, my ancestors' choice of enclave. They stood out even more because of their constantly drunk dad, whose stumbling figure wasn't *that* outrageous a sight in their part of town, but whose ten-dency to carry a knife while inebriated set him apart from his peers. Growing up in South Philly, the oldest in a family of five, with a father who made frequent weekend "business trips" to the drunk tank couldn't have been easy, which probably has a lot to do with how my mother is today—cold, aloof, and instantly disgusted by the smell of gin.

Once we were thankfully off the topic of my mother, Liv and I spent the next hour talking about how lululemon's pants *actually* changed the shape of your butt, gossiping about our mutual friends— namely, which Berkeley grads had hooked up lately and which high school friends were newly engaged—and conducting an intense debate about what to wear that evening. I wanted to save our cute-ness for the vacation, while Liv insisted that she was already on hers. But the whole time we debated whether it would be annoying if we both wore hats, I felt a sense of anxious expectation lurking in the back of my mind, threatening to take over the second I let down my guard. I was pretty sure that Liv could smell it on me—something was off. A few times I caught her looking at me closely in the mirror as she restraightened her hair and I attempted to tame my locks with something that promised "beachy waves," but delivered something that was more seaweedlike.

"My hair is out of control. I look like someone's crazy shut-in aunt."

"No, you don't." Liv laughed. "It's sticking up a bit in the back but I can fix that."

As she untangled my hair, I could tell Liv wanted to ask me what was going on, her best-friend senses working overtime. I felt the words on the tip of my tongue a couple times, but physically stopped them from rolling out. Besides, what would I say? *I'm scared to marry Sam. What's up with you?*

To be fair, marriage as a concept itself was a bit lost on me. When I got engaged I felt a bit like I was entering an anthropological study. I felt like saying to my single friends, I know, it seems crazy to me, too, but I'll infiltrate the natives and report back. It's not that I thought I was above the institution, or that it was antiquated or too sexist—although my Feminist Legal Theory professor could probably make a proper argument that it was, involving terms like *espousal rights framework* that I pretended to understand all semester. It was more about the fact that I'd never really pictured it happening to me. I couldn't imagine myself in the cupcake dress, shyly smiling as I walked down the aisle, or, God forbid, throwing the bouquet, carefully aimed to hit my most pathetic single friend. At my age I'd been that friend more times than I could count, which was only made more tragic by my lack of eye-hand coordination. This inevitably caused me to miss and the crowd to muse: *No wonder she's not married, she can't even catch.*

It took me a while to pick up that I was the odd man out on this. But after seeing enough romcoms featuring girls asking a Ouija board the name of their husband, and attending countless sleepovers planning my girlfriends' weddings down to the name of the golden retriever who would carry the ring down the aisle—a detail that seemed particularly uncritical at the age of twelve—I figured out I was for the most part alone on this one. It was kind of like when everyone was obsessed with the Backstreet Boys. I thought we were all kidding, a joke that all of America was in on. But when their song came on at the eighth grade dance and everyone screamed bloody murder I realized, alarmingly, that Backstreet was back, all right.

It wasn't that I didn't want to be with Sam, it was more that I was skeptical of the idea of forever. Marriage had always seemed a little like a sham to me, and those who believed in it slightly delusional. Part of me felt like the only reason people were able to get married at all was because the reality of *one person for the rest of your life* is so difficult to picture, they couldn't grasp how truly ridiculous, and nearly impossible, the concept actually is.

I even tried to bring it up with my intended once, but it hadn't gone very well.

"Sam," I asked tentatively one night, while we were eating

straight from the Whole Foods take-out boxes, him skimming film blogs and me distractedly watching *The Bachelor*, "how do you know I'm the one?"

"Is this a *Bachelor*-related question? 'Cause I don't really understand anything about that show except they bang in the fantasy suite."

"No." I laughed, encouraged by his banter to go on, although I probably should have shut the hell up. "I mean, aren't you ever scared? Being with me for the rest of your life? Staying together? Forever?" I looked at him for a response but his face was blank. He was probably suspicious that this was a Girl Trick, so I tried to reassure him. "I'm serious. Doesn't it ever feel like there's a noose around your neck and the second you walk down the aisle, there goes the slipknot?" I sensed that this conversation wasn't going very well, so I tried to turn it into a joke to loosen the tension (so to speak). To say that I'd misjudged the situation was an understatement.

"Nope, I don't," Sam said, shutting his computer and abandoning our couch nest of blankets and brown recyclable containers. "Night, Emma. I'm going to bed." As he walked by me, I tried to pull him back down to the couch to give him a hug.

"Buddy, are you upset?" I said, hanging on his arm. "It's not you, it's marriage in general. I love *you*. You know that. I thought maybe you felt the same way and wanted to talk about it."

He gave me a look that accurately noted this was bullshit. "It's okay, Em. I'm tired."

He was quiet for a couple days after that, and I engaged in the typical monkey dance of trying to make your mate less mad at you without actually addressing what's wrong. Eventually everything smoothed over and we went back to normal, but I still felt bad every time I thought about it.

The uncertain feeling still hadn't gone away. It wasn't about Sam, exactly. It was more about me, and the decision to commit my life to one direction, closing off all the others. And even more than that, Sam's decision to choose me. What if he changed his mind as soon as I got used to the idea? I found it utterly terrifying. Which led me back to marriage in general. How was it possible to ensure that such an unlikely plan would succeed?

Still, I wasn't ready to talk about any of it. Once I told Liv, it would be real. We would have to talk about it. And what if, after we analyzed it, I didn't feel better? Then what? No, all I wanted out of tonight was tapas, sangria, and some hilarious pickup lines from Dante that Liv and I would quote for years to come. That, at least, was foreseeable.

CHAPTER 4

"Emma Moon!" Dante jumped up from his seat and wrapped me in a bear hug as Liv and I entered the bar. "One week until you're my best-friend-in-law."

Dante was always incredibly sweet to me, most likely because we never had and never would have the opportunity to hook up.

"And of course, the gorgeous Olivia, in from the big city, I presume. How are you, darling? What can I get you two to drink?" Turning to Liv and giving her a kiss on both cheeks that each lasted a split second too long, he was instantly back in player mode.

After hugging Sam hello, Liv and I made our way around the high-top table and sat on bar stools in the crowded restaurant, Gjelina, hers next to Dante and mine next to Sam. The place was packed. It was the best restaurant in Venice, which meant long waits, incredible food, and frighteningly attractive hostesses. I loved it. I'd been going there for years, since I first moved to town and Val, one of Sam's producers, took me there.

I pushed her from my mind as soon as she entered it. After Sam sold his movie and introduced us, Val became my first friend in L.A., before she'd casually dismissed me from her life, quit her job, and moved to San Francisco to work as an executive at Gilt City without even telling me, presumably suffering the same Emma Moon disillusionment my mother had.

I brought myself back to the present and tried to adjust my skirt to hide the hideous pancake my thighs became when met with a tall chair with no footrest. Sam, however, didn't seem to notice. He was focused on my face, leaning in for a kiss, his adorable half smile just a few inches away. I leaned in and felt the same jolt of electricity I did every time his lips touched mine.

Sam looked the same now as he did on the softball field the day we met four years ago, happy to see me, relaxed, and ready to make me smile. He radiated an aura of comfort in his skin that made those around him feel comfort in theirs. I think they call that zen. Yet, as he reached out to pull me in for one more hug, I felt jittery, a passive guest in my own body, watching myself tumble down a path of uncertainty.

Sam gave me a funny look and cocked his head to the side. I shook my head to indicate that everything was fine and rejoined the conversation, which had moved to Liv's new apartment in New York, accompanied by an amusing rant from Dante about rent control in Los Angeles. Sam ordered a bottle of Sangiovese and some small plates for us to share, the arrival of which calmed me. If I relaxed and breathed, I told myself, everything was going to be okay.

"How goes the moviemaking, Dante?" Liv asked. Dante was a producer, primarily of Italian comedies that never made it to the United States, but it allowed him to live a life of leisure and work five months out of the year.

"Wonderful. I'm off to Europe for a few weeks to raise money for a new film," Dante answered smoothly, but genuinely. His life really was that fabulous.

"How does that work exactly, you just kind of stroll down the cobblestone streets asking for donations?" Liv teased.

"Pretty much," Dante said, smiling at her. "Last stop is Croatia, which I've heard is incredible. How can it be that I've never been?" Liv looked at me for direction, but I couldn't tell what the answer should be, so I gave a sort of noncommittal nod. This appeared to be the correct response because Dante continued. "Then I'll be back here looking for somewhere to live now that Sam's finally moving out."

"You can't keep your house?"

"Nah. What's the point? I'm only in town for half of the year, and, like this guy, I'm thirty-two years old. I'm getting to the age where I should probably have my own place anyway." I knew that, like me, Liv was fighting her inclination to vehemently agree, so we stayed quiet while Dante looked around poetically and his hybrid accent deepened. "It's the end of an era, though. Sam and I have lived together since uni."

"Wow, how many decades is that now?" We loved to make fun of Dante and Sam for being older than us even though in reality it was only by a few years.

"Ha. I'm a mere spring chicken, my dear. It has been almost ten years living together, though. Can't believe I'm losing my flatmate."

"Don't think of it that way. You're not losing a roommate, you're gaining a sofa to crash on," I said, a quarter meaning it. This was an extremely dangerous statement. When traveling, Dante was notorious for choosing to shack up at friends' houses for months rather than take the time to find a proper Craigslist sublet.

"I don't know about that," Sam chimed in.

"Emma and I will talk about it." Dante winked, probably automatically, while the waitress set down a few artisan pizzas.

Don't get me wrong, I love Dante like a brother. His only problem is that he consistently dates nineteen-year-old models whose personalities he doesn't like, and then gets confused when he doesn't like them. My twenty-seventh birthday was spent with Sam, Liv, Dante, and Lila, a nineteen-year-old model/actress who showed up halfway through a day of beers and burgers on the grill. One minute Dante was holding the spatula and carefully adding slices of cheddar, and the next his arm was draped across a shockingly thin brunette, who was eyeing the burgers suspiciously and referring to herself in the third person. "Lila doesn't eat dairy," she said. Which would have been fine, if any of us had any idea who the fuck Lila was.

Sam and Dante were funny together, like most best friends who've known each other since they were kids. Sam was the chill, funny one, and objectively (if not subjectively) Dante was the gorgeous one. But despite his ridiculous success with the ladies, Dante looked up to Sam as if he were still his new sixth grade lab partner, a cool American with an endless supply of Yankees gear.

"Is the honeymoon all set, Sam?" Liv asked.

"It sure is," Sam answered casually, while simultaneously stealing a crust from my plate. "Tickets have been purchased; rooms are booked. We're good to go."

"Really?" I said, somewhat surprised.

"Of course, Em. It's in a week." Sam laughed.

"Sorry." I squeezed him apologetically. "So, where are we going? Tell me."

My attempts at cajoling were fruitless as Sam turned back to Liv's questions.

"And how's the writing going, Sam?" she asked.

"It's pretty good. I'm finishing something up right now, which I'm really hoping the studio likes, considering they've tossed the last few versions of my blood, sweat, and tears to the side." Sam said this good-naturedly, but I could see the crack in his facade. His first movie, *On the Royal Road*, had been a surprise indie hit, but ever since then, Left Brain Productions, which had produced it and had options on the next three, had passed on his projects. There were some potentials here and there, some stuck in various stages of editing, but Hollywood is a fickle beast and the cash infusion from his first movie, which felt like winning the lottery at the time, wasn't going to last forever. He was already running through his savings, which had once felt so hefty.

I started to fall down the rabbit hole of money worries that I had traveled countless times since childhood. What if Sam never sold another movie? What if, as a result, I had to support us forever? Worst of all, what if he felt guilty about this and in turn got a job he hated and ended up resenting me?

I abruptly flashed back to an image of my mother and me at the bank when I was nine or so, before there were ATMs on every block. My mom was wearing a blue-and-white-striped sailor shirt and her blond hair was shining down her back. I remember thinking she looked pretty, like she should be hosting a party on a boat, and feeling extremely proud that she was my mother. After a short discussion, the teller politely informed her that she couldn't make the withdrawal with the form she had carefully filled out because her account had "insufficient funds."

Caro waved the dreadful words away, declaring it a silly mistake, and said she would come back the next day to straighten it out. After she herded me out of the bank, she took me to lunch at TGI Fridays. I was surprised: Eating dinner at a restaurant was a big deal in our household back then, and I didn't remember ever before eating out for lunch. My mom insisted I order the chicken fingers, my favorite, but I could barely choke down a bite. The breaded chicken stuck to my throat as I watched her stir her iced tea anxiously, with a big smile pasted on her face. I was a savvy nine-year-old, plus I knew what *insufficient* meant, having read it in one of my schoolbooks the week before. I'd asked my mom for the definition, and she'd answered "it means there's not enough." I swallowed hard, a garlicky fry adding to the painful brick of fear in my stomach.

"Anyway, it's all done," Sam continued.

For a second, I was lost, dizzy from my mental tailspin.

"Although we should shop for some new skis before we leave."

Oh, right. The honeymoon. He was joking. Not only did he

know how much I hated the cold, he was also aware that my klutziness would translate to certain death on the slopes.

"Emma skiing? That's a scary image," Liv said. "Em, come to the bathroom with me. I can never figure out where the flusher is in these chichi places." She wasn't far off. Here it was a pulley system a couple feet behind the toilet, suspended from the top of the stall. I was never sure what look they were going for: Wild West Saloon or ceiling fan chain.

"Okay, what's up with you, girl?" Liv said as we walked away. She flipped her hair to the side to curtain our discussion as we edged past the tables. "You're acting weird."

I sighed. "It's complicated. I don't know what's wrong with me. Sam is amazing. I love him. I'm probably just being silly."

"Yeah, Sam's great, but you're not crazy," she reassured me like a true best friend. "Getting married is a big deal. You have some good reasons for feeling nervous about it. Plus, it's hard for you to trust people. This may be the first stable guy you've ever dated."

She was right. Before Sam, I'd always felt much more comfortable dating damaged guys. I found stable guys intimidating. They were mature and communicative and made me look much worse when I went batshit. Dating a damaged guy is like settling into an already unmade bed. You don't have to worry about pulling out the carefully tucked-in bottom sheet or rumpling the pillows, because everything is already all over the place. Your only job is to snuggle under the duvet and try not to worry about the last time the sheets were washed. However, whether it was an accident or a thankful intervention from the sensible part of my psyche, I fell for Sam. Sam, for whom contentment is a baseline, and self-doubt and anxiety are rare. When Sam said everything was good, he meant it.

Ever since we'd met, I'd observed this odd state of being—Sam's inherent happiness—carefully. One morning several years prior, when he was lost in deep thought, forehead crinkled in concentration over morning coffee, I thought: Here's my chance! He's stressed! Maybe even, God willing, depressed! It's time to make my move.

I gently turned to him and asked what was on his mind, ready to discuss his relationship with his father or examine an existential crisis.

He answered thoughtfully, "I was thinking about bacon."

"You were thinking about bacon?" Maybe he was contemplating the unethical treatment of pigs in our country. "Um, what about it?"

"How good it is." Sam turned to me and smiled. The best part was, he probably thought he *was* sharing an emotional moment with me.

"Welcome back to the table, ladies," Dante said, sounding a bit tipsy, when Liv and I returned from the ladies' room. "You missed the arrival of the sunchokes."

"What are sunchokes?" Liv asked.

"I have no idea. Just go with it," Dante answered, refilling each of our wineglasses. "Emma, I know something you don't know." I looked at him questioningly. "The honeymoon location. Sam told me while you two were off powdering your noses."

"What about the mystery?" I complained. "I thought no one was supposed to know."

"Sorry, babe, I couldn't keep it to myself anymore. It's still a secret from you, though." Sam shrugged and pulled me closer to him. "If it makes you feel any better, maybe while you and Liv are in Napa, I'll go get us some mystery luggage, but I won't show it to Dante."

"We don't need new luggage," I said, instantly tense, hating the way I sounded, aware that I was changing the vibe of the table with my tone. "We can't afford it."

"My fifteen-year-old duffel bag isn't gonna cut it, Em. Not in the amazing location I've picked out for us . . . which I will in no way reveal."

"Sam, I don't know how to tell you this, but we can't get new luggage, and we can't build a room onto the house. Plus, aren't you going to be too busy writing all week to be shopping?" I tried to stop the nagging words as they were coming out of my mouth. I was certainly self-aware enough to recognize how bitchy and condescending I sounded. Part of me hated myself, but part of me was mad at Sam for putting me in this position. He knew I had money fears, and I was the only one making an income right now. How could his recent purchasing suggestions not freak me out?

Sam let his arm drop unnoticeably from my side. "Wow. Okay, Emma. Actually, scratch that idea, I'll get some burlap bags on Amazon. Would that be better? But do we still have Amazon Prime? I know we can't afford to pay for shipping." Sam doesn't get angry very often, but there are a couple things that set him off, and feeling criticized about his work was number one on the list. I saw Liv and Dante glancing at each other. They'd both known us too long to be truly uncomfortable in this kind of situation, but

I knew they wanted to defuse it. They were probably also thinking, like I was, that maybe two people who were about to get married shouldn't be having the money fight *right now*.

"I have Amazon Prime," Liv piped in. "You can use my log-in, if you promise not to judge my order history." We all laughed gratefully. The tension was alleviated although it didn't quite disappear.

We got through the dinner. Dante ignored the whole thing, got drunk, and sent a bottle of wine to the two girls at the table next to us. Liv kept the conversation going with stories about the Super Tall Banker, but it definitely wasn't as much fun as our usual foursome. At the end of the night, Sam pulled me aside before Liv and I walked home.

"I'm sorry, I didn't mean to snap at you," he said, standing close and opening his arms to pull me in for an embrace. I hugged him back.

"I'm sorry, too. I know how hard you're working."

"I know, Em. But what's this all about? You've been so distracted recently. Can we go somewhere alone for a little bit and talk?"

"And leave Liv and Dante alone? Too dangerous. Seriously, it wasn't about anything; everything is fine. I just don't think we need new luggage."

Sam gave me a close look. "Okay, no luggage it is." But he knew that wasn't it. Something was off, and he didn't know what it was. Unfortunately, neither did I.

CHAPTER 5

"Have you ever tried one of those neck pillows?" Liv asked. We were in line at the airport newsstand. She was loaded down with magazines, gum, and peanut M&M's, which she said we needed in case there was an emergency and we were stuck on the plane for eighteen hours with no escape. "Then it'll be every man for himself, like on that JetBlue flight where everyone was stuck on the runway with no food. Then you're gonna be glad we have these little suckers." I reminded her that our flight was forty-five minutes long, but she insisted we be prepared.

"Yeah, I got one for an overnight flight once. It didn't really work. I felt like I was wearing a neck brace the whole time."

"Ah, gotcha." We dumped everything on the counter and Liv turned to me. "Should we get some Reese's?"

"What about the 'every man for himself' M&M's?"

"Those are for emergencies, so we can't eat them unless there is one. What if we just need a snack?"

I grabbed a king-sized package of Reese's Peanut Butter Cups and handed the cashier a ridiculous amount of money to cover the cost of our pointless purchases. That morning, over croissants and lattes, Liv and I had analyzed my mini fight with Sam. In the light of day, I felt much better about everything. Still jittery, but less so. A normal amount, even. I had decided that, when it came down to it, sometimes luggage is just luggage.

I reminded myself of all the good things about getting married. For one, it meant that in seven short days I would be a Powell, which was a very good thing, far healthier than being a Moon. I was being invited into a clan where people not only liked, but also loved each other.

The problem was, I was slightly terrified.

Entering Sam's family would be like entering a real-world Pleasantville. You're really glad you jumped through the TV and you definitely don't want to leave anytime soon, but you're also pretty sure that any minute now you're going to turn into Technicolor and give yourself away. For example, last year I went on a two-week vacation with Sam and his family to Belize over Christmas. And for that entire two weeks, no one in his family had *one single fight*. Not one. During the day we participated in our chosen adventure—cave diving, kayaking on the Penchuc River, or, if you were in my activity group (population one), lying by the pool and reading. Every night, we met for cocktails and fresh seafood, drinking tropical concoctions with names like Panty Droppers (which became Panty Rippers as the more suggestive bartenders came on duty) until the entire group retired to bed in reverse age order.

Day after day, Sam's clan woke up fresh-faced and psychologically sound, ready to tackle the great outdoors and make new memories. Whereas I woke up ready to avoid the rain forest hike sign-up sheet and lie prostrate with a novel until it was an acceptable hour to drink a piña colada.

It wasn't that I was not having fun. On the contrary, it was one of the best times of my life, and I participated in everything I wasn't too uncoordinated to do without threatening major legal liability. But it was strange never to witness a negative moment, a hurt feeling, or a buried resentment brought to the surface. I think maybe there was one overly competitive game of Scrabble. Other than that, the days were filled with happiness, sweat, and general goodwill. We get it, people, you like each other. Now stop, 'cause it's starting to creep me out.

My own "family trips", which started during my teen years, when we were first able to afford a summer vacation at all, consisted of long stretches of time in the car, driving to the Delmarva Peninsula or the Outer Banks while my mom looked bored and I, in turn, plotted a not-too-bad car accident that would leave us both temporarily injured and the trip canceled. I usually got part of my wish, as we inevitably went home early.

In addition to gaining the name Powell, there was the somewhat frightening idea of losing the Moon. Sure, I'd never met Hunter Moon, but he had given me half my name, half my genes.

And by getting married, I was giving that away. Ending the Moon lineage, if you will. To join a family that was already formed, already together, already complete. It was starting to feel like the rashest of decisions, to dismiss an entire half of my identity and start afresh with a group of strangers. A healthy, well-adjusted group of people who would never leave their baby, would never skip their daughter's rehearsal dinner. How could I possibly become one of them?

"Reservation for Moon," I said, walking up to the tanned, lithe receptionist at the Calistoga Ranch in Napa. She was draped in a white silk romper, an ensemble that only the absurdly skinny can pull off. Her name tag read SIRI. I wanted to ask what it was like being named after an app, but I didn't think she'd appreciate the reference.

"Moon?" Siri stretched out the one syllable of my last name luxuriously as she scrolled down the screen of her sleek white Mac-Book Air. Idly, I wondered who was thinner relatively, her or the computer. "Here it is. We have you in a deluxe lodge, with a private deck and an outdoor Jacuzzi."

"Actually, I think we're in a regular suite," I said nervously, still feeling like a kid watching my mom balance her checkbook at the kitchen table.

"Your fiancé called and upgraded you as a surprise." That was really sweet, I thought with a flush, texting Sam a thank-you to show that I appreciated his generosity despite last night's freak out.

Siri picked up a paper-thin card—why was everything here so *skinny?*—passing itself off as a room key, and led the way outside. "I'll show you to your lodge."

On the way there, we passed a huge open space with a stone fireplace standing alone in the center of the room, surrounded by soft moss green couches.

"That fireplace looks amazing," Liv offered.

"You have a similar one in your lodge," Siri responded without missing a beat, leading us outside to a path running along a creek lined with huge, leafy pines.

The small cedar-paneled building was gorgeous yet cozy, with polished wood floors and deep-cushioned furniture, topped with floor-to-ceiling windows that held sweeping vistas of Napa Valley and filled the room with natural light. The French doors opened to a plunge pool, Jacuzzi and outdoor shower, surrounded by a tiny forest to ensure maximum privacy. On the other side of the patio was a private deck, with Adirondack chairs facing a peacefully lapping body of water, which Siri identified as Lake Lommel.

After Siri asked us what time we wanted our spa appointments the next day and explained how to request a car from the resort to take us wine tasting, she excused herself.

"This is amazing. Nice work, Sam," Liv said, starting to unpack. "Speaking of, are we ever going to talk about the marriage thing?"

"We talked about it this morning."

"We talked about the argument, which I know is nothing. But what about the general doubts you mentioned before the whole duffel bag nonsense."

"Oh, Liv, I don't know. Let's talk about it later."

"When? While you're cutting the cake? Were you planning on doing that whole 'are there any objections' thing? That could come in handy now."

I paused, unsure of how much to reveal. Liv knew my feelings about the silliness of weddings, and my natural bent for skepticism toward marriage in general. But there was something else on my mind, something I hadn't told anyone, not even Sam.

I sat down on the bed, thinking of the best way to phrase it.

"How do I put this? There's been something else on my mind."

"Well?" she pressed.

I took a deep breath. "Lately I've been thinking about my dad. About Hunter Moon. You know, the guy who skipped out on me before I learned to crawl, headed to California, and didn't look back."

"The idiot, you mean," Liv supplied supportively.

"Whatever he is, I've been thinking about him more and more, in relation to this marriage thing. Whether I have his gene for failure at relationships, his tendency to leave. Whether I'm too screwed up to make this work. And whether the fact that I've never met my dad and he's been this strange absent ghost in my life could hurt my relationship with Sam down the line or, I don't know, as cheesy as this sounds, keep me from knowing myself. I even thought about—" I paused here. This was something I definitely hadn't imagined verbalizing. "I thought about looking for him."

"Looking for him?" Liv's eyes widened. "Seriously?"

"It's not that I miss him or that I feel the need for a father figure exactly. I don't want to ask him to walk me down the aisle or anything. It's more like I have this unknown part of my past and I thought it might be good for me to try to find it. To figure it out."

"That makes sense." Liv paused. "Have you ever looked for him before?"

"No. Not really. I mean, I've Googled him and stuff. But his name is so weird that it's nearly impossible to sift through the Internet rubble. It's not like it's an actual possibility or anything. I just wanted to tell you why I've been acting so strange. There's nothing else really to say about it."

I slid down onto the absurdly comfortable yellow cushions, finally letting myself sink back, emotionally spent. "Should we find a bottle of wine or check out the Jacuzzi?"

"It's funny that Hunter lives in San Francisco and now we're up here," Liv said, ignoring my question. "He's less than an hour away. Maybe we'll even run into him. Would you recognize him, do you think? How smart was your little infant memory?"

Liv's question stopped me in my tracks. We were in Napa. Hunter Moon was in San Francisco. We had the next five days free from reality. Nothing to do. No obligations. The seed of an idea that had been planted in my brain for who knows how long— maybe years—was taking root. I looked over at Liv, at the smile slowly spreading across her face.

"What are you thinking?" I asked, suddenly nervous.

"I'm thinking what you're thinking. Let's go find him."

"I wasn't—" I began.

"You wanted to find him, let's find him. Maybe it will help you resolve some stuff."

I started to shake my head, but Liv held up her hand. "I know one thing. We aren't staying here eating grass and getting rubbed with Ayurvedic oil while your father is hanging out a few miles down the road."

"But we don't know that for sure. We don't know anything!" I protested.

"We're lawyers. All we do all day long is research. Emma, face it, we're going to San Francisco." She looked me straight in the eyes. "We're going to find your dad."

I instantly felt like I was going to cry, although I wasn't entirely sure why. "Really? You think it's a good idea? Are you sure? But weren't you looking forward to Napa? What about the plunge pool?"

"Sure, it's nice. Okay, it's heaven. But we can come here whenever we want. Well, when we've saved up another small fortune for one of the biggest events of our lives. But who cares? That's just stuff. Let's go find your dad."

I looked at my best friend, who wanted what was best for me. I thought about how long I'd wondered about my father. I thought about how much I might not know about Sam, and myself. I thought about the roller coaster of anxiety, fear, and inner chaos I'd been riding on for weeks.

"Okay," I agreed, a warm feeling growing inside me as I spoke. Liv squealed in response. "If you're sure you don't mind, I guess it can't hurt to look."

"Yes!" she cheered. "Now, should you break the news to Siri or should I?"

Grabbing our bags, we booked it out of the lodge as if we knew we wouldn't be able to leave if we looked back. When we got to reception we encountered a bewildered Siri, who was either performing meditation behind her glass desk or rarely blinked. We tossed the flimsy room key her way and sprinted to the door. I quickly explained that we were needed in San Francisco, and no, not to tell anyone where we went if they should call.

"Then what should I tell them?" Siri asked, her pale, slim shoulders raised in confusion, her face showing some kind of expression for the first time since we met.

"Nothing. I mean, take the messages and do whatever you want with them. But please don't give any information back. Look at it this way: You could always double book the room, keep the money, and go shopping. We won't tell the manager." I attempted a conspiratorial wink.

"I *am* the manager," Siri said, clearly insulted by our suggestion of insubordination.

"That's awesome, Siri," Liv said, jumping in. "You're doing a great job."

I took this as my cue to push us out the door.

"Um, bye," Siri called as we hustled out to the parking lot. Before that moment, no one had *ever* hustled on the premises of the Calistoga Ranch, unless it was to snag the last green tea smoothie after forest yoga.

"Why are we running?" I gasped for breath as I opened the passenger door.

"I don't know about you but I'm running from Siri," Liv

shouted. "She's gotta be a robot. No actual human being looks that good in a jumper." She slammed her door closed and started the rental car.

"I was thinking the same thing!"

Liv peeled out of the parking spot, opening her window and shouting, "Bye, organic pear and fig facial peel! Later, mustard seed body wrap with deep friction massage for an extra fifty bucks! Catch you on the flip side, organic milk bath!" I laughed at Liv's good-bye to our five-minute five-star experience and felt a ripple of excitement. After living in California for seven years, I was finally looking for my dad, who had been there all along. I was finally looking for answers to the questions that had been skirting around the edge of my mind for weeks. And who knows, I might even find them.

CHAPTER 6

"Can I ask you a question?" Liv said, glancing at me in the warm car, her figure outlined by a slice of orange sun about to succumb to the horizon. We'd been driving for close to an hour. After pulling up directions to San Francisco and locating an oldies station playing "the Seventies at Seven," we were on our way. In the background, Rod Stewart started to croon about Maggie May. I turned to face Liv to let her know I was listening.

"Why don't you ask your mom where he is? Hunter, I mean. I know you guys aren't close or anything, but maybe she could point us in the right direction. You know, 'He lives in Pac Heights in the yellow house on Fillmore'—that kind of thing."

"For one thing, she doesn't know. I overheard her talking on the phone years ago. She said after Hunter moved back to San

53

Francisco, she never heard from him. So really, this whole thing could be a crapshoot." I looked out the window. "And secondly, there's no way I'm getting her involved."

"Gotcha," Liv said lightly, turning up the music and singing along with Rod, who wished he'd never seen Maggie's face. Any knowledge my mother may have had about Hunter wasn't worth getting her two cents on this harebrained scheme, but I couldn't help being slightly embarrassed. Although I knew Liv loved me unconditionally and, to a certain extent, she understood the cold war between my mother and me, it wasn't exactly something I was proud of.

The funny part is, I vividly remember when my relationship with my mother went from best buddies to strained strangers. When I was little I would sit on the kitchen sink while she curled her hair for dates and we would dance around to Earth, Wind and Fire. When I was in kindergarten and I had a cat that seemed to have kittens every year, my mom let me keep the entire brood until I was able to give them away. In fifth grade, when my "friends" formed the I Hate Emma Club one day and told me I wasn't allowed to sit with them anymore (preteen girls, the true Axis of Evil), I came home the next night and my mom had put up a banner that read, *The I Love Emma Club*. The club had only one member, but hey, it was better than nothing. But those were the days when Caro was still getting her degree, volunteering at the lobby on the weekends and squeezing in waitressing shifts at the local pizza place to pay the rent. Once she started working full time and I went to high school, things irrevocably changed.

It was the summer before I started high school, when my mom graduated from her master's program and started as a paid staffer at the anti-tobacco lobby. She was able to quit her night shifts at the Italian restaurant on M Street, threw away her red linen apron—stiff from hundreds of washings—and lost the extra ten pounds created by the free pizza and calzones we subsisted on. Thanks to the new boost in income, we traded in the revolving door of temporary rentals and Georgetown apartments owned by friends who let us crash, for a small Cape Cod in Arlington, Virginia. For the first time, we had our own house, with a real backyard, replete with a dogwood tree and a hammock, where I could lie for hours in the shade and read. It was my own personal Glover Park, with fewer flashers.

This should have been good news, but for some reason as soon as we moved, this was when it seemed my mother morphed from Mom to Caro. All of a sudden she was out of the house all time, somehow even more than when she'd been waitressing, going to school, and passing out "Cough Twice for Philip Morris" flyers on Saturdays. Even though she finally had a salaried job and could presumably take a break from our ever-present money woes, she seemed more irritable than ever. Everything I did annoyed her, which wasn't helped by the fact that I felt less and less comfortable in my own skin every day. That summer I shot up to five feet, nine inches, getting clumsier by the second, while Caro stayed cool, sleek, and Reese Witherspoon sized.

A child's memory is biased, I know, but there are events from that time that stick out to this day, moments that I can point to and say,

Look, there it is, there's proof; my mother couldn't stand me. One night when we first moved in, our neighbor and the father of three younger boys from down the street, Mike Madigan, came by to welcome us. In only a few days, I'd already become familiar with the Madigan boys, who were always kicking the soccer ball around their front yard or having races in the street. Mr. Madigan worked as a government consultant, had a kind smile, and wore tortoiseshell glasses. He offered to fix loose cabinets and set up our cable box, as generic men in the suburbs are prone to do. I remember how nervous I was when he came over, the first ever visitor to our first ever house, as I chattered to keep him entertained.

I told him a story about my middle-school gym class, describing the annual line dance instruction, even impersonating the boys choppily attempting to grapevine. Our neighbor chuckled and I glanced at Caroline to see her reaction. She was watching me stonily and all of a sudden I saw her—quickly, imperceptibly—roll her eyes. It's subtle but powerful what an eye roll can do. Abruptly, I stopped speaking.

In the years following, when I wasn't at my new friend Liv's house, I hid in my room or outside on the hammock. I punished Caro by not telling her anything about my life. I didn't tell her when I got elected to student government. I didn't complain that I hated my chemistry teacher with a passion and I didn't invite her over to take prom pictures with the other parents. Over the years we became more and more distant, until we were basically two strangers living in the same house, reconvening to discuss Chinese food take-out orders.

Liv's family, on the other hand, was perfect. I idolized her parents, particularly Mr. Lucci, who in my mind was the perfect dad. He was the ultimate family man. He came home every night at 5:00 P.M. from his job at the State Department and cooked dinner for his family. I remember hearing a story about how he could have taken a job at a law firm and made ten times the salary, but he turned it down because he wouldn't have been able to make homemade fajitas every Thursday night. Mr. Lucci spent virtually every weekend puttering around the house, drinking decaf coffee, and reading the newspaper, reciting aloud any article he thought Mrs. Lucci might enjoy. It took him two hours to get through the Style section.

For Caro and me, things went from bad to worse. When I left for college, and then law school, and finally settled in Los Angeles, I think we were both relieved. To this day, she's never been to visit me, although the truth is she's never really been invited. She's only even met Sam a handful of times.

Of course, since I met Sam and the rest of the Powells, I haven't minded my mother's distance as much. My mind drifted unpleasantly to where I would be if I were to lose him. Back at square one, without a family, without anyone.

"Emma!" Liv shouted, interrupting my distress. "Look!" I looked up to see where Liv was wildly pointing. It was an exit for 280 South, toward *H. Moon*. I felt a sudden jolt of adrenaline, even though I had experienced this particular coincidence before.

"Yeah, that's weird, right? It stands for Half Moon—it's the freeway to Half Moon Bay. But that would be an awesome way to find him."

"I know it doesn't stand for Hunter Moon *your dad*," Liv said, rolling her eyes, albeit in a nice way. "But it's still a sign! We are heading toward H. Moon, literally!"

"Well, not *literally* literally, because that's not our exit."

"You know what I mean. Anyway, did you know they put the fake definition of *literally* in the dictionary? Now it says *literally* means either that something really happened or it didn't really but it's being used for exaggeratory effect. Isn't that funny? The point is, we're gonna find him!"

Despite being a practicing attorney with an eye for facts, Liv strongly believed in the power of positive thinking, and she gave a surprising amount of credit to signs, symbols, and other emblems of her destiny. I wasn't usually convinced, but today her excitement was contagious. There was a small part of me that held hope that we might actually find Hunter. Maybe things would turn out well. I let out a gush of air, resolving to be present and enjoy the adventure. I hadn't realized it, but I'd been holding my breath. "You're right," I said. "It's a good sign. Literally."

Liv laughed. "She's back to telling the dorky puns, folks!"

I sat back and wondered what had really happened to Hunter. I was six months old when he left. Did he hate changing diapers? Did Caro ruin his life and drive him away? Was it the Beltway traffic? Soon, I hoped, I would know.

We wound our way north through the city, to the place I'd reserved through Airbnb on our drive in. After a quick search with my phone, I'd found a three-bedroom Victorian in the Marina. It had what looked like a beautiful bedroom with a king-sized bed and an en suite bathroom, and it was available for an immediate vacation rental. I was a little unsure about a place that would have availability so last minute, but if the pictures were any indication, it would be perfect.

I directed Liv to the address, lost in thought, turning over the few facts about Hunter, the bits and pieces I'd put together about him, and even the rare mention of his name, overheard and collected throughout the years.

In truth, the most concrete memory I had of my father wasn't a memory at all. It was a story that my uncle Constantine told me, or rather, shouted near me, when I was nine years old. That year at Thanksgiving my mom decided that I should know more of her family, the majority of whom still lived in Pennsylvania. She invited them all to the small basement apartment we were subletting, while she was acting as temporary manager of the restaurant.

That day remains the only one I've ever spent with all of my mother's family. When I picture it, I remember a lot of shouting relatives and enormous bowls of pasta. Marinara sauce simmering on the stove and meat being patted into balls. And wine, lots of wine. No one mentioned a turkey, and I wasn't about to bring it up.

Uncle Constantine, who hadn't fallen far from Mickey Rigazi's tree, was drunk by noon, cursing the Steelers and the Raiders, which I realized years later were football teams, not a band of thieves committing breaking and entering. During grace, my grandmother gave a prayer for all the family who couldn't be with us that day.

Showing off, I added, "Like my daddy, Hunter." I didn't quite grasp the concept of divorce yet, much less abandonment, but I knew I had a family member who wasn't there, and figured pointing out his existence couldn't hurt.

Constantine looked directly at me for the first time that day, his small, angry eyes rimmed with red, a streak of sauce on the lower right of his chin, and pointed his juice glass of Chianti in my direction. I wanted to hand him a napkin, but something told me the gesture wouldn't be appreciated.

"Bite your tongue, Emily. Your father is nothing but a no-good, dick-eating louse!" he shouted. To this day, it was the oddest insult I've ever heard, which is probably why I still remember it. My grandmother tried to rein him in by patting his arm quickly and firmly in what appeared to be a Morse code pattern, but he wasn't to be silenced. Apparently my father was as unwelcome in this house as those burglars he hated from Pittsburgh.

"I'll never forgive him, Caroline," he went on. "Neither should you. After what he done to me when I come to the hospital to see *my* baby niece." He slammed down his glass. "That asshole kicks me out! Me!" he yelled, like the King of England thwarted from meeting his heir to the throne, rather than the uncle of baby Emily, who was, by the way, named Emma.

"Why?" I asked in a small voice. I couldn't help it. Caro looked wearily at her mother, who started dishing out the pasta and identifying meat versus eggplant as if a fat man sitting to her left wasn't turning purple with rage.

"For no good reason is why! Because he's a prick!" he shouted. "But I wasn't about to let this loser kick me out of my sister's hospital room, no sirree. I punched him right in the nose for that one. That taught him. Haven't seen him around here since, have you?" Constantine finished with a flourish, before turning back to the more important business of shoving an olive oil–soaked piece of bread in his mouth, seemingly a reward for setting the story straight.

Later that night after everyone had left, sensing there was more to the story—as would anyone with an ounce of deductive reasoning skill—I asked my mom why my dad kicked Constantine out of the hospital room. She never talked about my dad, but she had no choice after that little tidbit. Caro sighed mightily and said, "Because he was smoking in the delivery room. Constantine walked into the room and lit up a cigarette right next to a day-old baby. Hunter kicked him out. He was . . . protective that way."

I didn't ask any of the obvious questions. What way? Why would someone who was willing to get into a physical fight to protect his baby's tiny lungs leave said child mere months later? If he was so concerned about my well-being then, why hadn't he contacted me since? Instead I said, "I can see why he got mad," not clarifying whether I meant my father or Uncle Constantine, and continued bringing dishes in from the card table to the alcove kitchen, my mind swimming with questions and my heart hurting for a man who had once tried to protect me.

CHAPTER 7

We pulled up to a tall yellow Victorian with an unbelievably steep flight of narrow stairs, ensuring that all who lived there would curse themselves daily, and movers would charge them double their usual rate. Despite this, it was an incredible home, both historic and well kept. I reassured myself that this probably made the Airbnb somewhat legit.

I was struck by intense déjà vu.

"This block looks so familiar, doesn't it?"

Liv gave me an incredulous look. "You don't remember?"

"Did we come here in law school? Remind me."

Liv pointed to the bar on the corner of the block. "That's where we met Tony." I mentally reset the day counter where I kept track of how much time had passed since Liv last brought Tony up in conversation. Tony, also known as Sexy Tony Brown, or Liv's first love. The guy who stole her heart, ripped it out, and four years later still held a piece of it in his sexy hand. I calculated that it had been approximately six months since Liv last mentioned him, although I had to admit, this time it was probably my fault.

After huffing our way up what felt like a million stairs, we found the key under the mat as promised and slowly opened the door. The apartment was even nicer, if slightly messier, than in the pictures I'd seen. As we'd only given the owner one hour's notice, I mentally excused the mess.

According to the listing, the apartment was owned by Phillip C. Richardson, who had a list of positive reviews but no picture. He sounded quite distinguished. I pictured a harried workaholic who could afford a beautiful, well-kept apartment, discounted due to unfortunate stairway placement, but didn't have time to occupy it.

The apartment turned out to be a duplex. On the first level was our room, as well as an additional somewhat lived-in guest room, a kitchen, and a large open living room. The entire top floor was a master bedroom and office—Phillip's room, we assumed—which we decided not to check out, even though the place was empty. If we got caught, our snoopiness would surely result in a bad Airbnb review.

"There's a note on the kitchen table that says come to the bar down the street, not the Tony one, thank God," Liv intoned. I reset the Sexy Tony Brown counter once again. "To meet our host. What do you think? That's kind of weird, but nice, too, I guess."

"Why not? We can say hi and then do our own thing."

"Sounds like a plan."

After throwing down our bags and doing a final quick sweep of the apartment, we headed to the brewery where the apartment owner claimed to be. "Let's get some drinks, find a table, and start working on our Hunter plan of attack," Liv shouted over the din of the bar. "Then we can text Phillip and say we're here and at a table so we don't have to hang out with him all night." We positioned ourselves at either end of the bar, so we were guaranteed to be served first, whether the bartender preferred blondes or redheads. I attempted to smile at him flirtatiously, but he only glanced at me with a smirk that said he knew exactly what I was doing and served the person to my right. I immediately turned bright red and stepped back, slightly behind a tall guy with dark hair sticking out of a green baseball cap, who jostled me slightly on my right.

"Hey, sorry about that," he said, turning to apologize, giving me a direct view of his bright hazel eyes. He had that nice-guy look, with a friendly smile and eyelashes so long that had he been wearing makeup, he would have gotten mascara smudges all over his face. I sighed jealously. I *longed* to have the mascara smudge problem. Luckily for him, his face was saved from being boringly cute by a scar that looked like a checkmark under his right eye. It made his whole face look slightly asymmetrical, but the whole thing made quite a nice package, and strangely, I had the sudden urge to reach out and touch his scar. Was it because of its interesting shape or because I was a crazy person? I was unclear.

"Can I buy you a drink to make it up to you? And for your friend, of course," he said, noticing Liv walk up empty-handed.

"Sure, but only if it'll ease your guilty conscience." Strange thoughts about touching his face notwithstanding, free drinks were free drinks. I didn't want to give him the wrong idea, so I made sure my engagement ring was positioned facing out, and I ran my hand through my uncombed hair to give him a good view of it. Unfortunately, on the way down it got caught in my tangles.

"Are you okay?" he said, turning around to notice my awkward positioning, arm sticking out, elbow akimbo. "Are you . . . stuck?"

I turned pink with embarrassment as I tried to unwind my ring from my hair to avoid yanking out a chunk. "I'm fine, just got a little caught." I gave up on the delicacy of the operation and started freely tugging, my arm starting to fatigue. "It's okay, don't worry about it." I felt suddenly light-headed from having my arm up for so long and wondered what would happen if I fainted.

Liv stepped in, quickly removing the ring from my hand first so I could take my arm down, and then deftly guiding it out of my hair like an egg from a bird's nest. She handed it to me and everyone watched as I put it back on my left hand, which was bright red from exertion. Well, at least now he knew I was engaged.

"Two more beers," he said. "Do you guys have a preference?"

"Amstel Light," Liv piped in, at the same moment I said, "Allagash." Great. Way to make me look high maintenance, Liv.

"Done and done. I'm Dusty, by the way. We're also getting shots. Buttery Nipples sound good?" I nodded before he could say it again. There's only so much embarrassment a girl can take. He signaled to the snobby bartender that he needed two more shots.

"Can we order food up here?" I asked.

The bartender shook his head. "Someone will come around to your table." He slammed down the drinks and turned to the next guy.

"But we don't have a table," I said impotently.

Dusty picked up the drinks and motioned across the bar.

"We have one." Without waiting for my assent, he started heading to the corner of the bar with the drinks and I turned to Liv, who had already started following him.

"Do you want to sit with these guys?"

"Relax, Em. We'll see if his friends are cute, say thanks for the drinks, and then find our own table."

"What about Phillip?" I said to Liv's retreating back. She ignored me.

Dusty led us to a rowdy table with three other guys and pulled out two seats for us. I did a quick calculation: two Titleist hats, four legs clad in madras shorts, and one pastel popped collar. Jeez Louise, these guys were preppy.

"Do you guys live around here in the Marina?" I asked innocently, to amuse Liv more than anything else, because it was practically guaranteed that this group of bros inhabited the preppiest section of San Francisco.

"Yeah," answered Madras #1, who introduced himself pompously as Carrick, silently daring us to ask which rich grandfather he was named after. He had a surprisingly deep voice, dark eyes, and a sexy, wolflike set of teeth.

I lightly kicked Liv, ready to take our shots and get the hell out of there. But unfortunately, somewhere between Carrick's foxy smile and his Alec Baldwin impression, I'd lost her. I had to admit, there was something very appealing about the way Carrick's lips disappeared when he bared his teeth. It shouldn't be hot, but it was. Liv ignored my signal, flashing the boys a pretty smile. Damn it, I thought, she's gonna be nice to them.

"That's great. I love this area. We're visiting for the weekend."

"Where are you guys staying while you're in town?" Dusty asked.

I gave him the address, which caused Carrick to look up.

"Where?" he chimed in.

I repeated the street name and number.

"That's my building," Carrick said.

"And mine, for the time being," Dusty added. "I'm staying in Carrick's spare room until I find my own place."

"That's funny," Liv exclaimed. "It's an Airbnb place we rented out from a guy named Phillip. Is he your neighbor?"

Carrick laughed. "Nice to meet you," Carrick said to Liv, holding out his hand. "Phillip Carrick Richardson, but I go by my middle name. I guess that makes me your landlord."

My head swam. We were staying with these frat boys? Abruptly, I desperately wanted to be on my couch with Sam, with my legs in his lap, sharing a pint of chocolate chocolate chip Häagen-Dazs and debating which episode of *Friday Night Lights* we were on. As if on cue, my phone rattled on the table. *Sam Powell: iMessage.*

That's good news, I told myself, slightly cheered. We were still connected enough that he could sense something was off between us and intuitively knew to check in. I gave myself a mini talking-to. Everything is fine between you and Sam. You are with your best friend. You have a drink. You are having fun.

I held up my Buttery Nipple. "Are we going to take these or not?" The boys cheered in the affirmative, and the atmosphere at the table instantly changed from introductory to celebratory as we clinked our glasses and took our shots, each of us getting fractionally drunker and less self-conscious.

It turned out Carrick was a buddy of Dusty's from college. Dusty had recently moved out west from Manhattan and was, along with two other friends, creating a start-up much like Yelp, but targeted toward finding the holes-in-the-wall and neighborhood hangouts frequented by the city's residents. They were going to call it MyLocal.com.

"I love that!" I exclaimed genuinely. "Whenever I move to a new town I immediately search for my local—such a good name—coffee shop, bar, and bookstore. And trust me, I moved a lot growing up, so I know what I'm talking about."

"That's great," Dusty said. He was visibly pleased that I liked the idea. The more he talked about MyLocal, the genesis, the site design, and the investors, the more apparent it was that the company was his baby. My whole life I had always been interested in people with passions, no matter what those passions were. Ice hockey, street art, stand-up comedy, you name it. A person who cared desperately about what he did was cool.

"We still have a lot of work to do. Our office doesn't even have a coffeemaker yet. But when we do figure out how to turn on our computers and, you know, launch a company, you can be our first user." He smiled, flashing killer straight white teeth.

I wasn't attracted to Dusty and his perfect smile, I told myself. I wasn't flirting with him or enamored with his creative business savvy. I was one hundred percent still longing to be snuggled up with Sam and Coach Taylor. Despite this, I was having fun. With my new *friend*, I inwardly italicized.

"One more question for you, Emma," Dusty asked as my burger arrived and I heavily salted the fries that accompanied it. "Actually, two questions. Aren't you concerned about your sodium intake, and two, what are you guys doing in San Francisco a few days before your wedding?"

I'd given him the sketchy background of my relationship, but no specifics. Maybe it was the freedom I felt at that moment, temporarily untethered from the reality of my life, but, surprising myself as much as him, I told him the truth.

"I'm looking for my birth father," I said simply, reaching for the ketchup. "And I don't believe in the whole 'salt is bad for you' thing."

"I'm not sure it's really up for debate," he said, laughing, before he paused. "Please tell me if I'm overstepping, but you don't know your dad?"

"Nope," I said. "I've never met him before, never spoken to

him. I just know he's somewhere in San Francisco. Liv and I were supposed to be taking a bachelorette trip to Napa, but we made a detour. I guess I wanted to find him before I got married."

"That makes sense."

"It does?" I asked, shocked that he wasn't, well, shocked.

"Sure. It stands to reason that you would want to know your own family before you join someone else's. How are you planning on finding him? Do you have an address or anything?"

"I don't know, exactly. I guess I thought actually being in the same city as him would help; I'm not sure why. Does that sound ridiculous?"

"Nope, it doesn't. What kind of Internet searching did you say you've done?" Dusty asked thoughtfully. I explained the shallow depths of my research and how difficult it was to find a person whose name wasn't really a name, but two words.

"That's the problem," Dusty said, thinking out loud. "You need a search database that's only for people. Like Yellowpages .com. Something that won't cloud up the hits with half-moons and statistics on deer overpopulation."

"Why deer . . . ? Oh, Hunter. Exactly! Hey, this is your area of expertise. After you get MyLocal up and running, you should start a Who's My Daddy app for people looking for deadbeat dads."

Dusty laughed but looked like he was considering it. I made a mental note to invest.

"Have you tried LinkedIn?"

"No, only Facebook and Google," I said, feeling like a moron. "That's a really good idea. That would narrow it down to just people."

"Exactly. LinkedIn, Twitter, Meetup—something where you can put in a first and last name."

Dusty pulled out his phone. "Here, let me show you." Over the next few minutes, he quickly checked a few of the social networks he'd mentioned for Hunter's first name, last name, and any combination of the two, using HTML language and a search box I wasn't familiar with. This was ostensibly to make it go faster, although he might have just been showing off. I felt slightly less stupid when he also came up with nothing.

"I have to admit," I joked, "I'm glad we didn't find him on Meetup. It sounds a little too Tinder-y for my taste."

"Meetup isn't like that," Dusty said defensively. "It's for people who have hobbies like skydiving and who move to new a city and want to meet people who share their interests."

He paused.

I gave him a knowing look.

"Fine, I'll admit it. Carrick is the only person I knew when I moved to San Francisco. I joined to play Scrabble. And I know what you're going to say, but online Scrabble isn't the same! The sense of excitement is lost."

I genuinely had to bite my lip to keep from laughing. I excused myself to get another round of drinks with Liv, and we made a quick detour to the bathroom to have an official girl chat.

"You and Carrick seem to be hitting it off," I said cheekily.

"He's cute," Liv offered lightly. "I can't get over all of the coincidences today. First, our rental is on the street of the bar where I met Tony." I reset the counter. "Then we run into the guys who live there at the bar. What's next?" she said as she pushed the door open and turned back to look at me.

As if on cue, standing at the sink was Val Baby.

That wasn't her real name, of course. Her full name was Valerie Babbitt. Val Baby was her social media handle. More than that, it was what she encouraged everyone to call her. I am a firm believer in the fact that you can't give yourself a nickname. If a nickname comes your way, accept it. If not, sorry. But you can't tell people to call you A-Train or the Handyman; it either happens naturally or it doesn't. Thus spoke Emma on the Law of Nicknames.

But that was Val Baby in a nutshell. Ridiculously confident in her own skin, because at a size 2, with long black hair that fell down her back and almond-shaped green eyes so large that people often stopped midconversation to comment on them, why shouldn't she be? She had that exotic look that encouraged strangers to ask what her heritage was, as if her parents had the secret to impressive genetic combinations. I always wondered how these people planned to use this information, whether they asked out of genuine curiosity or solely in an effort to create the hottest match possible down the line. Oh, you're a Brazilian Italian, quarter Japanese? Hold on, booking a trip to Rio.

We were really good friends the first year I lived in Los Angeles. However, all at once, everything changed. The summer after we became friends, Sam and Val Baby left town to work on the aforementioned film, *On the Royal Road*, in South Carolina. It was based and shot in Charleston, his mother's hometown, which gave the script a sense of place so real it could only have been written by someone who spent every summer there growing up.

Twelve weeks later, after a long, lonely summer without my new boyfriend and my current closest friend, they were back. As soon as Val came back, however, she dropped me like a bad habit. First she stopped texting me updates, then she was always too busy to hang out. Finally, her birthday rolled around and I saw her tagged in a big group dinner, looking gorgeous as she blew out the candles. I'd kept the night free, figuring we would be doing something to celebrate, so instead I sat at home, watching reality TV and feeling sorry for myself. A couple months later her network and profession changed on Facebook. She'd moved to San Francisco without telling me.

That was why the second I saw my old friend, instead of being excited to see her, my nerves kicked into high gear. I observed her leaning forward against the wide metal sink, applying bright red Nars lipstick. When I walked in, Val handed the lipstick back to her friend—who, even glossier than Val, was practically glistening—and turned to face us. My shackles went up. Her shiny friend gave us what could only have been called a smirk. My fight-or-flight response said, *Get the hell out of this bathroom immediately,* but I had no choice but to acknowledge her presence.

"Oh, hey, Val! How's it going?" I reached over for the extremely fake one-armed hug made popular by gymnasts the world over, who were attempting to show their team spirit post performance, but who quite clearly wanted to shank each other.

"Hi, Emma. Long time no see. And you're Lydia from New York, right?"

"Olivia. You got two syllables right," Liv replied dryly. Val didn't seem to register the correction, lazily pushing up the sleeves of her three-thousand-dollar (give or take) off-the-shoulder cashmere sweater before beginning to apply another layer of mascara. *Unflappable.* The girl is unflappable.

"How are you?" I repeated nervously, my mind going blank from fear of confrontation. This was the first time I had seen her face-to-face in years. Val didn't respond, only stared at me, making me feel like an idiot in two seconds flat. Meanwhile, other girls were moving in and around the bathroom and I somehow managed to be in everyone's way at once.

Luckily, Liv stepped in. "I'm here for the wedding. I'm sure you heard, Sam and Emma are getting married."

"Next Saturday," I added unnecessarily.

"I did hear that, from some old friends at Left Brain. We were getting drinks and they mentioned they were heading to Santa Barbara next weekend."

"We're going to a wedding next weekend, too," Shiny piped in pointlessly. "In Turks." She didn't elaborate so I looked to Val, but she was busy blotting her perfect bow lips with something that looked like a mini toilet seat cover. She had told me once—when she handed me one and I, having no idea what to do, tried to dry my forehead with it—that it was a lipstick blotter. Val knew so much more than I did about feminine makeup maintenance that it made my head spin. Which was maybe why, in the brightest red lipstick ever, she somehow didn't look like a scary clown.

"Leaving tomorrow for a week," she explained, without turning from her own reflection. "I can't wait to be tan."

"Well, don't forget about skin cancer," Liv said, flashing Val a fake smile. "Good to see you."

Liv headed to a stall, reminding me what we were doing there in the first place. Val dropped the makeup she was holding into her leather fringed hobo bag, gave herself one last look of approval, and started toward the door, where I was still hovering.

"Bye, Emma. Good luck with the wedding." This didn't sound like the normal thing one says in the circumstances, but this wasn't the most normal of situations. She pushed her way out, back into the bar, and oddly enough, I followed her.

"Can I ask you a weird question?" I asked, raising my voice over the din. She was silent but paused, which I took as my cue to go on. "What happened between us? You know, when you got back from Charleston, I never really figured out why we stopped hanging out."

"Emma, that's ancient history," she said, glancing at the noisy bar.

"Did I do something to upset you?"

"It wasn't that," she said, moving her bag from one arm to another.

"Was it because of Sam? Because you felt caught in the middle or something? Did *he* do something to piss you off?"

"Emma." Val paused and sighed heavily. "Fine. You're right."

"What do you mean?"

"I did cut you off, and I'm sorry for that, but it was the right thing to do."

"What do you mean?" My inner voice told me to turn around, stop the conversation. I no longer wanted to know.

"It was because of Sam."

"What do you mean?" I attempted to keep my voice steady although my insides felt instantly sick, and my heart was beating out of its chest even harder than it had been when I started this idiot's mission.

"The truth is—and you might as well know now because I don't think you're gonna let me go until I tell you—we hooked up. In Charleston. I thought you knew."

No, no, no, no, said my brain. This is not true. This cannot not be true. Everyone stop talking *now*. I felt a cold chill wash over my entire body.

"Look, I'm sorry. I can't tell you how sorry. I have beat myself up about it and I debated for a long time whether to tell you. I decided that it wasn't my place, but it didn't feel right staying your friend. If it makes you feel any better, I think he felt really bad about it."

No, I wanted to scream, *that does not make me feel better!* Why was she saying this, part of me demanded, when it couldn't be true? It was impossible. Sam was a lot of things. He was messy, he was stubborn, and, let's be honest, when he unwrapped gum wrappers in a movie theater when it was dead silent, it made me want to stab him, but he wasn't a cheater. He was honest to a fault. He made me pay for my fifty-cent soda refills, for God's sake. What Val was suggesting was absolutely one hundred percent impossible. But as she stood there, staring at me, I realized that this wasn't a joke. She meant it. She was serious. Ashton Kutcher was nowhere to be found and besides, they don't punk real people, do they?

I felt like I was going to throw up. It was like I was watching myself have a nightmare, only I couldn't end it. Wake up, a voice in my head begged. Please wake up.

The weirdest part was Val's reaction. She was almost stoic. She looked slightly guilty, but not utterly ashamed. She looked like she'd just accidentally spoiled the plot twist in *Gone Girl*, not ruined my entire life.

"I don't know what to say, Emma. I didn't plan for any of this to happen. I don't think anyone did." She gave me one final look that said, *It wasn't my proudest moment, but the statute of limitations on feeling bad is up,* and simply walked away. I wanted to run after her, to stop her, to make her take it back. But she was already gone.

CHAPTER 8

I woke up on Sunday in an unfamiliar darkened room, startled from a terrible dream. In the dream, Sam was explaining that he was in love with Val and that he was leaving me for her. He asked if he could use our wedding to marry her instead. All of this took place on a train, but I didn't know where we were headed. I was desperate in the dream, pleading, begging him to change his mind, to give me another chance. But he was resolute; his decision was made. At one point the conductor came by and I realized in a hot flash of fear that I'd forgotten to buy a ticket. The scene changed. I was on the station platform, frantically attempting to make eye contact with Sam through the window and watching the train pull away. He never looked up as the train left the station and I dropped to my knees, crippled by the realization that I could do nothing to change his mind.

I woke up in the middle of a sob, gasping and blinking, slowly regaining consciousness. It was early, too early. So early you know that if you don't completely open your eyes you have a couple more hours of sleep in you. But the second you become aware of it, the game of chicken comes to an abrupt halt, and you're awake.

After losing the extra hours of sleep, I evaluated my mental state. For a brief moment I was relieved, realizing that the dream wasn't real, but then I remembered my current reality. I wasn't on a train, but I was definitely unsure of where I was going. Instantly anxious, and annoyed that my dreams couldn't be any subtler, I padded over to the window to check the weather. Pulling back the room-darkening curtains, I was slightly irritated to see the sun peeking through clouds. Right then the San Francisco fog would have been welcome.

I sat back down on the bed, careful not to wake Liv, trying to process what had happened the day before. But what *had* happened? I had no idea. I knew one thing. It couldn't be true. Val was either lying or confused, that much was clear. If this was a movie and a guy was falsely accused, I would be mad at the girlfriend for not giving him the benefit of the doubt. So I decided to. There was really no other option. It couldn't be true.

I had to hear him say it, I realized. I rooted for my phone inside my bag, then quickly scrolled through my recent contacts. There had to be some mistake. Maybe she'd mixed up the timing. Maybe they did hook up, but it happened before I even met Sam. My mind groped for this possibility quickly, hopefully, and I decided to hang on to it. For a moment, I felt the sickness start to subside and the mountain of ice in my chest begin to thaw. My heart started to beat more normally and I drew a full deep breath. Then, as quickly as it had appeared, this idea, and the accompanying hope, was dashed. Sam hadn't even met Val before he knew me. They met at Left Brain, after he sold his first movie, a month after we started dating. With that realization the sickness reemerged, rising like an ice cap, colder and sharper than before, piercing my heart as it fought to get back through.

My call went to voicemail.

Liv turned to me sleepily.

"What are we doing here, Emma?"

"What do you mean? We're in San Francisco looking for my long lost dad. It was your idea, remember?"

"Em, that's not what I mean. You have to talk to Sam."

"I tried to call him." I pointedly opened my suitcase to get dressed. "He didn't answer."

"Look, you have to deal with this. I'm as mad as you are, but this is something you guys can only fix if you talk about it."

"First of all, I don't know what there is to fix. I don't know anything. I don't need to start talking about fixing a situation that couldn't even be true."

"Fine, but we need to go back to L.A. so you can talk to Sam and confirm that."

"Actually, I don't. Not right now. I tried to call. I did my due diligence. I know it's not true, so there is no sense in making a huge deal about this by flying home to confront him."

"Okay."

"You know, I'm not surprised," I said, despite myself. "I kept waiting for the other shoe to drop and there it is."

It was true. My feelings about Sam and marriage had been twisted around each other for weeks. I blamed it on my background, and the persistent thoughts about finding Hunter, but here it was, another blow to the idea that marriage could ever possibly work. I didn't think there was any way that what Val had told me could be true, but the fact that this drama was even happening days before my wedding, wasn't that symbolic in and of itself?

In books and movies it's always so obvious whether or not people should be together. I could easily watch a romantic comedy and tell you within the first five minutes if the main characters would make it, or if she was really meant to end up with the scruffily hot next-door neighbor whom she thought she despised. Or, when reading a novel, I would think, That girl is so lucky to be with that amazing man— someone needs to tell her to stop acting like a dummy and tell him she loves him back, pronto! I would get stressed, wishing I could reach into these fictional worlds and tell the characters what to do. Yet in my own world, the real one, I had no idea what was right or wrong. In fact, I wasn't even sure if I wanted to know the answer.

I thought back to the beginning with Sam, when everything seemed so easy. When I first moved to L.A. after law school, I joined a Venice softball league for the sole purpose of making friends and meeting boys, as the thrill of competition (and coordination) are completely lost on me. During my first game, I was standing on the field trying to figure out how to get the team T-shirt on without taking my current shirt off, and Sam walked up. He smiled at me, offered his hand, and asked if I wanted to warm up, which I found funny, as I had no idea how one warmed up for a co-ed intramural softball game. I knew immediately that it didn't matter, though. What mattered was the way this guy was looking at me, and the way it was making me feel. You know how you can tell someone is attracted to you? I felt it. Instantly. In spades.

It's not that I'm naturally beautiful in that way where I can bat my eyelashes and get out of a speeding ticket, or confidently slip a guy my number at a bar, knowing he'll call. I would describe myself objectively by saying, I do it for some guys. With wide gray eyes, slightly too angular cheekbones, and a dimple in my right cheek when I smile, I'm a bit unusual looking. When I was younger people would often comment that I would "grow into my looks." It was the equivalent of the teacher's comment to a student's parents at a back-to-school conference that their child had potential, if only she would apply herself.

Before Sam, I've always had a type: dark. Dark hair, tanned skin, dirty stubble, and a wicked sense of humor. Kind of Robert Downey, Jr., postrehab. Which is why my instantaneous assessment when I met Sam was, Too bad he's blond, he's almost perfect. In the next thirty seconds, something happened. My type changed, or maybe Sam changed it for me. People debate all the time whether or not love at first sight exists. My opinion is, you don't believe in it if you haven't experienced it—which is technically true of a lot of things, like the magic of the Nubra and ghost stories, but I can speak from experience about this particular phenomenon. I fell in love with Sam, maybe not at first sight, but within about a minute. Maybe it was because he was so nice, picking out the one person on the team who didn't know anyone and making her feel included. Or because the second we started tossing the softball back and forth and chatting, I felt instantly at ease. Or perhaps it was because our pheromones were on fire and I wanted to rip his clothes off right there on the field of Penmar Park. All I know is, the first time I met Sam, I knew I loved him. It was a simple truth, like knowing the capital of Zimbabwe or how to make a proper martini.

I sighed sadly, overwhelmed by the memories, by Val's claims, and by Liv's insistence that I deal with any of it, which I was in no way ready to do. We'd been prepared for a *spa week*, for goodness' sake. I missed feeling normal. I missed feeling sure of my surroundings. I missed Sam. I stood up decisively, putting an end to this unhealthy train of thought. I had something far more important to worry about. I was here to find my father, who, once located, would make everything clearer.

I took some deep breaths and focused on the task at hand, searching my suitcase for my most appropriate "I might be your daughter" outfit. Who knows? We could find him today.

CHAPTER 9

The San Francisco Public Library is exactly what you would expect—colorful, welcoming, and more than a little offbeat. Upon entering on Sunday, Liv and I were immediately confronted with a cardboard cutout of a human-sized lime green iguana holding the second book in the Hunger Games series.

"Are you here to see the Lizard Lady?" asked an extremely tall man. He was sporting black-plastic-framed glasses and wearing a plaid collared shirt and Fair Isle sweater, topped off with a gray tweed blazer.

"Not today," I answered. "Out of curiosity, who is the Lizard Lady? I assume it has something to do with the iguana reading *Catching Fire*?"

The well-layered man, who was holding a stack of books for

reshelving and wearing a name tag that read RICK, grinned widely. "Sure does, although *Mockingjay* is her favorite." Rick gestured to the main sitting area, where a woman wearing a khaki safari jacket was pulling a tortoise out of her pocket to display to a group of squealing children gathered on a colorful patterned floor.

"She's kind of a lizard lady slash magician," he explained. "Everything these days has to be cross-promotional."

"Are you the librarian?" Liv asked, clearly surprised.

"Technically, I'm an archivist. But I can assist you with anything you need," he added, readjusting the display on Russian Cubism advertised for next month—did this library even have books?

"Actually, we would love some help, but it's kind of complicated."

"Take a seat," he said, pointing to two ergonomic chairs in front of a light blond wood circulation desk, and walking around to sit down behind the computer.

"Here's the thing, Rick," Liv explained once we took our seats. "We need to find someone." She paused meaningfully. "Someone who might not want to be found." Most likely this was a line she'd once heard in a TV movie, but it must have been the right thing to say because Rick leaned forward, his black frames slipping down his nose a fraction of an inch, looking back and forth between us meaningfully as if trying to figure out which of us was the fugitive.

"Who?" he nearly whispered.

"It's Emma's—this is Emma, by the way." I threw in a wave as Liv continued. "Her father." Rick looked at me for approval and I gave him a nod, feeling a bit like the mob boss who doesn't have to speak while his underling does his bidding.

"You don't hear that every day. Outside of Lifetime Original Movies, that is," Rick exclaimed, barely able to contain his excitement. "I can definitely help you look for him." He slipped back into professional mode, noticeably pleased that he wasn't being asked which reptiles would be in attendance today or for the library's wireless password. He opened his computer and quickly started typing.

"Do you have a current address or a street name? There's a reverse lookup system where we can cross-reference Google Maps with phone records."

"Unfortunately, no."

"Any past residences?" he asked, still typing and scrolling.

"We know he lived in D.C. at one point when Emma was little," Liv answered, glancing at me for verification. "I know that doesn't really narrow it down, sorry."

"We're pretty sure he lives in San Francisco now. That's basically all we have to go on," I said apologetically. "I really think he's out there, only I don't know how to find him." I realized as I said this that it was true.

"How about his name? Do we know that? Or are we going to have to do a DNA test?" Rick joked.

"Yes," I said quickly, glad to have finally gotten a question right.

I watched him print the name carefully as I recited the letters. "H-u-n-t-e-r M-o-o-n," he repeated, pushing his glasses back up and turning the pad of paper slightly to the side, as if by doing so he could shake out some information. "Got it. This should be easy."

After researching what felt like a thousand different paths on the Internet, Rick quickly found that wasn't exactly the case.

"We're thinking too big. We are trying to find him on these global networks, where there are either too many people or it would be easy to miss him by getting one little thing wrong. What about his membership in a smaller group?"

"Like a country club or something?" I asked.

"Exactly. One of the advantages we have is that he's in San Francisco. Let's use the city to our advantage." He rifled through some drawers and finally pulled out a stack of directories from the depths of his desk. *San Francisco Clubs and Organizations. Bay Area Golf and Tennis. Theater and Music of San Francisco.* The list went on. He handed Liv and me a stack each. "This is just the beginning. We have several shelves devoted to these local clubs in the archives, going back twenty years at least."

"Are you thinking we should call the organizations and ask if Hunter Moon is a member?" Liv said, quickly catching on.

"Or ever has been. If so, they should have his contact information."

"It's not a bad idea." I marveled at the relative simplicity of the plan. "And it really might show us stuff that isn't online."

"It definitely will. Groups like this don't keep their membership records online. Especially past ones." Rick looked back and forth between the two of us. "I think this is what they call good old-fashioned detective work."

Once Rick had set us up in a private reading room with two phones, we lugged the boxes of directories and spread them out to approach our task systematically. Rick was in and out for the rest of the day, helping us call, tending to the Lizard Lady, sneaking us sandwiches from the catered staff meeting. It was a slow-going, arduous process, but the fact that we were talking to real people made it at least entertaining.

Like when the guy who answered the phone at the SF Food Adventure Club accused me of being a spy from the NSA. "Sir," I explained reasonably, "if I were from the NSA, I would just tap your phone lines and be done with it. In fact, they're probably listening to us right now." He hung up shortly after that.

Another woman, who worked the front office of the Humboldt County Green Party, said she knew a Hunter once, who used to frequent the interpretative art scene, but readily admitted she'd done too many drugs to provide much more information than that. She had no clue what his last name might be. There was even one helpful, slightly bored-sounding man, who found a Moon listing in the membership records of the San Francisco Opera's Bravo! Club. When we called the number listed, however, Flowering explained that this was her chosen name, and she wasn't related to any other Moons, "in this realm at least."

"Emma, come here," Liv whispered loudly at one point, covering the receiver of the phone. She turned back to her call. "You don't have any record of one, but you *knew* a Hunter Moon? Uh-huh. He was your dentist?" She looked at me when she said this, raising both eyebrows. "When was that? Do you know if he's still practicing? Do you know his number or address, by any chance? Right, I understand. Let me give you our number in case you remember anything else after you talk to your wife. Thank you!" After scribbling down his number, she hung up and turned back to me dramatically.

"Hunter Moon was the name of his dentist about ten years ago, he thinks."

"How do we contact him? Does he have his number?"

"Oh. Well, no," Liv said, slightly deflated. "He doesn't remember any of that. And he said it might have been Harry. But it's a start!"

We scoured the Internet for every possible combination of *dentist*, *Hunter*, *Harry*, and *Moon*, but still nothing turned up.

While Liv was getting us some more coffee, and I was aimlessly scrolling through different organizations on the Web, I searched for Sam on the Writers Guild of America website, and reread his IMDB page. I'd seen it a million times before, of course, but I wanted to see his name again. I wanted to see if I felt any differently when I saw it. I read the entry critically. It was only when I got to *On the Royal Road* that I started to feel slightly sick. Would I ever be able to think about that movie again without wondering what may have happened in Charleston?

Val's disappearance after that summer had been unexplained, yet in some ways, it made perfect sense. We'd never had that much in common, and besides I didn't exactly match her effortless Hollywood style. No matter what kind of hair product/blow-dry combination I tried, my hair would never be as smooth as hers. When we hung out, we spent most of the night with her explaining who I'd been eating dinner across from for the last three hours—I had a serious problem with actor recognition—and the night usually ended with me begging off from the next bar because I had to cite-check a brief when I got home.

Despite that, when Val first got back from South Carolina and was ignoring my texts religiously, I was convinced I had done something wrong, that maybe Sam had unintentionally passed on some kind of miscommunication from me. I wondered if I was too needy, always asking her for advice while struggling with my first ever long-distance relationship. I couldn't figure out what I had done to upset her. I wondered if maybe something bad happened to her over the summer, if maybe she was going through something that had nothing to do with me and needed me to push through to show her I was there for her. So I did. I wrote her umpteen messages and e-mails to that end, all different versions of the question "Is everything okay?"

I told myself to drop it, that sometimes we never know why people do the things they do. But something had arisen in me, the old familiar feeling of being summarily rejected for no reason. It drove a pit of fear and anxiety into the lining of my stomach. It made me wonder what I was doing to drive people away. This led me to do something I'd never thought I would do. I signed up for therapy.

I attended for a grand total of three weeks. My therapist was named Dr. Majdi, a sexy Persian psychiatrist in Downtown Los Angeles who took my insurance and shouted at me while she posed meaningful hypotheticals that served only to confuse me.

"Suppose my only *familial* relationship was with a person who wasn't really capable of *being there*, who disappeared halfway through my *adolescence*. I would have an issue with *abandonment*," she stressed during my second session. I wasn't sure if she spoke this way because it was her general cadence, or because she was incredibly frustrated with me.

"That sounds awful. That happened to you?" I asked, genuinely concerned, sipping my water cup and relieved the attention was off me for a minute. I studied a bowl of Nature Valley granola bars she had set out on the coffee table. Did anyone actually eat those during therapy? They were so crumbly, that had to be a gigantic mess. There weren't even any napkins. It was a disaster waiting to happen. Although I supposed you could use a tissue if you were really desperate. There were certainly plenty of those.

"This is an *example*, Emma. No, this did not happen to me. It happened to *you*. I am trying to explain why you always assume the *worst*, why you always think everyone around you will fail you, will let you down, will *leave* you. Why you are terrified of being, and yet convinced you will be, *left*." As she spoke, she gestured wildly with her pen, but her carefully blown-out caramel-brown hair remained perfectly in place.

"Oh, right. Definitely. I completely agree." I wanted Dr. Majdi to know how much I appreciated her opinion and what a good job she was doing. I also wanted to ask her what wrinkle cream she used. She looked ridiculously young for a shrink. She stared back at me, as if I wasn't quite getting it. I suspected this was the case.

"Emma, when children experience any sort of *trauma* they blame themselves, because children cannot see the experience through any other *perspective*. They are not old enough to understand that people have other motivations, which have nothing to do with *them*."

"That makes a lot of sense."

Dr. Majdi stared at me and said, "Do you understand how this may relate to *you*?"

I bit my lip, stumped.

I wasn't trying to be difficult. I was genuinely there because I wanted to feel better. I wanted to stop obsessing about how I'd lost my friend, about what was wrong with me. I'd given Dr. Majdi the entire backstory when I arrived. I told her that I'd never met my dad, that my mom and I were practically strangers, and that despite my relationship with Sam, I was convinced I would end up alone. I explained with clinical detachment that whenever something good happened, I was basically waiting for it to be taken away.

Dr. Majdi looked concerned and even a little disappointed as I shared my background with her. I was pretty sure her reaction had something to do with my casual tone when I explained the situation, as if I were telling a story that had happened to someone else. As if I were reporting what had happened in the most recent season of *Game of Thrones* to someone who hadn't watched it. Not that I would hang out with an individual with such poor judgment.

In any case, I told her everything. I was honest. When she asked questions, or asked for examples of memories, I offered them up. In our second session, I told her about the time I was in a school play that was going to be performed on Father's Day. My teacher told our class that our dads would get to sit in the front row.

"Do you remember how you *felt* when you heard this, Emma?" she asked.

"Yes, I remember that moment exactly. I remember feeling sad and then saying to myself, Don't be sad about this, Emma. And then I wasn't," I reported proudly to Dr. Majdi. "I told myself to stop caring, and I did. I was fine."

Dr. Majdi sighed audibly, turned to a fresh page in her notebook, and probably mentally reorganized her closet to account for all the new pairs of shoes she was going to buy with my forthcoming insurance checks. Then she tried to explain that I wasn't really "fine." I just *told myself* that I was fine.

According to Dr. Majdi, we had two issues to tackle. I quickly organized them in my mind, like the lawyer on a lunch break that I was. There was one, my history with abandonment (father, physically; mother, emotionally, I subcategorized); and two, the neutral standpoint I'd adopted for coping with this history (in other words, my nonemotive explanation of the dad I'd never met and the mom who didn't really like me). The fact that I'd told myself not to care, so, accordingly, I didn't. Conclusion: This was unhealthy.

"You have may have *told* yourself that you don't care, Emma, and that you were *fine*. But this was simply a coping mechanism. The pain and hurt from those experiences, they *went* somewhere. A good one, I have to admit. You were a *strong little girl*. But that didn't make the pain go away. You braced yourself from the *pain*. You held it at *bay*. This worked at the time. But this approach will not *serve you well* in the long run."

What she was saying made sense, and it was probably good advice, but it made me realize that therapy wasn't what I needed, not at that moment, anyway. The ability to freeze my pain and tell myself not to be sad about my mom and dad was one of the things I was most proud of. Why would I want to break that habit?

I was honest about this when I quit therapy, explaining to Dr. Majdi that I liked the coping mechanisms I had developed.

"Why would I stop doing the thing that got me through life up until this point?"

"Because you don't *need* them anymore. You are not the same little girl. You have good friends, a job, a relationship. You have *security*. You need to face the bad things when they happen to you and when you *recall* the painful memories of your past, not *push them away*. Emma, you must turn *into* the wave of pain and let it wash over you. Because if not, someday after you have dived under these waves *time* after *time*, one will come along that is *too big* to avoid. And when it hits, you're going to be *flattened*."

CHAPTER 10

After Liv and I decided we'd done enough fruitless Hunter research for one day, we headed back, exhausted, to Carrick's place. Liv wanted to take a long shower, so I decided to go out for a coffee. Fresh air and a minute of quiet time sounded nice.

I walked to a nearby Italian coffee shop—the kind with a gorgeous awning and comfortable chairs that seem mandatory to San Francisco—and sat down at a wrought iron table by the window. Latte and scone in hand, I experienced an "I'm going to be okay" feeling, which I held on to desperately. The good news, I comforted myself, is that I'm on vacation and eating pastries at a lovely coffee shop, rather than in my office in Downtown L.A. with a Kind bar and a cup of lukewarm coffee, writing a motion for summary judgment, as I had spent so many weekends prior. I watched a mom at the next table silently hand pieces of croissant to her daughter, who was quietly reading a picture book. I briefly wondered what Caro would say if she knew what I was up to. I hadn't told her about the search for the simple reason that it wasn't any of her business. It would be like telling a current-day secret to someone who was your best friend in elementary school but you haven't seen since. Sure, you once held hands and shared graham crackers during snack time, but it's pointless if she doesn't know you now, if she doesn't know how much you hate your job or who the last ex-boyfriend to drunk text you was. It's the little things.

From the corner of my eye, I noticed someone familiar entering the café. He was wearing a blue-and-black-plaid shirt and looked almost too tall to make it under the fancy entrance.

"Dusty?" I called over to him.

"Hey! How are you?" he answered, heading over. This must be his local coffee shop, I figured quickly. It's just a coincidence. Despite that, I felt a slight flush at his appearance. It's because he's an attractive guy you don't know very well, I reminded myself. Don't be weird.

"I'm good," I said, when he reached my table. "How's your Sunday going?"

"Great. So, I have to admit, this isn't a random run-in," he said. "I saw the note you left for Liv. I don't have your phone number or I would have called."

"Oh, okay. What's up?"

"I wanted to tell you what I was thinking last night after we talked. About you—and your dad, the mythological Hunter Moon," he quickly added. "I wanted to tell you, but I wasn't sure if I should."

He paused then. I nodded encouragingly for him to go on. "The thing is, I've been there. I grew up with my mom and twin sister. I never knew my dad either. It's not exactly the same because I finally met him when I was sixteen—unfortunately, since he turned out to be kind of a bastard—but I get the allure of wanting to fill out your family tree." As he spoke, Dusty endearingly, if nervously, ran both hands through his hair and over the back of his neck.

"I made this huge deal out of finding him, and then when I did, he took me out to dinner and gave me his business card, like we were at a stupid networking event or something. He said to let him know if I needed money, or a college recommendation," Dusty recalled painfully. "He lives in Fairfield, Connecticut, with his new family. It's such a cliché. But I guess those are around for a reason, right?"

"Right," I said quietly.

"I never even told my mom or sister that I met him. Actually, I've never told anyone. It was too embarrassing. His reaction I mean." He looked at me. His face read unhappy but composed. He had accepted that this was the hand he'd been dealt, and he had it under control. It was a look I recognized. Also familiar was the way he lightened the conversation and changed its focus to me immediately after sharing his story. "So anyway, about Hunter Moon, great name by the way."

"I know, it's so silly," I said, with an odd flush of delight. It was definitely more fun to have an absent father with a catchy name than a boring one.

"Maybe it's fake," Dusty suggested. "And he's some San Francisco celebrity operating under cover. George Lucas? Gavin Newsom?"

"Maybe Gavin! I don't want to brag but I *was* in student government."

Dusty laughed, surely relieved we were back on a more comfortable topic. "I can tell. You have leadership skills."

"What about your mom? Can she help?" It was the same question Liv had asked in the car. It was the obvious one. It also happened to be my least favorite. Explaining my relationship with my mom is an inevitably painful activity. For one, it's semidepressing, and for another, it usually disappoints the person who's asking. Usually when people find out I was raised by a single mother they assume we were best friends, that it was "us against the world." It's hard to explain to someone that for me, the experience was like two pieces of bone rubbing together, with no cartilage to operate as buffer. Tense, sharp edged, and often painful. Gilmore Girls, we were not.

"We aren't close. Honestly, I don't even want her to know I'm doing this. Sorry, I know that's not what you want to hear."

"I don't want to hear anything," Dusty said. "That came out wrong." He smiled. "What I mean is, I don't have any expectations for anything you're going to tell me. Whatever you say is okay."

"Thanks. And Dusty, thanks for telling me about your dad."

"Of course. And seriously, I don't know if you need this, but I'd like to help you find him, however I can."

"Thanks, I really appreciate that." It was nice to have another ally in the search for Hunter. That he was a computer whiz who'd been in my fatherless shoes was a nice bonus. I felt a sudden surge of optimism. Maybe I really would find Hunter. And if I could find Hunter and get some answers, maybe I could find some peace. Figure out what to do about Sam.

"I still haven't gotten to the reason I came to find you. Last night, I was thinking how we came up with nothing when we did our searches. No hits at all. There's no record of this guy. Which isn't that weird when you think about it. He's old enough that everything he's ever done isn't online. Not like with us."

"Right. I mean, he could find me on the Internet in two seconds flat." I tried not to think about what this implied about how much my birth father might want to meet me.

"Exactly! That's what I was thinking. Then I thought, if he has one daughter who's easy to find, you know what else he might have . . ." He paused as it sank in.

"Another one," I answered slowly, taking in the realization. I was instantly filled with the same excitement reflected in Dusty's eyes. "He might be off the grid . . ."

"But maybe he has a *kid* who isn't." He sat back proudly.

"We shouldn't be looking for only Hunter, but for his potential offspring as well." I looked at him expectantly, and Dusty nodded. "Wow. That's a great idea, Dusty. But won't looking for any Moon still get a lot of hits?"

"Right, we have to run really specific searches. I was thinking, what about alumni or student databases? This guy could have a kid in college or grad school. And if he lives in California, where do you think he would send his kids?"

I held up my finger to say I knew exactly what he was getting to.

Without a word, I opened up the University of California's web page on my phone, where they had data on the gazillions of students who had attended the nine campuses over the years. I clicked on the link to alumni relations and typed in my password. I looked for the all-student search box and typed in my last name. One millisecond later, I had two hits. I gripped Dusty's arm so hard I practically pulled it off the table.

"There's me. And there's . . . Tyler Moon," I read aloud. "He's a freshman at Berkeley." I was suddenly terrified to be so close. Scared that it could be this easy.

"What's his home address?" Dusty asked faintly, equally shocked that his idea may have worked.

"I don't know, it only has his e-mail address." This could be it. This could be the moment I found my father. All I had to do was push play on the rest of the scene.

"Let's e-mail him," I said, before I could change my mind.

"Are you sure, Emma? What are we gonna say?" Dusty said, now looking nearly as nervous as I was. "We can't exactly ask for parents' contact information."

"Oh, yes, we can," I said knowingly. "You want a college kid's address? All you have to do is ask where to send the bills."

"Whoa. You're good," he said, thoroughly impressed. I felt inordinately pleased by his compliment.

"Can I borrow this?" I asked, pointing to Dusty's phone. I figured Tyler wouldn't question an e-mail from Dusty, given the ridiculous amount of information sharing that goes on these days, whereas emma.moon@gmail.com might alert him that something was up. I quickly typed an e-mail requesting his home address for some overdue tuition bills.

For the next few minutes after I sent it, Dusty and I tried unsuccessfully to make small talk, both of us distracted by the existence of Tyler Moon across the bay. Finally we heard a small *ping* of incoming mail on his phone and nearly jumped out of our seats. Dusty grabbed the phone.

"'Hey. Sure,'" he read slowly. "'You can send all bills to my home address below, so I don't get stuck with them. ROFL.'" Dusty paused. "What does that mean?"

"Rolling on the floor laughing. It's stupid. Keep going."

"Then he lists a home address, which is less than a mile from here." I felt my heart jump as Dusty scrolled. "Okay, Tyler, we don't need the full zip code. Holy shit, Emma. There is one more line at the end."

"What?" I demanded. "Read it." Dusty cleared his throat.

"'By the way, the bill should be addressed to my dad. His name is Hunter Moon.'"

I burst back into the room to tell Liv about our breakthrough. "I think we may have found him, Liv! I really do. Dusty had this great idea. It's a long story, but I feel really good about this."

"Dusty, as in our roommate? That is amazing, Em. You can tell me all about it over dinner because I am starving, but before that, you need to do something else. No arguments, Emma, I'm putting my foot down. I'm not eating until you call Sam."

"You're going on hunger strike?" I laughed, still giddy about our discovery.

"Yes. You have to deal with it, Emma. You have to ask him what happened with Val. You have to talk to him."

CHAPTER 11

S am answered the phone after a single ring.

"Hey, babe! How's the trip going? I miss you," he said.

"Hey. I miss you, too," I said, ignoring his question.

"How's Napa? Are you girls wrapped in seaweed right now and debating which *Real Housewives* series is the best?"

"No, we both know it's New York," I answered automatically. "Although Beverly Hills is a close second."

"I miss you," he repeated. "Tell me about Napa." I looked around the small park I found down the street from the apartment to make my call as I considered his directive. *Okay, well, how about, I skipped out on the fancy lodge you surprised us with and came to San Francisco to go on a secret mission to find my father. Oh, and I have doubts about marriage in general. Does that about cover it?*

"I'm so glad you called," he continued, oblivious. "I was worried at dinner the other night. The money fight. And I know you were upset on Friday morning when I mentioned adding another room on to the house. I want our home to be perfect, but I didn't mean to make you worry. I know how that stuff stresses you out.

"You didn't call me back last night," he went on, without a trace of accusation, only confusion. "Is everything okay?" Instantly, he sounded nervous, his usual steadiness shaken. I wanted to say yes, everything is fine. I wanted to hang up and worry about all of this another time. Actually, I wanted to ignore it for the rest of my life. But the fear had become too much; the dread in my chest had expanded to the point that I could no longer properly breathe.

"I ran into Val," I said, before I could consider the wisdom of bringing her up.

"Who? Which Val? Valerie Babbitt?"

"Yes." I was silent, losing my nerve. Before I could talk myself out of it, I blurted out, "She said some stuff about you guys hooking up. While we were together." When he didn't respond immediately, my stomach started convulsing. As the seconds ticked by, the uneasiness turned to full-throttle panic. He wasn't denying it. Why wasn't he denying it? I wanted to cry, or scream, or find the nearest black hole and fall into it. Because at that moment I knew. The second he paused I knew that Val wasn't confused, crazy, or lying. I knew it was true.

"Emma. I don't know what to say. I am so sorry."

"You're *sorry*? So it's true? What is going on?" I exploded, feeling myself lose control as the words escaped my lips. All I could think was, *No, no, no.*

"I can't begin to tell you how sorry I am. I would love a chance to explain it all. If it makes you feel any better, I have felt sick about this since the day it happened."

"No. It doesn't. Not at all. How could this be true, Sam?"

"I don't know. But it is," he said miserably.

"Why didn't you tell me?" I cried. "Why did I have to find out like this?"

"I don't know, it was wrong. I was wrong. It was the biggest mistake I've ever made. I panicked. And I lied because I was scared."

"You lied because you were *scared*?" I said, as meanly as possible.

"Yes. I didn't want to lose you. I thought if you never knew, it would be better. It meant nothing. It was nothing. Please believe me. Charleston was such a stupid, meaningless mistake. I was freaking out. I thought we were about to break up."

"I don't care *why* you did it. I care *that* you did it," I practically wailed, thinking that I finally understood the true meaning of the term *gut-wrenching*. I was pretty sure that if I looked down, I would see my guts down there, lying on the ground. "I thought it wasn't true." The last thing I'd been pinning my hope on, the hope on which my entire future depended, was washed away. On the other end of the line, Sam was silent. The only thing he could say that would have made it better—that this awful thing that had happened wasn't true—was impossible. "But it's more than that," I told him. "She was my friend, Sam." I shuddered visibly. "How long was this going on?" I asked the question before I could change my mind, even though I was afraid the answer might kill me.

"It only happened once," Sam answered immediately. "I never did anything like that before or since. I made a huge mistake, but it was only once."

"Maybe that's true. Or maybe you're lying. I have no idea. What else don't I know?"

"Nothing. I didn't want you to know because it meant nothing. Less than nothing. I didn't want to hurt you. Because it didn't matter." My heart sank even deeper as I started to fully register that there was no possibility this whole thing was a misunderstanding. It was true.

"If you didn't want to hurt me, you shouldn't have cheated on me," I spat out. "I have to go. I can't talk to you anymore."

Sam paused, as if assessing his options and choosing the logical and reasonable path.

"I understand," he said quietly. "I'll give you some space to think this through, but please know that I love you. And there's more to say. More to explain."

"I have to go, Sam. I can't . . . I can't do this anymore," I said, not sure exactly what I was referencing. "I have to go," I repeated, hanging up before he could respond.

In the law, most crimes require that the person had a certain level of mental involvement at the time of the offense, in addition to the physical action, in order to be found guilty. The Latin term for it is *mens rea*, which technically means "guilty mind." This means that what you were thinking or intending at the time you "committed a crime" may determine your level of guilt. Depending on your *mens rea*—did you do it on purpose, by accident, or because you were being lazy or stupid?—you can be found guilty of a different crime, at a different level of seriousness. This is true despite the fact that each crime requires the same physical component.

For example, if you intentionally shoot a teller while robbing a bank, that would be murder. However, if you shoot a gun into the sky at a festival to start a footrace—seems unnecessarily dramatic, but maybe you're in Texas—and it falls and hits someone innocently buying a funnel cake, you've committed negligent homicide. But if you're cleaning your malfunctioning hunting rifle and someone pushes you, causing it to fire against your will and shoot your neighbor Stanley, that's an accident. All of the acts are the same— shooting a gun and killing someone—but the mental component, and the resulting crime (and accompanying jail time), is vastly different.

However, there are also crimes that don't require any level of *mens rea*, called "strict liability" crimes. It doesn't matter whether it was your intention to commit the crime, if you had any idea what you were doing was illegal, or if it was completely unavoidable—if you committed the physical act, you're as guilty as they come. One of those crimes is statutory rape. You can tell an officer of the law until you're blue in the face that you didn't know she was under the age of consent and, in fact, you met in a bar where patrons have to be twenty-one to get in. Doesn't matter. Congratulations, you're a rapist. Another example is traffic law. If you committed the crime, it doesn't matter if you *meant to* or not. So the next time you think about telling the officer you didn't know the speed limit, try crying instead; that's far more likely to get you out of the ticket.

Sam's crime of sleeping with Val would be, without a doubt, a strict liability crime. Maybe he didn't intend to break my heart, much less for me to find out about it the week before our wedding, but it didn't matter. It didn't matter that maybe Sam's *mens rea* wasn't present when he committed the crime, that his intentions were more stupid and weak than intentionally evil. So what if he didn't *mean* to hurt me this badly, or *intend* to cause the resulting pain? He was totally fucking guilty.

After I hung up with Sam, I walked down the street like a zombie. I was in desperate, aching pain. The pain of a person who would give anything to alter the current reality. For several minutes I inwardly begged any god I knew to make the entire thing a joke. When I was about to completely break down, I stopped dead in my tracks. I pushed stop. Stop crying, I told myself. Don't let him do this to you. Just stop. I managed to push the pain slightly out of reach. And that was when the tears in my throat morphed into a mountain of white-hot rage.

I wanted to hurt them. Both of them, Sam and Val. I wanted them to feel as badly as I did. All of the revenge fantasies I'd ever had in my life—the one about slashing the tires of the guy from Expedia who kept me on hold for an hour, or planting porn on the computer of the TA in college who gave me a D in my Intro to Nineteenth-Century European Art class—seemed like child's play. I wasn't going to cry anymore. I was going to break things. I pictured showing up at Val's new office, lowering my pitch-black sunglasses, and saying mercilessly, You ruined my life, bitch, now it's my turn to ruin yours. I pictured taking all of Sam's stuff and starting a bonfire in the middle of his yard. For the first time in my life, I understood the urge to commit arson.

When I finally made my way back to Dusty and Carrick's, I crept past the quiet living room and found Liv sitting on the bed of our large room, ready to go. She took one look at my tear-streaked face and asked what had happened, her voice filled with dread.

"He cheated on me, for real." I choked out the words, collapsing on the bed.

"No. Are you sure?"

"He admitted it. It happened when they were in Charleston. Just like Val said. Val, it turns out, was the only person who was honest with me. This is an actual nightmare."

"It is," Liv agreed quietly. "I'm so sorry. I wish I could do something."

We were silent for a few minutes. Me lying there, wishing I were dead. Liv looking at me nervously, trying to figure out how to make everything better.

"How about some food? Tony's Pizza in North Beach? A carafe of red and a large margherita pizza?" Liv suggested. I doubted anything would make me feel better, even Tony's pizza, which Liv knew I considered the best in the world. Maybe I could eat enough pizza to make me fall into some kind of gluten coma. I would eat pizza until I passed out, I decided. Every day, for the rest of my life. I closed my eyes, trying to will myself to stop picturing Sam and Val together, and trying to picture crusts dipped in marinara instead.

As my eyes focused, I saw Liv looking at me closely.

"Are you doing that thing where you decide you're just going to eat pizza for the rest of your life?"

"Yep."

"That's probably best." She swallowed and looked at me seriously. "I'm sorry, Em. I don't know what to say. I want to kill him."

"Me, too." We sat there in sad companionable silence. "I feel like such an idiot."

"You shouldn't. If it makes you feel any better, I didn't believe it either."

"Really?" I asked, sitting up slightly, momentarily comforted until I remembered that it didn't matter whether or not we had believed it or not, it had still happened.

"Yeah, not for a second. What should we do now? What would make you feel best? We can do anything you want."

What I wanted was to get under the covers and sleep until they invented a time machine so I could go back to before this all happened. But no, I told myself forcefully, there was no way Sam was going to take my dad away from me, too. Not when we'd come this far. And if I did find Hunter, maybe he'd want to kick Sam's ass himself. I entertained the image of a beefy man who somewhat resembled me slamming one fist into the other expectantly, ready to smash Sam's nose in, as soon as I gave him the go-ahead.

"I want to stay. I want to try and find my dad."

"If you're sure." We sat there in silence for a few minutes until Liv spoke up. "Speaking of Hunter, I tried Facebooking him again while you were gone." Liv pushed the open computer screen toward me. "All that comes up are some weird groups with pictures of wolves howling at moons." Liv scrolled through the page of one of the Facebook groups, absentmindedly clicking.

"Did you know his name is an actual moon phase?" she said, sounding fascinated. "Well, almost. It's called hunter's moon." Great, like there wasn't enough to worry about, without considering how astronomy could be affecting this whole thing.

"Apparently, it usually occurs in October. 'It's the first full moon after the harvest moon,'" she read. "It says here that the hunter's moon is especially bright and yellow. Which is good for hunters . . . the bright autumn moonlight . . . stocking up for winter . . . et cetera. Makes sense." Liv clicked on the profiles of some of the likers. "Also, how is it possible that some people still don't understand privacy settings? I'm looking at this random girl's 'moon appreciation' pictures from St. Martin right now. I mean, that's ridiculous. Ooh, that's a cute bathing suit. Do you think I could pull off a bandeau?"

As I listened to Liv try to keep me entertained, I felt myself drift back to what I'd learned about Sam. I could still barely believe it, but the stabbing pain in my heart was slowly spreading into a sickening realization that it was true. I had to press my hand against my heart, as badly as it hurt.

I thought about the last time my heart had truly been broken, when my study abroad boyfriend, Laurent, a beautiful Parisian with huge mahogany eyes and milky skin, broke up with me.

Laurent and I shared a lust that was born of passion, given that we never actually discussed anything beyond each other's favorite body parts, and Hemingway. We would spend entire days lying prostrate in Le Jardin du Luxembourg, his sweater under our heads and our hands intertwined as we discussed how much he loved my ass, me his eyes, and both of us, *A Moveable Feast*.

Every day in Paris was a new adventure. A backdoor viewing of the Musée Picasso, a trip to get falafel that somehow turned erotic, him reading French poetry to me in the last row of the bus with his left hand holding the book and his right hand up my skirt. When he took me to the countryside for the weekend to his family's vineyard, the potent combination of utter desire and champagne vinegar was almost painful. And when he said good-bye in May, on the same street where he first stopped me six months earlier and begged me to have a glass of wine with him—I think he thought the whole thing was very poetic— I thought my heart would stop beating.

Liv, who was studying in Florence at the time, tried for weeks to help me regain perspective. First from afar and then by actually coming to Paris with two American guys, one of whom I was expected to make out with, an idea that only made me more depressed. There was no way I was going to get over Laurent with some dude from Chicago named Matty who thought Paris was "pretty neat" despite the fact that "they don't put ice in the pop." When that didn't work, Liv tried another tactic, listing people who had it worse.

"At least you aren't a victim of vaginal mutilation," she pointed out. "Or a soldier in Vietnam who lost both of his legs and, as a result, his self-worth."

"Are you talking about Lieutenant Dan?" I responded, annoyed that she was trying to cheer me up by cheaply using the plot of *Forrest Gump*.

In the end, the only cure was, as they say, time. (I don't know who they are, but they really know what they're talking about.) I mourned for Laurent over the entire summer I was home before my senior year of college, eating only oatmeal, the one thing I could stomach, and studying for the LSAT. The morning I took the LSAT in October, I woke up, ate the requisite test banana, which I'd been eating before every standardized test since high school, and realized that, against my will, I was over him.

But Laurent was no Sam.

It wasn't going to be that easy to heal from this wounding revelation. Without warning, I was struck by the strangest feeling of nostalgia, and for one quick moment, I had an overwhelming desire I hadn't felt for a long time. I wanted to call my mom.

I wanted to be little again. I wanted to be taken care of. I wanted it to be one of the long-ago Sunday afternoons from my childhood, when we would go to the Georgetown movie theater that showed black-and-white classics. Caro always let me pick the movie, and beforehand we would load up on popcorn and Reese's Pieces. After all, she always said, we need to fill both our salty and our sweet stomachs. No matter what movie I picked, Caro had inevitably already seen it—a fact that I found extremely impressive as a child— and as we walked home she would reminisce about the first time she saw the film, as if she had just visited an old friend, recounting who she'd been with, what she first thought of it, even what she'd worn. But like so many other things, when she finished school and we moved to Virginia, those trips stopped.

This was brought starkly into place one afternoon a few weeks after we moved in when I ran into our neighbor Mr. Madigan, who mentioned that a small movie theater showed old movies outside on Saturday nights in the summer and fall, a program called Screen on the Green. That week the movie was *An Affair to Remember*, a favorite of my mom's. I knew for a fact that she saw it for the first time at the shore with her girlfriends. Mr. Madigan explained that everyone in the neighborhood went and brought a picnic. He told me that you could buy kettle corn and root beer at the park and encouraged me to come along. We could bring the Reese's, I thought to myself.

I came home to find Caro hanging up from a conference call and furiously highlighting documents. After grabbing a soda from the fridge, I tentatively perched on the arm of the sofa and suggested we go. She looked immediately annoyed, then stressed, then she flat-out said no, claiming she had a work fund-raiser that would take up all of her time that weekend.

When the Madigan family, laden with picnic baskets and old, scratchy blankets, stopped by on Saturday night to see if we were going, I made sure to walk out to the safely darkened front porch to meet them, so they couldn't see my face while I lied. My mom was indeed at work—whether because the excuse was true or because she was using it as a cover, I'll never know—but, too embarrassed to tell them this, I said I didn't like old movies, but thanks anyway.

Mr. Madigan looked at me questioningly, as if mentally recalling the day when I'd said the opposite, but he quickly let it go, mentioning that I should let them know if I changed my mind. Next week, he said, it was *Jaws*. For a minute I thought he was going to ask where my mom was, and his eyes shifted in the direction of our house, but then he simply smiled and told me to have a nice night.

I never did find the opportunity to tell the Madigans that I wanted to go to Screen on the Green. As the fall weather turned cooler, every Saturday night I watched the family of five stroll to the park, struggling to carry their canisters of steamy cocoa and their baskets stuffed with Cape Cod chips and homemade brownies, but I never said anything or asked to come along, even though I desperately wanted to. One week I even bought a carton of lemonade in secret, planning to run out and casually join in when they walked by. But week after week, I didn't move, I just watched. And after that first day, they never asked again.

CHAPTER 12

A s any good attorney will tell you, you can trust the testimony of an eyewitness to a crime about as far as you can throw him. This isn't only because witnesses can be liars or because of the inherent problems with mistaken visual perception. It's more than that. It's the things we miss when we think we are observing carefully, the things we choose to focus on, and, most of all, the things we automatically use to fill in the gaps.

If you saw a man in a broken-down Chevy parked across the street from where your neighbor's child was later kidnapped, upon reflection, yes, he did look suspicious. But was he dressed in a blue shirt, as the kidnapper was proven to be wearing? That sounds about right. Minutes later, you're positive. It was robin's-egg blue—not unlike the one you *actually* saw on your grocery store checker that morning.

Also, did you notice a rattling tailpipe, which would explain the sound the car made during the ransom drop-off? Yes, that makes sense, your brain says, because the image of a broken tailpipe fits in with the look of the car you actually saw, and *poof*, it becomes your memory. Before you know it, an innocent man has been convicted, all because you chose to go to Whole Foods that day instead of Trader Joe's.

As psychologists have discovered, and lawyers of the accused are quick to point out, the paradigm of how you expect the world to appear, combined with what you actually see, determines what you observe. Memories are not entirely accurate records of our experiences and what we see *isn't* always what's right in front of our eyes. We are influenced by biases, beliefs, and an automatic attempt to structure events into our existing worldview. Thus, what we observe is often a distortion of reality, but one that makes sense to our imperfect human brains.

That's probably why, when the strong oak door on Powell Street swung open on Monday morning, I knew exactly who was staring back at me. On the other side of the threshold was an attractive older gentleman in his sixties with thick salt-and-pepper hair, striking blue-gray eyes, and a dimple in only his left cheek, a mirror image to the one in my right. The second I looked into his eyes, I knew he was my father.

"Good morning," I said robotically. "Are you Hunter Moon?"

"It is I," he said, a stickler for accuracy like his grammarian daughter. My heart jumped. We had to be related. I couldn't wait to discuss our favorite dangling prepositions.

"I was wondering if we could have a few moments of your time. We're here from the Democratic National Committee," I heard myself say randomly. Where did that come from?

I felt Dusty turn to look at me slightly. Liv had woken up that morning with a migraine, mostly likely brought on by the several carafes of wine consumed at Tony's the night before. I could tell she felt terrible, but there was nothing she could do but climb back into bed with a hot washcloth on her head and a handful of Excedrin. Luckily, I passed Dusty on my way out, who was heading to work but offered to take the morning off and accompany me to Hunter's, pointing out that as the boss he could do that kind of thing on a Monday morning. I was nervous enough to agree, and now, considering how wacky this situation was becoming, I was glad I did.

"Ah, canvassing on a Monday. You young people certainly are passionate. I was about to sit down for a second cup of coffee. Would you like to join me?" he said, in a friendlier tone than I would have predicted, almost like he was expecting us. But then again, maybe he was. Maybe he was feeling the same thing I was, the father-daughter connection zapping between our identical lopsided dimples.

Ushering us inside, he offered us mugs and poured two cups of coffee, taking his time to offer us milk, sugar, and even fresh pastries. I noticed he was also a two percent milk devotee. Genetics sure had done a number on us. No wonder all I got from Caro was her hair. The rest of my DNA code was used up before she even had a chance.

Hunter turned the radio down, but not off, leaving the news on low in the background. I approved. I'd always preferred a radio to a television in the kitchen; it made me feel old-timey, like a line cook from the 1950s. I surreptitiously studied my surroundings. Gorgeous, brightly colored Le Creuset pots hung from the ceiling above a long white island, which we sat around on high stools. In the back of the kitchen there was a window seat overlooking a small backyard brimming with bougainvillea.

As Hunter turned around to fix his own cup of coffee, I nervously bit into my croissant and tried not to think about how much Sam would love the cookware. He was a sucker for a heavy ceramic pan. Perfect for bacon frying. My stomach tightened. I shook my head, annoyed that despite my resolve not to think about him, he kept creeping back in.

"Are you here on a fund-raising mission? Or is this a courtesy call, may I ask?" Hunter inquired politely, taking his own seat at the white granite counter.

What was he talking about? Oh, right, the DNC thing. Oops. I turned to Dusty and remembered, Hey, he's done the whole "find your dad" thing before, he can take it. Throwing him as far under the bus as I possibly could, I answered, "Actually, Dusty, why don't you explain?"

Without missing a beat, Dusty smoothly began to ask Hunter some generic questions about his voting habits. I watched, surprised, as the conversation naturally transitioned into one about family. Within minutes, Hunter was describing his two sons, a freshman and a senior in college. I was the older sister of two half brothers, I realized with a jolt. I could give them advice on their girl problems and tease them about their facial hair experiments. One attended Berkeley (Tyler, I had to stop myself from adding) and the other,

Kyle, went to Stanford. Apparently, they were engaged in some healthy sibling rivalry, both majoring in the combined sciences, molecular biochemical physics, or similar. Okay, so maybe they wouldn't need the girl advice.

Hunter also described his wife, who taught at a Montessori school in Marin County. She sounded like the perfect antidote to my icy, bureaucratic mother. I wondered if she would want to attend the wedding. I made a mental note to ask if she would prefer the fish, steak, or vegetarian meal. Finally, Dusty and my dad discussed the recent local election, which I supposed was meant to establish our believability as party-toting Democrats. I was quite impressed by both of their depth of knowledge of Nob Hill parking structure ordinances.

Having realized that my search was over, I started to relax. It was a feeling punctuated by the occasional jolt of recognition in the way Hunter spoke and the expressions he made when he laughed. We look alike, we talk alike, we sometimes even act alike, I sang in my head. As I watched the conversation unfold, I collected each piece of knowledge Dusty gathered, to pull out for closer examination later. A thought occurred to me—Powell Street. Hunter lived on Powell. Sam's last name. I felt a sudden rush of longing for him to be there, quickly followed by a gust of regret that I hadn't told him I was coming in the first place. We could have found my dad together, on Powell Street, then gotten married and become Emma Powell and Sam Powell, and our lives would have been perfect, you know, if he hadn't cheated on me and ruined everything. I started to feel slightly ill.

"It's been lovely chatting with you two today," Hunter slowly drawled, bringing me back to the present. For the first time I noticed that he had something of a lisp, which I quickly threw out as unnecessary judgment. Who cared? I ordered myself to stop being so superficial. What was more important: a couple of questionable "you thoo's" or a family? A family, I decided loyally. I would tell Hunter the truth as soon as he finished his thought. I wondered if he would cry.

"But I have to admit"—*thoo admit*—stop it, Emma!—"I think I know why you're here," Hunter continued, pouring his third cup of coffee. Three cups, wow, I thought. Isn't he retired? What's with the caffeine intake?

"You do?" I replied, smiling nervously.

"Yes, and I understand why you came here today, but I made up my mind about this and you can't do anything to change it." He shook his head regretfully. Hunter took in our puzzled faces and looked slightly apologetic as he continued. "I'm sorry if this comes as a surprise, but citizenship is important to me. My ancestors came over here on the *Mayflower*. I take my status as an American very seriously." Hunter might as well have been speaking gibberish. "Isn't that what you're here about?"

"I'm sorry, Mr. Moon, we're a little confused," Dusty said. "A lot of stops on the Democratic train to make today. What exactly are you referring to?"

"To what am I referring, you mean, son," Hunter corrected him.

All right, enough with the grammar.

"I assume you're here about me changing my party affiliation," Hunter said defensively. "I voted Democrat in California in every election since Jimmy Carter, so I understand why you were surprised when I switched parties in 2008."

Dusty, so chatty before, was completely silent, stumped by this tangent. "Of course, sir. Why did you switch parties, for the record?"

"Because, young man, Barack Obama is not an American citizen!" Hunter exploded, grateful to finally get it out. My mouth dropped to the floor, shocked by this crazy right-wing birther posing as my father. Did they even allow those in San Francisco?

"Hold on," I interrupted, a thought suddenly occurring to me. "You voted for Jimmy Carter in California?"

"Yes, I did. As I was saying, until I was forced to switch parties, I voted Democrat in every election since I moved here in 1976," Hunter finished, annoyed to have the spotlight stolen from his big announcement.

My mind spun. I knew one thing for a fact. My father, Hunter Moon, lived in D.C. at the time of my birth, married to a mother who made me memorize every president by election year before I was six. So in 1976, when the lispy Hunter Moon was in San Francisco dropping acid and supporting the Carter-Mondale ticket, my real father must have been still on the East Coast, still years away from having baby Emma. This Hunter Moon, despite the dimple, the grammar, and the excellent taste in cookware, could not be my dad.

CHAPTER 13

A large red-and-white Muni bus pulled up on the opposite side of the street, and Dusty and I hightailed it over, waving it down like you can only do in a city where everyone is overly nice. As we boarded, I noticed that the plump middle-aged bus driver had a dog-eared Sidney Sheldon novel tucked into his side pocket, which I assumed he read on his breaks. Or brakes. The inexplicably touching image of this sweet man paging through a thriller while he ate a sandwich during his twenty-minute lunch tugged jerkily at my already weak heartstrings.

Unaware of my observations and over-the-top emotional response to them, the driver waited for us to board, motioning for us to deposit our money in the fare box and move to the back. The bus slammed into action, gliding down the electrical wires, while I searched for cash and attempted not to fall. Finding a few dollars in the side pocket of my wallet, I was struck with an unexpected childhood memory.

My mom asking me to go upstairs to our landlord's room to look for loose dollars because I was small enough to fit under the bed. Me gathering up all the money I could find and delivering it to my mother, my face hot with shame, wanting to get the eleven dollars—I would never forget the number—off my hands as quickly as possible. We needed gas money. I shook my head to rid my consciousness of the uncomfortable memory.

"Plans tonight?" Dusty asked as I slid down in the seat next to him.

"Not really. More searching for Hunter, I guess, although who knows how."

"I have an idea. Take a night off. Carrick's band has a show at a pretty cool bar in the Mission. Why don't you and Liv come along?"

"Hold on—Carrick is in a band?" I laughed despite myself. "I thought he was a venture capitalist."

"He is, but music is his true passion." Dusty grinned. "They're actually pretty good. Maybe it'll be good for you to take your mind off things."

Dusty had no idea how right he was about that.

"You should have a little fun while you're here, shouldn't you? I don't know if you've realized this yet, but I'm really fun."

Was he flirting with me? Or just being funny? Did it matter? After all, I was engaged to be married to someone who had cheated on me and lied about it for years. The feelings of anguish rushed back, but I held them at bay. I would not start crying on a San Francisco city bus. I focused on his invitation instead. I did love live music—any kind. And despite the fact that I couldn't imagine having any *actual* fun, possibly ever again, it might be an okay distraction. Plus, Liv would probably love it, considering her smiles and hair flips in Carrick's direction the other night. Flirting or not, I couldn't spend another night with only the painful jumble of my emotions invoked by Sam and Hunter. I just couldn't.

"You know what?" I said before I could inwardly debate it any further. "That sounds great. Let me check with Liv, but she texted me that she was feeling better, so I bet she'll be into it, too. Thanks for the invite."

I turned back to face forward, my eyes settling on an alert from the San Francisco Police Department. *If you see something, say something! Under recently passed law, there is a duty to report in San Francisco. It is your legal obligation to report it if you are witness to a crime!* I'd read about this. In some cities not only was the crime itself illegal, but they were also putting a burden on any witnesses who failed to report the crime.

Without warning, my interaction with Dusty was washed away and a new distressing thought occurred to me. What about Sam's crimes? Was it possible that other people knew about those? My mind quickly flashed through a list of possible witnesses. Other friends in Venice? Dante? Some actress on their movie? I pictured this amorphous group of people shaking their heads behind my back, but not telling me a thing, and was struck with a fresh wave of rage at Sam for making me look like such a pathetic fool. There should be a duty to report this kind of behavior, I thought for the first time in my life. It was necessary for a proper functioning society. If you were betrayed, you had a right to know. You had a right to expect someone, anyone, to tell you.

As we walked down Guerrero Street on Monday night, I contemplated how many of the dive bars from a few years before had gained a line out the door and a black-and-white photo booth inside. I couldn't believe how much had changed, but, as disconnected from reality as I felt, I barely cared.

"Are you sure you're okay?" Liv asked as we walked quickly through the cold night to the bar where Carrick's band, the Springfield Isotopes, was playing. It was nighttime in San Francisco, which meant we were subjected to practically subzero temperatures, but everyone was pretending not to notice.

"Yes, Liv, I told you, I'm fine. Part of me feels like crawling into a little hole and never coming out, and the other part wants to go down to L.A. and start exacting murderous revenge on Sam, but other than that, I'm fine."

"You sound fine."

"What about you? Migraine completely gone?"

"Yep. I napped and self-medicated. While you were gone I even stopped by Equinox—there's one right down the block from Carrick's—to see if I could take a yoga class or something, but they said my Manhattan membership didn't transfer."

"That's ridiculous."

"I know! But I love it there. And they have Kiehl's. I do it for the Kiehl's." She sighed.

As we approached, Liv took out some lip gloss to freshen up. I considered asking her for some but then I realized it was pointless. There was no one I wanted to look cute for, nothing I cared about. My heart felt heavy at this thought. I vaguely considered running down the street and back to the room, so I could cry into my pillow all night.

Before I could make my getaway, I realized we were next in line, being gently pushed into the warm bar filled with people. The bar had a homey, lived-in feel. I felt the immediate urge to drink a martini, and surprised myself by being slightly comforted by the vibe. Maybe if they had pillows, I could cry into them here.

"You guys made it!" Dusty exclaimed, walking up. He was holding a beer and looking cuter than I remembered. I noticed that his green T-shirt hung perfectly on his broad shoulders. I inwardly checked myself. Did I need lip gloss now? Nope. The verdict was in. I no longer gave a shit.

"Hey, Dusty!" I attempted to summon some energy, even though all I wanted to do was lie down on one of the couches lining the wall. I reached for my inner steel core and reminded myself that if I was sad it would mean Sam had ruined my night once again. I forced my expression into a smile.

"Need a drink?" I asked. "We owe you a round or two from Saturday night. I'm headed up there anyway. You had Sierra Nevada the other night, right?"

"That would be great, thanks." He smiled.

I headed up to the bar, relieved to have a task to perform and an excuse to take a break from people for a few minutes. My phone vibrated in my purse. Without a doubt, it was Sam. He had been calling and texting all day. So far I had successfully ignored his overtures, although I was leaving my phone on vibrate instead of silent, so I suppose one sick part of me was still interested in knowing how often he was contacting me. Was that a sign that I wanted to talk to him? Or did it just mean I was human? I settled on the latter.

I approached the bar behind a man dressed in a western shirt and worn jeans. The cowboy had longish sandy blond hair and appeared to be in his late thirties. I sidled up next to him, thinking how if he tried to hit on me right now, he would most certainly get slapped. Without warning, my adrenaline rocketed. It was one of those moments where you're certain something big is about to happen. All my senses were on alert. I knew implicitly to pay attention to my surroundings, but I wasn't sure why. He turned around and that was when I realized, *That's no cowboy; that's Sexy Tony Brown.* For a beat, we stared at each other in disbelief.

"Emma Moon?" he finally exclaimed, leaning in for a kiss on the cheek, which I attempted to resist as much as possible short of physically pushing him away.

"Hi, Professor Brown." My mind worked frantically, trying to think of ways to get him out of the bar before Liv noticed him. Tell the bartender he roofied me? Then I'd have to play dead the rest of the night. Scream fire? That might involve jail time. "What are you doing here?"

"I live here, remember? And, Emma, you know you can call me Tony."

"Right," I said robotically. He lived in the Bay Area, of course. But I'd never even considered we might run into him on this trip. What was I supposed to say to him? I no longer had to be nice to him, I realized. He wasn't my professor anymore. I gave him the meanest look possible, narrowing my eyes in a way I'd only read about in books.

"Is there something in your eye?" he asked, concerned. I dropped the look.

"No, I'm fine. Are you still at Berkeley?"

"Sure am. Still teaching Torts to 1Ls who don't know what a tort is, just like you," he teased. That joke again?

"I can't believe you still remember that. Good memory." What I really wanted to say was, Get a new schtick, asshole. Isn't that what his class was for? To teach us? I hated him. "How are the kids this year?" I tried to make being a law professor sound akin to babysitting, in an attempt to win some ground.

"We've only just gotten started, but they seem great. Although, it's been much less interesting since you and Olivia left, I'll give you that."

I fake laughed and turned toward the bar, managing to get the bartender's attention in record time—that's the trick, I inwardly noted, you really have to *want it*—and ordered a beer and two martinis, one gin, dirty, and the other vodka, with a twist.

"Vodka martini with a twist?" Professor Brown looked at me and raised an eyebrow knowingly.

Fuck. I forgot that Liv's drink was a dead giveaway.

I thought as quickly as possible, pretending I was in the back of his classroom being asked to recite the facts of a case I didn't read. Say something, Moon!

"You guessed it," I said awkwardly. "Actually, we're here to see some guy who's in love with her. He's in the band," I added, hoping that would intimidate him.

"Oh, really?" He laughed. "This I have to see."

As I paid for the drinks, Professor Brown picked up his own, as well as Liv's, and indicated that I should lead the way. Dammit, I'd gotten cocky. I was trying to make Liv look hot and unapproachable in a way that I would tell her about later, when we were safely blocks away from Sexy Tony Brown and his odd western attire, but I'd crossed the line and piqued his interest. The scary part was—and I'd never admit this to Liv—he was somehow even more attractive than when we were in law school. Maybe it was the longer hair. Or the snap buttons.

I picked up my overflowing martini glass and Dusty's beer and walked back to Liv, trying to signal to her with my eyes that there was a surprise in store for her behind me, and not a good one. She looked up from the conversation, midlaughter, and glanced at me expectantly, until she noticed my face. But before my eyes could get out the full sentence, she saw him. You know how people say theatrically, "all of the blood drained from her face"? At that moment I realized it wasn't just an expression. It really happens. On making eye contact with STB, Liv looked like she had seen an *actual* ghost. Which I guess, in a sense, she had.

"Olivia, it is wonderful to see you," said Professor Brown, kissing her cheek far differently from the way he'd kissed mine and placing her drink in her hands. Despite the circumstances, he was in control and comfortable, as always.

"Hi, Tony. This is unexpected." Liv looked unsteady as she spoke, most likely vacillating between shock and pure, full-throttle attraction.

"A wonderful surprise. You look beautiful," he said softly, giving her a look that I was embarrassed to witness. I felt Dusty turn to me and looked up to meet his surprised face. I shrugged, pushed his beer toward him without a word and turned my attention back to the lovebirds. I felt I had to intervene but I wasn't sure how. This guy may have been my number one enemy of all time, but he was still my professor at one point. I couldn't exactly yell at him to go away. I cursed my inherent respect for authority.

"How are you?" Dusty asked me, attempting to reclaim my attention. "What's on the agenda for tomorrow? I have to work in the morning, but I could take the afternoon off and help out."

I paused, surprised by his offer, which made me feel both better and slightly uncomfortable. Was he asking to hang out with me, or was he asking to help me find my dad?

"If you and Liv need another assistant, I mean," he added hurriedly. He's just being nice, I chided myself, embarrassed by my awkwardness. Stop thinking that every time he offers to run a Facebook search he's asking you on a date.

"We're thinking we might check out the library again in the morning. Maybe look up some old newspaper archives, Ashley Judd style. You know, for the headline *Newly Single Billionaire Moves to*

San Francisco in the year of my birth. That kind of thing. Otherwise, sure, you can help us start combing the streets." San Francisco was, what, seven miles across? How hard could it be? Although it seemed like half of the population was in this bar, I thought, getting jostled from every angle. Should I just try yelling "Hunter" and see if anyone answered?

The music from the speakers started fading out. The band was about to start and if I didn't cut in soon, Liv was going to forget all about our purpose in coming tonight and fall back in love with the asshole. All at once, the merits of Carrick and his wolflike smile were ever so clear.

"Hey, Liv," I said, pushing into their conversation, "maybe we should get a little closer. You know, so we can throw our underwear at Carrick like proper groupies." I looked at her and Dusty encouragingly for support.

"Yeah, let's get closer," Dusty said. "I, for one, would enjoy seeing that."

I reddened slightly. Luckily, I heard the band tuning up and looked up to see Carrick taking the stage, along with his bandmates. I was pleasantly surprised to see him carrying a bass. I'd fearfully pictured him as an obnoxious lead singer, filled with teenage angst. Bass players were cool. My hope blossomed for Carrick and Liv's imaginary future, born from a base hatred of STB.

Meanwhile, Dusty used this opportunity to grab my left hand—the one not holding my drink—to guide me forward. The switchboard for my nerve endings reacted. It's because it's unfamiliar; it doesn't mean anything, I scolded my oxytocin levels. You don't like this guy. Tony turned back to me and started to say something—but he stopped when he noticed my hand.

"Emma Moon, are you engaged?" he asked, glancing at the antique diamond ring Sam had given me the previous November.

The memories came, unbidden. Last fall, on a cool L.A. night, Sam took me to Bruno's, my favorite family-run Italian restaurant where they serve wine in gorgeous handmade ceramic jugs and homemade spaghetti on paper placemats with not-to-scale maps of Italy. After dinner he suggested we sit by my fire pit, took both my hands in his, and asked me to spend the rest of my life with him. It was perfect. This memory, obviously, made me want to throw up.

Tony, who clearly had no idea the emotional hole he'd pushed me down, gave Dusty a sidelong glance, using his cheating sixth sense to instantly determine that this was not indeed my fiancé. I'm not like you, Professor Dickhead! I wanted to shout. I decided right then and there that it was time to grow a pair, for Liv, if not for myself.

"Hey, Liv, I think I left my card at the bar. Come get it with me," I instructed, not giving anyone a chance to cut in. The music was starting, and it was actually pretty good, rock with a hint of a reggae beat. "Be right back," I said forcefully, dragging Liv behind me and leaving STB and Dusty with no other choice but to head toward the stage.

"We're leaving," I said, definitively, when we reached the bar. Liv was staring down sadly. She absentmindedly picked up and shuffled the pile of decorative coasters and free postcards advertising events and other bars in the area.

"Some of these are kind of cool," she said, examining them.

"Liv, focus."

Of all the bars in the freaking Bay Area, why did we have to run into STB? What an awesome vacation this was turning out to be. First Val, now Tony. I pushed my own issues down, which kept bobbing to the surface against my will, and handed her the last drops of my drink. Despite the emotional beating my soul had taken recently, right now she needed it more than I did.

"Come on, let's go," I said. It was time for this day to be over. I took the postcards from her hand to put them back on the bar. When I turned them over, the one on top caught my eye. It was an advertisement for an art show at a gallery in Hayes Valley. In bold blue letters, oblivious to the heart-stopping reaction they were causing, it read:

THE SELECTED WORKS OF HUNTER MOON

I searched frantically for a date. The show was tomorrow.

CHAPTER 14

"Is it weird to be the first one there?" I asked nervously. The Magic Postcard, as we'd taken to calling it, stated that the show started at 11:00 A.M. We weren't going to waste a second. I checked out my slightly bohemian outfit, a striped sweater, patterned jeans, and ankle boots. As an artist I thought he might appreciate the mixing of patterns. I hugged this thought to myself. Was my dad an artist? That would be the coolest thing in the world.

"Yes. But it's also weird to traipse across the country looking for your dad and find his name on a Magic Postcard," Liv pointed out.

The night before, as soon as we got home, we'd tried Googling *Hunter Moon* and *artist*, hoping he might have a website, but the only thing we could find were some small mentions of shows at various galleries in the area. The good news was that he appeared to be real and in San Francisco. Despite what had happened the day before, I couldn't help but feel positive. This had to be him.

"Hello!" boomed a loud voice as we walked in the open doors of the small funky gallery on Chestnut Street. "Are you here for the show?"

I looked up and saw the huge smile of a man I assumed was the gallery owner inviting me in. I couldn't help but smile back. He was notably tall with an open, cheerful face, freckles splattered across his nose, and curling blond hair. He looked to be in his early fifties and slightly resembled Robert Redford with his lean figure and boyish attractiveness.

After ushering us in, he continued straightening pieces of artwork in preparation for the show, which had technically started three minutes earlier. Around us were huge, expensive-looking landscapes and wire sculptures hanging from a vaulted ceiling. I heard Jacqueline Taïeb, a French singer I loved from the yé-yé era, singing her whispery lyrics in the background. It was lovely. I decided this was a sign to dive right in.

"Yes, we are. Is this Hunter Moon's show?" I asked.

"It is!" he answered cheerily, fusing the words to give them a British lilt, although he was definitely American. He smiled at us like he was on the verge of laughing at a joke, which made me want to tell him one.

I felt instantly more at ease. But despite his welcoming manner, my throat was dry and my heartbeat had tripled its normal rate. Was it possible to get a heart attack at the age of twenty-nine? I cursed myself for quitting, after a single torturous session, those barre classes Liv had made me sign up for the last time she was in L.A.

"You can find Hunter's works scattered around the gallery among some of the permanent collection," he explained. "It's a bit informal here, as you can see," he added quietly, with an odd hint of disapproval in his voice, given that it appeared to be his gallery. "Are you looking for anything in particular?"

"Actually, yes," Liv cut in. I gave her a warning look. She motioned for me to start talking. I faltered, but then remembered how many pastries I had consumed before realizing that Hunter #1 was a right-wing extremist the day before. Maybe it was best to get to the point.

"I'm looking for the artist. Hunter Moon, himself." I paused, unsure of how much information to provide. Suddenly, the story of Dusty's first meeting with his dad flashed through my head. I held up my finger and dug through my purse. I found a business card and pushed it into his hand. He studied it for a minute, slightly perplexed.

"Unfortunately, Hunter's not here right now," he explained. "He went to get a coffee. He should be back in about five minutes."

"Look, I know the artists don't like to talk to the collectors at these types of things," Liv said, jumping in, "and I get it. But this isn't about the art—although your gallery looks amazing." He tried to cut in, but Liv plunged ahead.

"Just between us, and this is a crazy story, Emma *Moon* here"— she pointed at the card still in his hand—"is trying to find her father, who she's never met. And she's here today because she's pretty sure that Hunter *Moon*, who is showing today, *is him*." There was a pause while we all three absorbed her explanation.

"I am so sorry," he said, turning to me. "But I'm afraid there's been a miscommunication—I'm not the gallery owner."

"Oh. Well, that's okay," I answered, unclear about the importance of the distinction.

"That's the thing. I don't work here. My name is Leo. I'm Hunter's partner. I have been since before you were born." He said this empathetically, and I caught the slightly Midwest twang in his voice that must come out only when he shows emotion. He seemed genuinely regretful to have to deliver the next sentence. "There's no way that he could be your father. Hunter Moon is gay."

I was stunned into silence. When I finally was able to find the words, I choked out, "Right, of course." I didn't know what else to say. In all the times I'd gone over in my head the ways in which this afternoon could turn out, this was the one twist I hadn't anticipated.

"Thank you for your time. I'm really sorry," I said, my voice trailing off in embarrassment at both the unnecessary drama of the situation and my icky hetero-assumptions.

"Don't be sorry, please. Do you want to come in and chat? Hunter should be back in a minute. You can explain to us why you, beautiful girl with the amazing cheekbones, are searching for your father. *Scandal* wasn't on last night and I'm dying for some good gossip." His eyes twinkled hopefully, begging me to cheer up.

"That's okay," I answered, too disappointed to even smile in response. "Thank you for being so nice, but it's not that interesting a story."

"I cannot believe this!" Liv exploded, as soon as we hit the pavement, startling a couple sharing the sidewalk.

"What do you mean?" I replied wearily.

"Where *is* he? Why can't we find him?" Liv peppered the air with questions, throwing up her arms in frustration and nearly smacking another passerby in a suit. "We're not total idiots, right?" Assuming this was rhetorical, I shrugged in response. I was too tired to join her outburst. I understood why she was upset. This was her first time almost finding Hunter. I, on the other hand, was used to it.

Was it possible that I was wrong about Hunter living in San Francisco in the first place? Could the right Hunter Moon be living happily in an adobe in New Mexico or a condo on Miami Beach? For the first time, I wished I'd started the search earlier, tried harder. I needed this entire ridiculous escapade to be worth it. A thought occurred to me. What if my father's legal name wasn't Hunter at all? What if it was short for something, like Hunterson? Ew. I hoped not. Or was it possible that my mom had made him up entirely? I certainly wouldn't put it past her. But no, I'd seen the birth certificate and marriage license once when I'd been snooping. Hunter Moon was my father, that much was for sure. So where was he? My mind settled on the dentist, Hunter Moon, DDS, who may or may not have been named Harry. Could there be something more there?

"Maybe we could put out an ad in the paper," Liv suggested.

I wanted to respond positively, since Liv was trying so hard, but seriously, did they even have those sections of newspapers anymore?

"Or how about Craigslist Missed Connections?" I joked. "Baby seeking father, met briefly in the nursery of Georgetown hospital circa thirty years ago."

"You better not be giving up on me," Liv said. "We have to believe. There is a powerful energy in this city and it's leading us toward something. We just have to keep looking."

"I don't know. There have been some pretty bad coincidences this week. Maybe the energy of the city is telling us to leave."

"Not all of this week has been bad," Liv protested.

"Really? Finding out Sam cheated on me? Bad. An enormous fight days before our wedding? Really bad. Running into your married ex-professor/ex-boyfriend who clearly still has a thing for you? Even worse." I looked at Liv, who was quiet.

"I'm sorry to bring him up; I just hate that guy." When Liv still didn't respond, I asked gently, "How was it seeing him?"

"It was weird," she admitted.

They met the weekend before law school officially began. Liv and I moved into our apartment in Berkeley on a Saturday morning, which we decorated sparsely with brightly patterned throw pillows from Target, a toaster oven, and the remnants of each of our college dorm rooms.

We were twenty-two, tan, and rested from a summer of bartending in Adams Morgan, and ready for a brand-new adventure. This time together.

Early Saturday afternoon we headed over to the law school to find our way around and check what section we were in, the group of people you have every class with during your first year of law school. Those I knew who were already in law school had repeatedly stressed to me the importance of "getting in a good section," which seemed strange, since we had no control over it whatsoever. Classes were held either with your section alone or combined with others, so they could be as small as the original thirty or up to four sections combined, to form a 120-person lecture.

That afternoon in late August, we tentatively walked the wide, hallowed halls, named after various successful alums, brilliant legal minds, or millionaires who decided their money was best spent on getting their name on a plaque in the hallway next to the library, until we finally stumbled on the posting. It stated that Liv was in section C and I was in K, which meant nothing to us. What did mean something was that sections C and K had a class together: Torts, Monday, Wednesday, and Friday from 9:00 to 9:50 A.M. We were thrilled. Law school was scary enough, but at least we knew that when Monday morning and our first class rolled around, we would be together.

That night, after unpacking the necessities and eating a power meal of Easy Mac, Liv and I came to the mutual decision that we had to go out one last time. Who knew when we were going to be released from the library in the next three years? Plus, we were still at the age when you could get hammered one night and feel good enough to attend your first day of law school thirty-six hours later.

"Let's avoid any of the law school bars we've heard about, in case we want to make fools of ourselves," Liv suggested wisely as we dug through each other's closets looking for things to wear.

We ordered a cab and when the driver arrived, honking outside our apartment building, we asked him to take us to a bar slightly off the map, one that students didn't typically frequent. We explained that we were new to town and didn't know anyone, or where to go. At twenty-two, we were still naïve enough to say things like this to strangers without worrying about being sold into sex slavery. The driver said he knew just the place. He drove us over the Bay Bridge and into San Francisco, dropping us at a small boutique hotel in the Marina that he promised had a great bar.

As soon as we got inside we declared it our secret bar, loving the dark décor and leather club chairs, where people sat drinking malt liquors and having *real* conversations. It was more of a lounge than a bar, somewhere you wouldn't be surprised to see a jazz band or a gentlemen smoking a pipe, if that had been legal.

We sat at stools by the bar and ordered two martinis, dirty gin for me, and vodka with a twist for Liv. I was on a tangent about how I wanted to work as a public defender, speculating that I *might* have to work in corporate law for a year to pay off my loans, when I noticed that Liv wasn't really paying attention. In fact, she had been glancing at the same spot above my right shoulder the entire time I made my altruistic, yet clueless speech.

"What's going on behind me?" I finally asked.

"Promise me you won't turn around."

"I can't promise that." I shrugged. "Not without another martini to focus on."

"Okay, but you know what my dad says. One martini, good; two martinis, drunk; and three martinis . . ."

"Pregnant. I know," I said, finishing the joke Mr. Lucci had told at their family Christmas party every year since I'd known him. It was the one time of year he consumed more than a single beer, which was usually during a Redskins game, and the point in the party in which Mrs. Lucci ordered him to bed.

"There's a really hot guy—actually, he's probably properly described as a man—behind you," Liv said coolly, signaling the bartender for two more drinks.

"A silver fox? I like it. With anyone?"

"Not quite silver. Probably midthirties. He keeps looking at me. He's with some lady but she looks super boring. They're not touching or anything. Okay, they're saying bye, and she's getting up; looks like a bad date," Liv reported as softly as a golf commentator. "Now he's alone."

Emboldened by my second martini—Mr. Lucci really was right about those—I swiveled my stool around to search for Liv's guy. She wasn't exaggerating. He was definitely attractive and definitely a man. He looked dangerously confident, like he had a secret and if you were lucky, he'd share it with you. I gave a small but friendly wave. The man saluted back. Then he said something to the bartender, picked up his beer, and walked over.

"How are you two ladies doing tonight?" he said. I remember

distinctly thinking it was the first time I'd even been called "lady" and that I didn't really like it.

"We're great," I answered, waiting for Liv to chime in, but she didn't say a word. I looked to her, ready for some kind of adorable introduction that would make him fall for her instantly, as I'd seen her do so many times, but she only nodded. Was she really tongue-tied, for the very first time, in front of this man-child?

"I couldn't help but notice that you two seem to be having the most fun in the place. I'm Tony," he said, offering his hand.

"I'm Emma, and this is Olivia. We moved to town today."

"Can I just say," he said, turning directly to Liv, "you have the most beautiful hair I've ever seen in my life? Promise me you'll never straighten it."

Finally Liv found her voice. "I promise," she said coyly.

Over the next hour Liv and Tony discovered all sorts of bland things they had in common. They had both traveled to and loved Cinque Terre (because most people hate it there?), they both had had appendicitis when they were twelve, and they both thought anyone who preferred Milky Ways over Snickers was crazy. ("But they're certainly not nuts," I added. No one laughed.) Typical of two people who were instantly attracted to each other, they became overly excited about unmeaningful coincidences, when the most important thing they had in common was that they wanted to see each other naked. Finally, after they marveled over the unbelievable fact that they both preferred biographies to fiction, I got the hint.

"Liv, I'm gonna grab a cab home. I want to get a good night's sleep for Monday."

"What's Monday?" Tony asked. Hard to believe we hadn't yet explained the reason we'd moved to Berkeley, but John and Yoko had been too busy comparing favorite toothpaste flavors.

Liv quickly changed the subject. She had this rule about not admitting that she was in law school until absolutely necessary. She thought the lawyer thing made her sound uptight and stuffy and didn't represent her true self. Although the feminist in me objected, she had a point.

When Liv got home much later that night, she didn't think twice about waking me up to tell me everything. Apparently they'd closed the place down, sat in his car for an hour talking, and then went to IHOP—ironically, of course—for Tater Tots drenched in ketchup, *both of their favorite midnight snack.*

"We didn't even kiss, but I've never felt more sexual tension in my life," Liv said, lying back on my pillow and grabbing another one to hug while she talked. I hoped she wasn't about to start demonstrating on it. "I think we have to call him Sexy Tony Brown 'cause that boy is sexy."

I laughed sleepily. "I wouldn't exactly call him a boy. Did you ask him his age?"

"No, Em, that would have been so weird, but he got all of my pop culture references, so that's all that matters. I'll get more details for you next time I see him, Nancy Drew." She paused for a minute. "This is embarrassing, but I can't wait," Liv said happily and I smiled with my eyes closed. I hadn't heard her this excited about a guy in a long time.

"That's great. But be careful. He is older." I didn't know exactly what I meant by this, but sensed it was good advice.

"I know, I know," she replied without listening, starting to fall asleep next to me, presumably dreaming of eating Tater Tots with Sexy Tony Brown on the Italian Riviera.

A day and a half later, Liv and I entered our very first law school class. We sat on either side of the huge lecture hall to keep ourselves from talking or giggling—a true sign of maturity—to find a man facing a chalkboard, scrawling case names. He kept writing and I unpacked my laptop nervously.

At precisely 9:01 A.M., the chalkboard guy—our professor, I assumed—turned around, scrolled through his class list, and without missing a beat looked up and said, "Ms. Moon? Where is Ms. Moon? Can you please tell the class, what is a tort?"

I sat silently, flummoxed, and momentarily unable to form any words. Finally I raised my arm to identify myself. My nerves weren't helped by the fact that I didn't have a clue what the answer was. Sexy Tony Brown *was* Professor Brown.

When he recognized me, a short look of surprise passed over Tony's face, but he continued his cold call smoothly. After it was clear I didn't know the answer, he moved on and asked the same question to the girl on my right, dressed in argyle, who perkily stated, "A civil action leading to legal liability, not involving a contract." Suck-up.

Three hours later, after rushing from class to class, without even a second to discuss the turn of events with Liv, I sat in Criminal Law with my small section, only thirty students. Without warning, Tony's, I mean, Professor Brown's, bad date rushed in and started handing out syllabuses.

"Good morning, class, my name is Professor Gray. You may

have had Professor Brown for Torts this morning, but I assure you, my class is far more demanding than my husband's."

She looked much better than she had on Saturday night, in a dark jacket and skirt, over a royal blue shirt that brought out her sharp sapphire eyes. She looked sexy and serious, her straight black hair pulled back in a bun and her black heels impossibly high.

Confused, I turned to a guy from my section, sitting next to me. "What did she say about Professor Brown?"

Looking at me like I definitely didn't belong in law school, or kindergarten for that matter, he answered, "Considering she referred to Professor Brown as her husband, I'm pretty sure she's his wife."

For the entire three years of law school, Liv and STB kept their relationship a secret from everyone else, and even with me she was reluctant on the details. I had enough of a rough sketch to know that nothing physical happened that first year—although emotionally she was hooked—but things progressed our 2L year when she was no longer his student and Professor Gray took a sabbatical to assist in writing a new criminal law textbook in New Haven with some law professors at Yale. STB told Liv his marriage was over, and the sabbatical cover was a polite way to end the marriage without causing a stir at the university. Like so many others before her, she believed him. This, of course, ended up not quite being the case.

Before tonight, the last time Liv had seen STB was at our law school graduation.

The weekend started with a Friday evening cocktail hour to honor the graduates. After Liv's family gathered at our apartment, we all headed over to the reception hall, with her parents and two brothers in tow. Caro couldn't make it to California until the actual ceremony on Sunday, so as usual, the Luccis had taken me under their wing, inviting me to tag along with them for the weekend. (Unsurprisingly, my mother ended up not coming at all, when the lobby's head researcher was called to testify in one of the many court battles going on at the time and she was asked to spend the weekend prepping him.)

The first person we saw when we walked into the Friday cocktail hour was Professor Brown: Torts, as his name tag read. With his charming personality and good looks, he was often chosen to operate in this function, greeting parents and representing the faculty. In my opinion, he'd only gotten the job at Berkeley in the first place because he was married to Professor Gray, who was a legal superstar, and this was one of the few things he offered the school.

While Liv's dad and brothers went off in search of beers, STB approached us, warmly shaking Mrs. Lucci's hand, telling her what an intelligent and special daughter she had. I could feel Liv smiling next to me, proud of him in a secret, palpable way. Mrs. Lucci didn't seem quite as impressed, maybe because her mom sixth sense was flashing red. Then, clad in a fitted white Theory dress and holding a lime-spiked cocktail, up walked Professor Gray: Criminal Law.

You'd think we would be used to this by now. But Professor Gray didn't attend many social law school events and she'd been on the East Coast for the entirety of our second year. After that first time, neither Liv nor I ever took a class with her again. Actually, I realized, the only other time we'd been in the same room with STB and his wife was that fateful night in the hotel bar.

The introductions made me feel ill. I was at the same time sad for

Liv, while also painfully ashamed of the position Professor Gray was in, not to mention livid at STB for being such a spineless jackass.

The rest of the weekend didn't get much better. STB distanced himself from Liv, seeming to take the cocktail party as a warning from the universe to check himself. As he ignored her through the picnic and softball game on Saturday and ducked out of the fancy graduation dinner early that night, I saw Liv slowly start to panic. I could tell that the reality of the situation was dawning on her with increasing intensity, and soon it would hit her squarely in the face.

I awoke in my bed on Sunday to the sounds of her sobbing through our shared bedroom door wall. I heard her call Tony and convince him to meet her before the ceremony. Shortly after, the front door opened and closed, and forty-five minutes later she returned. They'd met in Tilden Park, a lookout in the forest of the Berkeley Hills with a panoramic view of the city. Sitting on my bed while I rubbed her back and encouraged her to alternatively take deep breaths and drink the tea I made her, she explained that for the first time ever, she'd given him an ultimatum. He had to initiate divorce proceedings or it was over.

"What did he say?" I asked, ignoring the fact that we had thirty minutes to shower and get to the ceremony at the Hearst Greek Theatre.

"No," she said flatly. "He chose her. I thought this was going to be it, our time to be together finally. I didn't tell you this yet, but a couple months ago he got asked to come teach at Seton Hall for a year. We were going to get an apartment together in the city. I love him, Emma."

"I know you do."

"The worst part is, after he said no, I started to backtrack. I suggested maybe they separate for now, but he still come to New York. Then he said no, I was right, this couldn't go on. Even after that, I still tried to convince him that we could stay together long-distance. It was so embarrassing. But it didn't matter anyway. I couldn't change his mind." She looked wild-eyed and desperate. "This isn't possible. This can't be how it ends. He can't just decide to end it."

But that was the thing about relationships. He could. Although I didn't blame her one bit for feeling that way, and I had certainly experienced the same frantic loss of control myself, I knew she was wrong. He could make the decision. He could decide to end it all on his own.

I've noticed that when someone gets his or her heart badly broken, this is usually the first reaction, citing these pledges of commitment. "She said he would love me forever," or, "He swore he would never do this." Sometimes even, "I gave him another chance because he promised this would never happen again." But, at the end of the day, these are only words. There really isn't any guarantee that these vows will be kept. And when it comes down to it, people are going to choose their own happiness over a promise they made to someone else, every day of the week.

This brought me back to the present, to my own situation and the sense of powerlessness and confusion I was feeling. I couldn't change what Sam did in Charleston. Now, however, the tables were turned. I *could* break up with Sam. I didn't have to marry him. I didn't have to forgive him, or try to understand, or even ever speak to him again if I chose not to, and he couldn't stop me. I could make that decision all on my own.

CHAPTER 15

"Do you remember senior year of high school, when I wanted to join the dance team?" Liv asked, as our waiter plunked down two extra-spicy Bloody Marys.

We had walked to North Beach, my favorite part of the city, due to the beautiful views, stunning churches, and welcoming parks, not to mention that it was home to the best part of San Francisco: Little Italy. Liv declared that we needed a drink and a bite in order to figure out our next move, and I wasn't about to disagree. She pointed us toward a beautiful restaurant on the water with a back deck exclusively dedicated to day drinking and staring into the blue water of the San Francisco Bay.

"Of course I do."

"Do you remember how I forced you to try out with me

because I didn't want to do it alone? And we came home after school every day for two weeks and practiced the routine over and over." Liv looked way too excited about this unimportant footnote in our friendship.

"Yeah, to the Spice Girls' 'Wannabe.' And your CD player kept skipping, so we made Benny hold it for, like, three hours a day." Her little brother so was thrilled to be included that he would agree to anything, even pressing pause and play when we screamed out instructions. Liv and I really had no business trying out for the dance team. We couldn't do a pirouette to save our lives. But we were seniors and it was spring semester, so they'd pretty much let anyone in our position shimmy on the gym floor for a few minutes during pep rallies.

"You didn't even want to do it, but I couldn't try out alone, remember? I was too embarrassed, so you did it with me. And then, once we made the team—and I use that term loosely—I decided I wanted to do the musical instead and ditched you?"

"Yes, of course. I blame Mrs. McCarthy, who lured you away with the promise of a solo—although you were a great Golde." Liv may look like a floppy bird when she does the running man, but the girl can sing. Despite the aging makeup and long cotton layers, her performance in *Fiddler on the Roof* ensured that every drama guy in school fell in love with her immediately.

"Thanks, I think it was all that practicing for a bat mitzvah that my Catholic parents wouldn't let me have," Liv reflected, taking a swallow of her Bloody. "But wait, I haven't gotten to why I brought this up!" She took a pause as if to recapture the seriousness of her point. "The point is, even after I quit, you stayed on the dance team."

"That's true . . ." I said, completely lost.

"You didn't need me! I couldn't possibly have gone through something so embarrassing without you, but you had no problem doing it alone."

"But you did the musical instead," I said, trying and failing to get her point.

"I'm a good singer—the musical was no sweat—plus, I had a crush on Tevye so I was really convincing. But we had zero experience dancing. We looked completely ridiculous, no offense. It was going out on a limb and really taking the risk of looking really silly. To do that, I needed you, but you didn't need me. You just went for it.

"Here's the thing, Em," she went on. "You talk about not having family in your life, and I disagree to a certain extent, because you do have Caro." I guffawed. "Okay, maybe she's not the warmest person in the world, but you always have me, and the Luccis. And Sam— which I know is complicated right now. But that's one of the amazing things about you. You're independent. You moved to L.A. not know- ing a soul! I only agreed to go all the way to Berkeley once I knew you were going, too. Do you know how much I wish I could do that?"

"I guess." I wasn't sure how to feel. It was nice, but it was com- plicated, too. Plus, the thought of *having Sam* hurt so deeply it took my breath away.

"Emma, no matter what happens with Hunter and Caro, or your relationship, or your job, for that matter—"

"What's going on with my job?"

Liv ignored my joke and finished, "No matter what happens, you will be fine. You can take care of yourself. Emma, you're brave."

"Thanks, Liv," I said quietly.

There was something very true, and also somewhat sad, about what she was saying. I liked that quality in myself. I knew I would be okay on my own, despite life's up and downs. To be honest, it was one of the things I was most proud of, my ability to be alone but not lonely. But I didn't like thinking how I got that way, or what consequences that might bring.

The summer before, I'd chosen to go on a vacation to Hawaii alone. Sam had to work, Liv was in arbitration, and I had vacation time, so I picked somewhere that I'd always wanted to go and went. I spent ten days in Paia, a tiny surf town on the north shore of Maui, eating at Mama's Fish House, tearing through novels, and learning that water sports were no different from the terra firma variety—I sucked at them. Even so, it felt like heaven.

From an enjoyment standpoint, the adventure lived up to expectations. But there were certain points in the trip when I felt almost *too* proud that I was doing it on my own, too eager to show myself and the rest of the world that I didn't need anyone.

Everyone who heard about it was overly impressed about my decision to travel by myself, which definitely wasn't why I did it, but it gave me a certain measure of pride. When we had to fill out the arrival card at Kahului Airport, I'd been tempted to write *proving a point* in the space that asked our reason for travel. There was something about the experience, and the joy I took in it, that made me wonder if all those years of not needing anyone had made me unable to truly want anyone. If maybe I couldn't adjust to the steady presence of another human being in my life. I thought about how long I'd kept the secret of wanting to look for Hunter, even from Liv. As well as the feeling of relief I got when I realized I could leave Sam forever, start over on my own, that it was my decision to make. It all felt related.

"Thanks, Liv. It means a lot that you think that." When she kept staring at me, waiting for more, I confessed what was holding me back. "Only sometimes, I wish that I needed other people a little bit more. Sometimes I get nervous that, at the end, all that independence is going to leave me all alone with my cat, who isn't even really my cat!" I was referring to a stray cat that lived in my yard and I fed. I bought her organic cat foot, rubbed her belly, and named her Sausage, and she, in turn, hissed at me regularly. It was a symbiotic relationship.

"It's funny how often the things we like the most about ourselves are also the things we want to change," Liv remarked. I knew what she meant.

"There's something else . . ." she added. Liv looked like she was in pain. "I've been wanting to tell you." She looked hesitant, like she was wrestling with herself. Finally she closed her eyes and plunged in. "Emma, my dad cheated on my mom." Liv's eyes were practically closed, either from the pain of the memory or in an effort to avoid my reaction.

"What? No. You're joking. Why would you joke about that?"

She was silent a moment, giving credence to her statement, which didn't make an ounce of sense.

"I'm not joking," she said in a raspy voice.

"Why are you telling me this? Because you want me to forgive

Sam?" I said impulsively, regretting my words as soon as they were out of my mouth.

"No, Em. I'm telling you this because, for one, I've kept this from you for over a decade and I've been wanting to tell you for as long. And two, because I know how you feel about my dad. I mean, not in a creepy way. I know that you think he's perfect, and I think you should know that no one is, you know, before you meet your own dad. I didn't even think about the Sam thing."

"I'm sorry, Liv. That was stupid. Start over and tell me what happened."

She sighed like she regretted even bringing it up.

"When I was sixteen and we were juniors, do you remember when my dad went to that immigration trial in Florida for a couple months?" I did. Mr. Lucci—I couldn't help but call him to this day—was called out of the blue to go to Jacksonville for a six-week trial that year. I remember thinking that the life of a lawyer was unbearably exciting and pictured him arguing in a huge sunny courtroom objecting loudly, with white sandy beaches in the background. Once I grew up and drove through Jacksonville on the way to Key West, the image changed, but my perception of Mr. Lucci never did.

"They made that up. Actually, the entire time my dad was staying in a hotel in Alexandria. My mom kicked him out after she overheard a phone message some woman had left on his"—she choked the words out—"car phone." There was a long pause, and I struggled to take this in. "Remember car phones?" she added. "Weird."

I nodded and looked at Liv, who wasn't meeting my eyes,

reaching for what to say. "I am so sorry. That is beyond terrible. Do your brothers know?"

"Nope. My parents didn't tell anyone. The only reason I know is because I caught my mom crying one afternoon after he left and she confessed everything. I think she was really relieved to tell someone, but to tell you the truth I wish I never knew."

"But they worked it out, I guess?" I said tentatively.

"Yeah. I don't really know the details, but I think the woman went overseas for a diplomatic appointment—that was where my dad met her, at the State Department—and eventually things went back to normal."

After looking at me for a second, as if to make sure her words had had their required impact, she motioned the waitress for another round. I suppose she'd had a dozen years to get used to it, so she wasn't feeling the same level of shock I was, but I was dumbfounded.

Why would Mr. Lucci, a man so seemingly happy, threaten everything—his family, his marriage, his *Washington Post* weekend edition, for a random woman he worked with? It was abruptly clear that I knew much less about life than I thought I did.

After spending hours analyzing the bombshell Liv had dropped, drinking several rounds of Bloodys, and brainstorming increasingly absurd ways to find Hunter—the subject of Sam, his cheating and our impending marriage studiously ignored, as I requested—we realized that the warmer than usual Indian summer afternoon was coming to a close.

"You know what we should do tonight?" Liv said mischievously, as we stared out into the slowly darkening sky. "Something we haven't done in forever. Find the diviest karaoke bar in the city and sing until we forget our troubles."

"On a Tuesday?" I said skeptically.

"Yes," she laughed. "Drake says! Plus, we're on vacation! There are no Tuesdays on vacation. What else are you gonna do? More Hunter research? Call Sam back?"

As I'd had enough fruitless Hunter searching for the day and I wanted nothing less than to talk to Sam, analyze his texts, or think about what he had done and what I was going to do as a result, I had no choice but to agree.

"Excellent point. Let's do it."

CHAPTER 16

"How about 'Time after Time'?" she asked, flipping through the plastic pages of the karaoke song book.

"I feel like we can do better than that. But no Journey. I hate how excited people get about Journey."

"I know you do. I've got it, 'Love Shack,' I'll carry the vocals." Without waiting for my response, Liv flipped her red-and-gold-streaked waves and headed to the deejay booth to sign up and no doubt convince him to bump us up in the order.

"Hey, Emma," I heard an extremely deep voice say from behind and felt a tap on my shoulder. I turned around and found Carrick and Dusty, owners of the voice and hand, respectively.

"Hi," I said in barely concealed surprise. "What are you guys doing here?"

Carrick produced a rascally smile and pointed toward the deejay booth. "Liv texted us, said it was a karaoke kind of night and to consider this her official tryout for the Isotopes." Carrick motioned to Dusty in boy sign language and headed off to the bar, presumably to grab some beers.

"I take it Liv didn't consult you?" Dusty asked. "She kind of implied you had a hard day and needed a fun night out. Is it okay that we're here?"

I turned to look directly at Dusty and took in his dark hair curling in the warm room, his wire-rimmed glasses, which must be replacing contacts as I hadn't seen them before, and his kind expression. He really was adorable, especially with the glasses. I inwardly cursed Dean Cain for influencing my prepubescent desires and making me susceptible to lookalikes.

"It's fine. It's good to see you!" I said, slightly too brightly.

"How are things?" he asked, with an emphasis on the "things."

"You mean, Hunter things? Well, it appears he doesn't exist!" I tried to laugh, but it came out more like a rattling cough. Gross.

"What do you mean?" Dusty guided me toward a table that he seemed to locate as if by magic.

I sat down and faced him. "I've found two Hunter Moons, neither of whom was him, one because of you and another because of a Magic Postcard. I've looked everywhere else. I've combed the Internet and called every organization in the city. He's not out there. Or, at least, I can't find him."

"That really sucks," Dusty said genuinely, his eyes crinkling worriedly behind the wire rims. I shrugged in silent agreement. "We don't have to talk about it if you don't want."

"Yeah, that would be great, actually," I said, relieved to be off the hook. I heard the distinctive notes of "Don't Stop Believing" in the background as the entire bar erupted in cheers. The large screen lit up with its fluorescent green words, as Liv and Carrick walked up and handed us beers.

"People really love this song, huh?" Dusty commented. "It's pretty annoying actually."

I laughed despite myself. "Agreed."

We clinked bottles, and I realized I was glad Liv hadn't told me she was inviting them. My knee-jerk reaction would have been to say no, and in the end, I was kind of glad I wasn't given a vote. Tonight might actually be fun.

By closing time, Carrick had crooned three rock ballads—turned out he was musically gifted with or without the bass—Dusty and I had performed Captain and Tennille, and Liv had sung numbers from *Grease* with pretty much everyone in the bar and positively killed "Rhiannon." The pain of the afternoon was completely gone; the alcohol had loosened the tightening in my chest and convinced me that, for the moment at least, I didn't really care how much the men in my life had failed me and how much, to a certain degree, I was failing them.

When we got home from the bar, Carrick put on some music—not his own, thank God—pulled out a deck of cards, and asked if we knew how to play hearts. Liv, who had a secret talent for counting cards and once hustled the entire cast of *Music Man* playing backstage during rehearsals, said we'd love to.

It was the perfect plan, since I didn't want to be alone with Dusty and it gave Liv and Carrick an opportunity to flirt—taking peeks at each other's cards and laughing at each other's stories. A couple tricks in, Carrick asked me how the father-finding mission was going. Dusty looked guilty, but rather than being annoyed at him for revealing my secret, I felt touched that Carrick inquired. Also, drunk. I felt drunk. But touched nonetheless.

"Pretty bad, actually. I didn't find him." I felt a wave of sadness wash over me, but it didn't take my breath away like it had earlier in the day. Maybe saying it out loud was the key. I tried again. "I can't find him."

Carrick nodded but didn't look up from his cards. "You know what, I've known my dad my entire life, and the only thing I've ever gotten from him is constant confirmation that I'm a disappointment and the occasional comment that I'm 'definitely no Seger,' so maybe it's not such a bad thing." He proceeded to lay down the queen of spades, successfully shooting the moon and making me wonder how much attention he could have been paying to the topic at hand. (Nice one.)

"Carrick!" Liv exclaimed, although I wasn't sure whether it was a reaction to his statement or the fact that he'd earned the rest of us each twenty-six points. "No one could ever be disappointed in Emma."

"No, I know what he means. And it's very possible he's right. I only wish I knew one way or the other." I handed my cards to Dusty, who was gathering them up for a new round. He looked thoughtful, like he had something to say, but stayed quiet.

"Maybe he's in jail," Carrick suggested, looking up to meet my eyes. He stretched back, his arms in the air behind him. We were around the coffee table, Dusty and me on the couch and Liv and Carrick in armchairs opposite us. When no one responded, he looked defensive. "It's possible, right? It could explain why he's fallen off the map."

I remembered a TV movie I'd once seen, where a girl found out that her normal, suburban father was a serial killer, and shuddered. The girl in the movie went crazy, tormented by the fact that she was related to someone so horrible, and overwhelmed by the anguish of seeing her father locked up in an orange jumpsuit. That would definitely be worse than not finding him, I decided. Fortunately, I reminded myself, there would be arrest records and court documents if that were the case. (Was it possible I punned more when drunk?)

When someone went to prison, they did the opposite of fall off the map. Maybe when it came to Hunter, no news was good news.

Dusty passed the stiff blue and white cards around our small circle. I glanced at Liv and Carrick over my cards. They weren't listening at all, engaged in a fake fight about him beating her in the last round, which would surely lead to an obnoxious makeup. I turned to Dusty. "What were you going to say before?"

"How could you tell?" He smiled. "It was nothing. It's not my place."

"Are you kidding? After you argued local politics with the birther?"

"Okay, but stop me if this falls into the category of unsolicited advice." I nodded encouragingly so he would go on. "I'm not saying you're necessarily the same, but when I was sixteen and looking for my dad, I realized after I found him that I was really looking for something else."

"What?"

"I don't know, exactly. Answers about who I was? A role model? I'm not sure. It was only after I met with him that I realized whatever I was trying to find, he wasn't it." Dusty turned to look straight at me. This close, I could see his eyes better, hazel with flecks of green.

"Emma, I know I might not know you very well, but in the short time since we've met, I've found you to be completely amazing. If you don't find Hunter Moon, then it's his loss, not yours." I was abruptly aware of the silence in the room. Liv and Carrick were gone. I had no idea where, probably upstairs to his room to transition to strip poker. Part of me was jealous of Liv. Not because I wanted to be with Carrick, of course, but because of the fun she was having. I wanted to feel good about something, I thought, my booze-addled brain pushing all rational thoughts to the side. I was sick of being sad all the time.

I turned my body to face Dusty's, inching closer on the couch. He looked incredibly nervous, which I took as a compliment. Slowly and tentatively, he put his arms around me. As his nervousness eased, he held me tighter and tighter. I sank into his embrace, allowing myself to lie down slightly, to fall into the soft couch. I was aware that I was allowing my drunkenness to make decisions for me, knowing that my sober self would have sat up, said good night, and gone to bed. Still, I let him hug me. I tightened my arms around his neck. I closed my eyes, just for a minute, letting the pleasantness of the moment wash over me.

CHAPTER 17

"It's time to get up," Liv called, reaching under my thin veil of sleep.

"What time is it?" I asked, disoriented. Painfully vivid dreams of Sam had been rolling through my subconscious on a loop all night. Sam. For a few seconds, I let myself think about how sometimes I would wake up to a note from Sam that said how pretty I looked when I was sleeping. I quickly dismissed the thought and reddened as the memories of the night before trickled back, particularly memories of Dusty and my intimate hug.

I had woken up halfway through the night alone on the couch, covered with a blanket, and crept back to bed, surprised to find Liv sleeping peacefully. I guessed nothing had happened with Carrick. Whereas I must have fallen asleep in Dusty's arms, and then he covered me with a blanket. How incredibly embarrassing.

As I let the steaming hot water of the shower run over me, the events of the day before settled over me in an unhappy haze that felt completely misplaced for this time of day. These kinds of gloomy feelings should be accompanied by a glass of wine after work, or lying in bed at night questioning the day's decisions. The morning was for bagels, optimism, and baseless cheer. I attempted to reach for some faith that things were going to turn out okay. But what exactly did that mean? That I would forgive Sam? Was there something to be gained by trying to see his side, or at least listening to what he had to say? I thought of the twelve ignored calls from the day before and the unread texts and e-mails.

Unfortunately, I couldn't think about how often he'd been in contact without also remembering why. There was no *seeing his side*, I reminded myself. He'd cheated on me and never took responsibility for it. His side didn't deserve consideration. It wasn't my fault that the truth came out a week before our wedding. I wasn't the one who'd cheated. Let him be the one to worry about how everything was going to work out for once. As I started to spin, I reminded myself to focus on Hunter, the slightly more emotionally manageable hurdle. The Sam problems receded ever so slightly into the background. I was finally able to take a deep breath. Despite the disappointment of the day before, I couldn't give up now. I needed a plan.

I'll wash my hair, I decided grandly, for starters. I scrubbed my favorite shampoo into my scalp and began to relax. I took a deep breath and let the water pour over my closed eyes. Attempting to condition my frizzy mane was a slightly less calming process. As I pounded the almost empty conditioner bottle in an attempt to squeeze out a couple more ounces, Liv, who was in and out of the bathroom getting dressed, realized what I was doing and shouted at me over the water.

"Use mine, Em. It's full. Don't cut corners when it comes to conditioning. Didn't your mother ever teach you anything?" I knew she was teasing me, but, still stuck somewhat in my funk, I couldn't help but take her literally. No, she didn't. Caro and I were barely on speaking terms by the time I was old enough for hair maintenance to be an issue. If I ever had questions about blow-outs or leg shaving, I went to Liv, who in turn asked her mom and reported back. No wonder I was mystified when Val handed me the lipstick blotter or whatever the fuck it was.

For the millionth time I wondered what was wrong with me. Why didn't Caro have any interest in her own daughter? And if it was all her problem and not mine, if she really was the one woman in history who didn't care about her offspring, then how was I to explain Hunter's similar behavior? It had to be me. It was the only logical conclusion.

I sighed heavily, my melancholy deepening. In truth, I knew the real reason for my bad mood. I knew why I was so sensitive and feeling so raw that morning. It was because, the night before, I'd dreamed of Sam and our first date. I reached for the memory with both hands, allowing all my other gauzy dreams from the night before, which were still hanging at the shadowy edges of my subconscious, to slip away.

Four years earlier, one week to the day since we'd met, I met Sam at the Venice Beach bar he'd suggested, exactly eight minutes late. I remembered the intense feelings from the softball field, but I wasn't sure if they would stick. The second I saw him, however, I knew my feelings were not fleeting.

When I walked in, he texted me immediately, so I knew he'd been watching the door waiting for my arrival. *I'm sitting at the bar, in case you forgot what I looked like.* I looked up from the text, straight into his smiling blue eyes, reflecting the last light of day, unusually bright in the magic hour. He was so cute, with his wry half grin. I knew immediately that I wanted to kiss him, and that I probably wasn't going to want to stop.

It had been about six months since my last breakup, with Jared, a hot but angry classmate I met in my Wrongful Conviction Death Penalty clinic. We had a passionate, explosive relationship my last year of law school, as we partied, studied, and celebrated our final months of idealistic utopia, but I knew it was over the night his parents took us out to dinner and he spent the entire meal arguing with his father, a federal judge, over minimum-sentencing requirements. It wasn't only because his entire vigilante belief system was so clearly born from rebellion that it became trite, but also that he would fight with his father while the man treated us to a meal at Saison. That was just plain rude. I broke up with him a few weeks before graduation, citing distance, as he was moving to Brooklyn to become a public defender and I was heading to Los Angeles to bill hours, and for once, he didn't fight me on it.

By the time my first date with Sam rolled around, I was single, happy, and ready to date someone different. A nonlawyer, preferably a nonangry person in general, who would get along with the general public, his parents, and, especially, me. Within minutes, I knew I had found exactly what I was looking for.

As we sat down with our beers, at a table outside, facing the ocean, Sam's dancing eyes and relaxed tone put me instantly at ease, as he had on the softball field. Whereas Jared was always gearing for a confrontation, whether it was about the library's appalling study carrel reservation policies or the rich assholes gentrifying Oakland, it was immediately clear to me that Sam tended to live and let live. I forced myself to stop comparing them and to enjoy what was right in front of me. This resolution was easy to keep, and thoughts of my ex easily floated away.

For the rest of the night, we didn't stop staring at each other. After dinner at Oscar's, a nearby Mexican restaurant, where Sam's friendly demeanor got us seated in minutes, he walked me home and, without hesitation, I invited him in.

We started kissing the second I handed him his glass of wine. I felt like a vixen as I untied my dress and climbed on top of him on the couch, straddling him while continuing to kiss him urgently. He clearly didn't know what to make of me, but wasn't about to look a slutty gift horse in the mouth, so he carried me into the bedroom. We did it, as Lionel Richie would say, all night long. It was the sex of a single person who hasn't gotten any in months and has met someone she can't keep her hands off. It was perfect.

But, of course, given that I possess two X chromosomes, I panicked in the morning. As I lay in bed, listening to Sam's steady sleeping noises—he even slept like a content person—I reasoned with myself. Sex on the first date: Obviously this was a huge mistake. I would never hear from him again. Fine. The good news, I reasoned, was that there were a lot of cute guys in L.A. I'd met a great one in about five minutes. There had to be more! Plus, it gave me a good excuse to quit the softball team. I was terrible.

As I brainstormed what to do with my Sunday nights going forward, I noticed that the sleeping noises had ceased. Damn it, he's awake, I realized frantically. I should have spent the last twenty minutes trying to make myself look presentable, rather than pondering whether taking up knitting is too *Goop* for me.

"Good morning," Sam said sleepily. "Get over here." With that he pulled me from my side of the bed to his, wrapping his arms and legs around me until I was in a lovely body lock. As we hugged and kissed with both the comfort level of two people who have been dating for months and also the excitement of our first morning together, he casually asked, "Have you ever been to the Getty Villa?"

The dream started there, a replica of the morning after our first date. There was a hazy sequence of us at Patrick's Roadhouse in Santa Monica, where Sam laughed as I assigned personalities to our breakfast items, defending the charge that his frittata thought it was superior to my omelet, and listening to me wax poetic about the relationship between my jam and butter. For the record, they had a falling-out because toast was two-timing them. Somehow, Sam thought this geeky rant was funny.

Then, in that fuzzy, dreamlike way, we were at the Getty, no travel time required. In real life, the Getty Villa is a towering museum on the northern cliffs of the Pacific Palisades. The villa itself is a work of art, a palatial white mansion framed by a series of huge white columns, full of Green and Roman antiquities. In the dream, it was even more incredible. The building was hundreds of stories high, practically in the clouds.

As Dream Sam and I walked over to look at a beautiful painting of the San Francisco skyline, with the Coit Tower in focus and the rest of the drawing foggy and nebulous, I looked down and realized it was actually a window. I turned to him anxiously. Why was he showing me this? I wondered. He looked back and shrugged, saying, "I only slept with her once," and pushed me out the window. The last thing I remembered was falling, plummeting down toward a rushing Coit Tower.

Without warning, the water stopped abruptly. I looked down and saw that Liv had reached her hand around the curtain and cranked it off. We really had to talk about boundaries.

"Come on, girl, you've got to be clean by now," she shouted as she left the bathroom. I got out and closed the door tightly, to trap in the steamy condensed air.

"Let's get going." Liv kept talking from the other side of the door. "It's already Wednesday. We're flying out at five, and Hunter's not going to find himself. I think we should go back to the library, maybe look into that dentist thing. We never found anything on that, right? Also, your phone is buzzing like crazy out here. Either Sam is calling or something embarrassing you did went viral on YouTube." She paused. "Dang, it's him. I was hoping for public embarrassment."

"Where the hell are you?" Sam demanded into the phone.

"What are you talking about?" I replied, taken aback by his tone.

"Well, I know you're not in Napa. Do you know how I know this? Because I flew there yesterday. And you weren't there."

"You did what?" I stuttered, standing up and starting to pace around the room, grateful Liv had decided to go grab us coffees to give me some privacy.

"I went to the hotel to find you," he responded. He paused, waiting for me to explain. I was silent. "To the Calistoga Ranch. When you weren't there, I practically had to bribe the manager to tell me where you were. She said you checked out before you even checked in."

I knew Siri would give us up—well, I guess it wasn't her fault, she was programmed to respond to questions.

"So I guess you guys left? I called you repeatedly, probably a million times, and of course you didn't answer, so I turned around and flew back home. Where are you? Are you in L.A.? What is going on?"

"Do you seriously think I owe you any kind of explanation right now?"

"No," Sam said, calming down slightly. "I'm glad to know you're safe, though."

"I'm safe," I said flatly.

"Okay, so I guess you're not going to tell me where you are. But either way, Emma, you can't just run away from me. You have to give me a chance to explain." I considered this. Did I? I remembered the terrible dream from a few nights earlier, watching the train pull away from the station. Did that mean I should leave him, or that I was a fool to push him away? Maybe it stood for the fact that it was over before I even found out about Val. Maybe it was over the second I started having the doubts. The second I started looking for my dad without telling him. Maybe it was over the moment I was born the child of Caroline and Hunter Moon. Maybe I never even had a chance.

"Please. This is me, Emma."

Who was he, though? My boyfriend, my fiancé, the guy who'd cheated on me, the one who scratched my back if I was having trouble sleeping or felt inexplicably itchy, the person with whom I'd watched every episode of *The West Wing*, the guy who'd kept a horrible secret from me for years, the one I'd kept an important secret from for weeks, the man who knew my faults, my strengths, my favorite ice cream flavor depending on the time of day, and what funny dance moves made me laugh the very hardest. My lover, my friend, my almost life partner. Sam.

"The night that thing happened with Valerie, I was in a horrible place. We hadn't talked for a couple weeks. I don't know if you remember this, but you essentially stopped answering my calls when I got to Charleston. I thought you were going to break up with me." He paused to let this sink in.

"But I didn't," I added quickly.

"You're right. But I was convinced you were going to end it. I was freaking out, mostly because it upset me so much. I started to convince myself that it was over. I thought *we* were over. I went out with the crew. I got blackout drunk, passed out, and when I woke up, she was there. Waking up the next morning was the worst I've ever felt in my life."

I considered his words, although hearing the details cut into my heart like a machete. Some of what he was saying was true, truer than I would have liked to admit. I was ignoring his calls when he got to Charleston. I remembered that time distinctly. I even remembered the decision to distance myself. As soon as Sam got to South Carolina, I started to feel insecure about his absence and did the only thing I could to regain some control. I pushed him away. He was right to think that we were on the rocks. The truth is, I was very, very scared. I didn't think we could make it through the distance or the time apart. I was sure Sam would meet some nubile young assistant or quirky props girl. Someone who knew all about movies, who knew about what was going on in his life, and mostly, who was there. Then I would lose the first guy I really loved, the only one ever who made me feel like I'd found my place in the world.

But I was right, wasn't I? He did turn to another girl the second I turned my back, one who happened to be my friend. I was infuriated, all over again. Why was he so weak? Why couldn't he have just sucked it up and told me how he felt? Or dealt with a couple weeks of weirdness? Why did he have to resort to cheating on me? And now, what, he was blaming me? This was bullshit.

Sam, unable to read the turn my thoughts had taken, continued. "The day after it happened, I knew it was the last time I would ever put our relationship in jeopardy again. I bought a ticket and came home the next weekend and convinced you to stick with me, remember?"

"Yes, I remember. You convinced me it could work despite the distance. After you *cheated on me*. Sam, you didn't tell me the whole story!" I finally exploded. "Sure, that was a nice thing to do, flying home, and I'm glad you realized I was the person you wanted to be with, but you didn't tell me that you got there by sleeping with Val!"

"I know. And for that, in addition to everything else, I am so ashamed."

Was he trying to make me feel sorry for him? If so, it wasn't working.

"I didn't think there was any way you would take me back if you knew. I convinced myself that the circumstances, and the fact that I was too drunk to even remember what happened, made it unimportant. I physically could not make myself tell you the one thing that would make me lose you forever. But I was wrong. I should have let you make that choice."

I was silent in response, causing him to anxiously add, "How do you feel?"

How did I feel? Anyone who has ever had her heart broken knows, there is no worse feeling in existence. You can't get a deep breath without crying; every single thought and memory makes your chest ache with sorrow. It's like your own insides have turned against you. But it wasn't only my heart that was broken; my trust and belief in what we had and who we were was smashed as well. It was as if the fragmented pieces of my heart had twisted and coiled into nameless, shapeless objects, rendering them useless, capable only of scratching my insides raw every time I shifted. That's how I felt.

"Emma, are you still there?"

"Yes." The rage that I felt when we started the conversation had settled into an exhausting sadness. He'd given me his explanation and I didn't feel one bit better.

"Can I ask you something?" he said tentatively.

"Okay."

"You don't have to tell me. But where are you?"

"I'm in San Francisco, Sam." I sighed sadly. "I'm looking for my dad."

"What?"

As I explained the story, how we'd gotten here, what we'd found so far, Sam listened quietly.

"Have you talked to your mom about any of this?" Sam asked as soon as I was finished.

"Caro? Are you joking?" I responded sharply, my chest instantly compressed. There was something distressing about him bringing up Caro, a person that made the questions about my father, and the fact that I didn't know him, all the more painful. I recalled the one time I brought Sam home for Christmas. We actually had a pretty nice time. It was nothing like the Christmases spent with his family, long dinners full of drunken toasts and cold walks to get last-minute presents for his countless cousins, but it was much better than expected. We had a cozy Christmas dinner by the fire, Sam and Caro chatting comfortably over a bottle of red wine in the Georgetown apartment she'd inhabited since I left home.

"Em, I have an idea. Let me come up and look for him with you. You were supposed to fly home tonight, right, but this is more important. If we have to, we can postpone the wedding. I know we can find him. And once we do, everything will be better." He paused. "It'll be like the rain shadow. Completely different on the other side." Wow. Now he really was pulling out all the stops.

Sam and I had only been dating for a few months when we took an impromptu trip to Palm Springs for the weekend, stumbling on Korakia Pensione, a glorious Mediterranean-inspired bed-and-breakfast, with gorgeous, sparse rooms that had heavy stucco walls, huge beds, and scratchy record players. We spent the entire weekend having sex on the absurdly soft thousand-thread-count sheets, playing cards at the outside wooden tables, and reading the thick novels they provided in stacks around the white stone infinity pool.

The only time we even left the grounds was one morning to bike to the Palm Springs Aerial Tramway, a rickety-looking gondola that rose 8,500 feet, which picked up travelers at the barren desert floor and deposited them in a forest at the top of the San Jacinto Mountains. It would turn out to be the source of one of my most amazing and most terrifying memories ever.

This was mostly due to my incredible fear of heights, forever preventing my submission to any reality show, but it wasn't helped by the fact that the tram was designed to spin in circles, like a rooftop hotel on acid, as you ascended the mountain. This design move was actually pretty genius. It meant you could see the view from every angle as you traveled up the edge of the mountain. Unfortunately, this detail was difficult for me to appreciate so near a panic attack.

To calm me down, Sam rubbed my back—not in circles, thankfully—and quietly explained how it could be so dry on one side of the mountain and so green and lush on the other, why the landscape appeared so different as we approached the peak. In a low voice, he explained the concept of the rain shadow.

"The rain shadow is created because of the mountains; they block the rain-producing clouds from crossing over," he explained simply. "Because of this, one side of the mountain is desert, and the other is forest." He looked straight into my eyes as he explained, holding my gaze.

I can say without a doubt that was the moment I realized I would love him forever. Not because he was the guy who knew a little bit about everything or because he was sweetly using the same tone you'd use on a mental patient, both of which were true, but because as he explained it, he knew not to point down *at* the rain shadow. He wasn't thinking about transmitting an interesting fact or trying to get his point across, he was simply trying to distract me from looking. Rather than focusing on the anecdote, he was thinking about how I *felt*.

I got what he meant. Sam thought that finding my father together could be like crossing the rain shadow, starkly different on the other side. It could bring us to a new place in our relationship. Well, I thought, strangled by pain, you could also say that finding out that Sam had *cheated on me* and *lied about it* was like crossing the rain shadow. I couldn't in a thousand years have imagined what it was like over here, or how it could be so different, but once I crossed over, I couldn't get back.

"Look, Sam, I can't do this right now. I have to go," I said, hanging up on him for the second time that week.

In an incredibly famous case in 1891, *Vosburg v. Putney*, one boy lightly kicked the leg of another boy in class, presumably innocently horsing around. His kick shattered the other boy's bone, due to the fact that it was already nearly, although not visibly, broken.

The court held that Putney, who'd always seemed like a bit of a bully to me, was responsible for all of Vosburg's damages, despite the fact that they were inordinately extreme. The injuries may have been improbable, but they were actually suffered by the person the defendant chose to kick; thus, the consequences were entirely his fault. If he was responsible for *some* of Vosburg's damages—which undoubtedly he was, as he had blatantly kicked him—he should be responsible for *all* of them. As the opinion stated, "a defendant takes a plaintiff as he finds him." In other words, don't kick the guy with the bad leg, because you'll probably have to pay for a new one.

The eggshell plaintiff rule was born.

Maybe Sam couldn't have predicted the level of pain his act of betrayal would cause, but he was responsible for it. All of it. He knew what he was getting into. He knew my history. Emotionally, I was an eggshell plaintiff, ready to break the second you tapped the surface.

He should have been much more careful.

CHAPTER 18

After once again telling Liv that I didn't want to talk about Sam, we headed back to the library, where it seemed so many good ideas came from the first day. First, we tried to crack the dentist mystery, searching the California Dental Association online membership directory, as many insurance providers' dentist listings as we could think of, and several find-my-dentist websites. We even called a few local practices in the area to ask if there was any other way to find an errant dentist, but they pretty much only pointed us back to Google.

This dead end gave us the idea to search other professional membership sites. We perused the State Bar of California—I briefly wondered if he would be proud or horrified to have another lawyer in the family—and the Medical Board of California. Next, we tried the

California Vital Records site, an idea that Carrick had mentioned to Liv. If Hunter were married or had a kid (other than me, that is), that information would be in there. We almost jumped out of our chairs when we found a single entry—for Hunter Moon, the father of Tyler and Kyle Moon. I wanted to scream.

"Seriously, now what?" Liv turned to me, shaking her head in frustration.

"I have no idea."

"Let's think of it this way. What do people do in life? They get married, they have kids, they have a job, interests, hobbies . . . what else? We have checked any possible database where anyone who did those things would show up."

I felt the germ of an idea sprouting. What else *did* people do? Where did they put their names? Where did they check in? Day in and day out . . .

"The gym!" I practically shouted. "People go to the gym."

"They do," Liv said emphatically. "Especially in San Francisco. Emma, that's a great idea. You are totally right. That just might work." I wasn't exactly sure what she was referring to, but I let her keep going as something was clearly clicking for her. "When I went to Equinox the other day to try and take that yoga class, they looked me up on their database and instantly knew I was a member in Manhattan, so they must have all the records in the same place. If your dad belongs to any of the locations, and there are loads, we could find him!" Liv got up and started packing her bag, ready to put our newest plan into action.

"Hold on. What makes you think they're just going to give us that information? I'm sure there are privacy rules and stuff."

"Oh, they'll give it to us," she said, mysteriously confident. "Let's just hope your dad's the type to overpay for a gym membership."

"Excuse me," Liv said to the buff, blond man at reception who bore a striking resemblance to Westley from *The Princess Bride*, wearing a name tag that somewhat amusingly read FRANK. The name didn't exactly fit. "Hi, Frank. I'm a member—I came by yesterday, I don't know if you remember."

"Of course I do," he said quickly, turning slightly pink. Oh, here we go, a new card-carrying member of the Liv fan club. Now I knew why she was so sure she could get the information out of him. That saucy little minx, God bless her.

"I was wondering, Frank, could you look up someone for us in that handy computer of yours? We need to find out if he's a member here," she said sweetly.

"I'm not supposed to," Frank said nervously.

"Frank, it's a really long story, but I promise we will never tell a soul, and it would mean more to me than you would ever know. I wouldn't ask, but it is so very important," she whispered conspiratorially.

He looked conflicted, but in the end, Liv's hotness won the day. As usual. I think her record at this point was four thousand to nil. "Okay. I'll do it, just this once. You won't tell anyone?" We shook our heads vehemently. "What's the name?"

"First name, Hunter; last name, Moon." We waited a few precious seconds while he typed, until he started to nod slowly, still looking at the screen.

"Yes, I see one listing for a Hunter Moon," he said. Liv let out a little chirp, and I grabbed her hand.

"Thank you, Frank!" Liv said gaily. "Does he live in San Francisco?"

"Yes, he's in the Bay Area, but unfortunately I can't give out any information beyond that."

"Why not?" I asked in a strangled voice.

"Please, Frank," Liv pleaded.

"It's not that I don't want to—I really can't. It's not in the computer. We only have addresses on file at the locations where the members belong." My mouth dropped and I had a mental image of leaping across the desk, grabbing the computer, and throwing it out the window.

Luckily, Frank went on before the impulse got the better of me.

"But I would suggest you try the Marin County Equinox; they might be able to help you."

"Marin?" I repeated.

"Marin," he confirmed, glancing down once more. "Can I help you with anything else?"

"No, Frank, but thank you. You have no idea how much I appreciate it."

He bowed his head slightly and turned back to his computer. "As you wish."

Liv and I immediately jumped in our rental car and made our way up and around the city to the Golden Gate Bridge, hugging the peninsula with its steep hills on our left and the placid azure bay on our right, stretching out to the steely gates of Alcatraz and beyond.

We chugged past the Marina Green, filled with happy young moms pushing their baby strollers over the well-tended grass and kids of all ages running around wildly, with the strings of kites wrapped tightly around their fists. I wondered why they weren't in school in September. I figured they all went to those alternative charter schools that took breaks throughout the year. The realization that I had no idea how the school system worked anymore made me feel both old and young, straddling the gap between being a kid and having one. I thought about the blond curly hair I'd assumed our kids—Sam's and mine—would have. We hadn't decided anything official, but we knew we both wanted two, and, like every couple, we liked to throw names around. He loved the name Pearl, after his grandmother, which I thought was beautiful, and I liked Henry.

I'd pictured our family so many times, a serious little boy and fun-loving little girl, both with curly blond mops and a dad who loved to throw them into the air, that it was incredibly painful to realize it might never come to fruition. This potential loss of the life I had imagined with Sam hurt almost more than the loss of Sam himself.

After we passed through the Presidio, we finally arrived at the dusty entrance of the Golden Gate, slowly inching toward the bridge until we were making our way across, to the North Bay of San Francisco and Marin County, where my third potential father currently resided.

"We should call *this place* Dude Island," Liv said, as we rumbled over the planks of the prettiest suspension bridge in the world.

I burst out laughing. "What made you think of that?" Dude Island was what a group of our guy friends called their house in law school. Hosting flip cup tournaments and weekly after-parties, they lived their lives like they were still in a fraternity and we, in turn, used their house for similar purposes. At their parties, it was considered a victory if we didn't lose any of our girlfriends and collectively made it back to the mainland for the night.

"San Francisco is the *real* Dude Island," Liv said pensively, as if her comment had added substantially to string theory.

"How so?"

"Well, in law school they called it Dude Island to be funny or whatever, but here on San Francisco, an *actual island*, is where every important dude in our lives ends up." Liv smacked the steering wheel for emphasis.

"Agreed, there are a motley crew of men in residence on this . . . well, technically it's a peninsula—Dude Peninsula, if you will. But you're right, STB, my dad . . . Can we count the hot Equinox guy?"

"Of course Frank counts. It's the energy, I'm telling you. That's how it works. You start to think about something, and when you put that thought out into the universe, that's when you start to find it. How else do you explain the fact that you've never encountered another Hunter Moon in your life, and now, you find three?"

"Well, I've never looked before."

"That explains some of it, sure, but there's more to it. You are *ready* to find him. You finally realized that, and then asked for it. And now you're going to get it."

"Maybe," I added, to avoid the possible jinx.

"Plus, what about Dusty and Carrick? They're dudes. Add them to the list."

"I guess if Frank counts, they count," I said lightly, looking out the window. If I was going to be perfectly honest with myself, I'd thought about calling Dusty as soon as we left the gym, to tell him about our new lead, although it hadn't occurred to me to contact Sam. Maybe it was because I simply wanted to talk to someone who had been in my shoes. Or maybe it was because of whatever we'd shared the night before. I shook my head to rid that moment from my memory, still embarrassed by the full-body hug I'd instigated.

In any case, I'd restrained myself from calling him, if for no other reason than because it was a Wednesday morning and I didn't want to bother him while he was Gchatting and listening to Spotify like a true young professional.

Now, though, in a moment of impulsivity, I pulled out my phone. Before I could change my mind, I typed a note to Dusty. *Going to see another Hunter, after Liv seduced a gym receptionist for the info . . . Long story. Wish me luck and Happy Wednesday!* The final exclamation seemed to give it the casual edge I was looking for, and while I didn't really consider myself an ellipses person in text, it felt right. Maybe now we could forget my weird behavior from the night before. My phone buzzed. *Can't wait to hear it. Good luck! Let me know if you need a ride to the airport later.* I felt a wave of relief wash over me. At least my relationship with one islander was completely normal.

I quickly closed my phone before I could read the multiple texts from Sam. I also noticed that I had a couple missed calls from a 415 area code from that morning. They must have gotten mixed up in the dozens of missed calls from Sam that Liv initially thought (hoped) were evidence of a humiliating video of me trending on the Web. It was probably someone from the UC's San Francisco fund-raising office calling to ask for money. They tended to call obsessively for a few weeks every year until I gave in and made a pledge.

The melodic clanking of the bridge's planks against our tires abruptly stopped and we were deposited on the other side of the bay. The second we crossed, I started to feel different, like when you go on a tropical vacation, step out of the plane, and breathe in the humid air, instantly removed from your normal life. Maybe it was because the North Bay looks so physically different from San Francisco proper. Lush and dark, with pines and redwoods forming the thick green canopy of Muir Woods, it almost feels like a forest. A forest of really rich people, I thought as I spotted a lavish real estate property hidden among the trees.

"Holy shit, look at some of these houses," Liv exclaimed, reading my mind. "I hope your dad has a good view of the bay. Where are we heading?" She checked the gym's address in the rental car

GPS. "Tiburon? Isn't that where we used to go and day drink on Sundays sometimes?"

"The very same," I answered. When we lived in the area, every once in a while, we would wake up early on a Sunday morning, drive over the Bay Bridge, rent bikes in the Marina and bike over the Golden Gate Bridge. It was a long, but very fun adventure. We would slowly make our way to the other side, past the sparsely beautiful beach and through the quirky town of Sausalito, until we found ourselves in Tiburon. A tiny town whose main attraction is a sprawling blue-painted stucco restaurant, Sam's—which now felt like some kind of unreadable omen—standing firmly on the edge of the sea, crowded with dozens of picnic tables providing the best view of the water for miles. The tables were inevitably occupied by like-minded twenty-somethings shouting happily over their breakfasts. We would order mimosas and eggs, which we'd really earned at that point, rehash the same topics that we'd been rehashing for the previous ten years, and, hours later, ferry home with our bikes.

"What exactly are we going to do when we get to Equinox?" I asked.

"We are going to reason with them. And explain that one of their gym members is your long-lost father and you need a kidney."

"Liv!"

"I feel good about this, Em. Maybe he'll even be working out."

Despite the false starts, my confidence was back up. I was once again struck by the incredible idea that my dad could be physically *at* the place where we were headed. I just hoped he wouldn't be on the elliptical. That felt like an awkward angle for a father-daughter reunion.

"But first," she added, "I really need some brunch. Do you mind?"

"No, I'm starving. Let's go to that place up ahead; it looks great."

Liv swung the car into the right lane and pulled up to a small diner housed in a cottage, the middle in a row of several equally tiny, equally adorable retail establishments. Something about the place looked delicious. Maybe it was the name, Bluegrass Diner, but I knew immediately that the scramble would be fabulous and the biscuits even better. We slowly climbed out of the car and took deep breaths of the bay breeze, stretching like we'd run a marathon.

As we walked inside, it only got cozier. Brightly colored quilts hung on the walls, giving it a warm, welcoming feeling, almost like you were under the covers. The rustic hardwood floors were scuffed from age and wear, and the waitresses were huddled around the coffee machine gossiping. A sign sassily instructed us to order at the front so they could call our names when our meals were ready.

Liv and I dutifully got in line and each ordered a BLTA with a side of fried potatoes, adding a thick piece of cornbread to split. It seemed only polite. We found a perfect table in the corner to plunk down our steaming cups of coffee and stretch our legs. I added a generous dose of cream to my cup, silently congratulating the establishment for not switching to milk and thus forcing me to choose the less healthy option. After they called my name and I grabbed our plates, we tucked in to our feasts for a few minutes, in pure eating bliss.

"Moon?" the waitress called from the counter, startling us both.

"Geez, what else did you get?" Liv teased. "Bulking up for winter?"

My eyes shot up to meet Liv's. "I didn't give them 'Moon.'"

"What?"

I started blinking nervously. "When I ordered. I gave them 'Emma,' remember? They're talking about a different Moon."

We both glanced up quickly to see a man walking up to the counter to get his lunch. My mouth went dry. "The waitress called out 'Moon' and he answered. That guy's name is Moon." I looked at Liv for verification.

"It's gotta be," she said with the same astonishment that I was feeling. I've heard of people feeling alertly aware of all of their senses but never really understood what that meant until now. It was as if I was zoomed in on the picture of us. I saw the pepper spilled on the red-and-white-checkered tablecloth, I smelled the bacon frying behind the counter, and I heard the customer apparently named Moon ask for sriracha sauce, but I didn't feel connected to any of it.

"Go talk to him," Liv urged. "This is your chance. And it means we won't have to stalk him at the gym. This almost looks like a coincidence!"

"This is a coincidence," I said robotically.

"That's true! Even better." Liv gave me a look and I realized that I had to get it together, especially since Liv was acting kind of crazy herself. What was my problem? I'd already done this twice. This was why we'd come all this way. I stood up slowly and turned toward the man with my last name, who was now sitting at his table. I took my time to push in my chair and examine him.

He was utterly normal looking, but at the same time strangely familiar, with brown hair, a mustache, of average height and build. He sat with a newspaper spread out before him. What was it about him that I recognized, I wondered, wracking my brain. Then I realized it with a start: He looked like a dad.

"Sorry to interrupt," I said faintly, after approaching his table and waiting for him to look up. He quickly skimmed the rest of the sentence he was reading.

"Yes?"

"I didn't meant to overhear," I started, unsure of how to start, "but is your last name Moon?"

"Yes, it is."

"Is your first name Hunter?"

He frowned. "Yes, although I usually go by my middle name. H. Collingsworth Moon, DDS," he said, reaching out to shake my hand. "How can I help you?"

I returned the handshake but felt my mouth go dry again and my breathing become shallow. This had to be it. I looked around to Liv for guidance, but instead made eye contact with the two women at the table next to us, who were watching the interaction unabashedly.

"Can I sit down for a second?" When he nodded, bewildered, I sank down and lowered my voice. "This is going to sound very strange. It might even sound made up. But I promise this isn't a practical joke or anything like that." He closed his newspaper and waited for me to go on. "I think it's possible that you're my father." I waited for some kind of reaction, but his facial muscles didn't move an inch.

"My name is Emma Moon, I'm Caroline Moon's daughter, and my father is . . . well . . . he has your name, Hunter Moon. I came to San Francisco to look for him and found out that he—well, maybe you—belongs to Equinox and I was headed there now to see if we could get his address, but then I heard the waitress here call your name, Moon, and I thought I'd try my luck." I trailed off, watching him for any look of recognition or familiarity, or perhaps the guilty realization that he'd been tracked down after all these years. His face was still curiously blank. "So, could that be you?"

"Caroline Moon?" he said, apparently still grappling with the facts.

"Yes! Do you know her?" My already rapid heart rate doubled.

"Are you asking if I was married to someone named Caroline Moon?" To my dismay, he did the last possible thing I expected. He laughed. "No, I'm sorry, but no. I don't mean to laugh. It's the absurdity of it all. No, I don't know a Caroline Moon and I've never been married. What's more, I can't even have kids. I'm sterile," he added bluntly. "Although I do belong to Equinox. So that's me. At least you saved yourself a trip."

I was completely at a loss. Here was the magical gym member and the elusive dentist from the phone call, all wrapped up in one. And he wasn't the guy. Something didn't make sense, though. Why couldn't we ever find him in any dental listings, even under the last name Moon alone? After all, he must have been licensed by the State of California. Were we doing something entirely wrong in our searches? Or was it possible he was lying?

"If you need a dentist, though, my practice is right next store." He pointed to a sign visible from the window: *H. Collingsworth Moone, DDS.*

Moone—with an *e*. The one thing we hadn't looked for, in any of our searches, ever, was a Dr. Moone. I cursed myself for not spelling out *Moon* for Frank, who'd inadvertently sent us on this fool's errand to storm the wrong castle.

The last Hunter was uncovered. The last stone unturned. And he wasn't my dad. The hazy idea of finding my father, the fantasy I always hoped would gel into a solid reality, vanished up in smoke before my eyes. It was over.

I felt like an utter failure. I'd been trying to prove them all wrong. Sam, Caroline, even Uncle Constantine. To prove my father was out there and wanted something to do with me. To show myself and everybody else that the last twenty-nine years of absence had been due to a mix-up, a lost telegram, a secret super-hero identity—anything to give lie to the theory that my father simply didn't care.

When I was a kid, and I realized the significance of having a dad who'd abandoned you, I knew that I had a choice. I could wallow and long for him. I could ask my mother furtive questions about whether I had his nose, make curious inquires about their wedding, check the mail hopefully every year, longing for a Christmas card. Or I could choose not to care. Until age eleven, I'll admit, I cared. I didn't come out and ask direct questions about where he was, but I collected details on the sly, fantasized about all the fantastic adventures he was having, and dreamed about the day he would show up at the door of our apartment.

Every year on my birthday, when it was time to blow out the candles on the cake, or pecan pie, whatever was on sale at Safeway that day, I would wish for my father. Then, on my eleventh birthday, I was sitting in front of a coffee cake with a slightly smushed right side, and my mother, tired from her shift at the pizza place but happy to be with me, told me to make a wish. I screwed up my face and realized that for ten straight years I had wished for Hunter Moon. And for ten straight years, I hadn't gotten my wish. It was getting old. Instead, I wished for the new Baby-Sitters Club Super Special. And guess what? I got it.

From that day until essentially the past few weeks of my life, I'd cut any longing for Hunter out of my system like a suspicious mole. If a new friend questioned where my dad was, I waved the question away and made a joke. When coworkers asked where my parents were from, I said Philadelphia, ignoring my California connection. The day my sixth grade art class made Father's Day cards, I claimed I had a stomachache and spent the afternoon in the nurse's office.

As Dr. Majdi had declared, I told myself not to care, and for the most part I didn't. It was only when my wedding started to creep up on me that the tug returned. The insistent tug that asked: Where did Moon come from anyway? Who is he? And what happened between him and my mother that made them both so hell-bent on pretending they'd never had a daughter?

CHAPTER 19

We need to talk, said an iMessage from Sam that lit up the screen.

I don't have anything to say, I quickly responded.

I do. Answer me please. The phone rang.

"Hello?" I said, picking up and quickly walking out of the apartment, where Liv and I were packing up our things. Our flight back to L.A. was in two hours and we had to leave for the airport any minute.

"Emma, I need to tell you something. Something I should have said from the beginning." He took a deep breath. "You don't need to find Hunter, because you have me. I'm your family now."

"My family?"

"Yes," he said firmly. "You can come home because you don't

197

need to look for him to find that stability, the one you've always craved yet also always convinced yourself you'll never find. You have it with me."

Something snapped when Sam said that. It was probably a combination of how true his words were, how deeply he understood me, and what he'd done to betray that understanding. I suddenly realized that I shouldn't have been surprised that looking for Hunter was a failure. After all, my relationship with Sam was a failure. Our marriage surely would have been, too.

"Let me ask you this, Sam. Do you think one *family member* would do this to another? Hurt them like this?" My voice was getting higher and louder and I had a sudden flash-forward. This was not going to go well.

"I made one mistake. One!" he said forcefully, more upset than I'd heard him possibly ever.

"*One?* Every single *day* that you lied to me about this was a mistake. One mistake? Every time you kissed me since then. Every time Val's name came up and you didn't tell me the truth."

"I see, so you're going to use this to push me away? I get it."

"*Use* this?"

"Emma, I'm talking about marriage, about spending our lives together. We said we would be together through thick and thin, that we would be there for each other for the rest of our lives, and you won't even consider forgiving me for one mistake that I made, that I acknowledge was awful?"

"Actually, we haven't made those promises yet. We haven't said our vows, Sam. Looks like I found out the truth about you just in time."

"I really hope you don't **mean that.**"

"I do mean it," I said, gaining strength from the power of my words. "We could never be a real family now."

"And you think if you find Hunter, that's real? He left your mom when you were a baby and hasn't been in contact since. You know what, Emma? You've always had one foot out the door. You've always been waiting for me to screw up, to prove your theory that you will end up alone. This is just the newest way for you to push me away."

I exploded. "I knew you *wouldn't get it.* And you never will." Tears burst out of my eyes and streamed down my face, racing past my mouth and chin as I shouted. I could taste their salty warm familiarity. He would never understand what it was like to be abandoned. Or to be cheated on, I mentally added. The memory and pain associated with the loss of my father and with what had happened with Sam and Val Baby seemed at the moment to be one and the same.

"It's over, Sam. It's done. I can't forgive you. I can't marry you. Good-bye."

Back in the rental car, packed up and heading toward the airport, I felt the full weight of the week's emotions on my shoulders, pulling me down. I couldn't begin to deal with any of it. I was relieved that Dusty and Carrick were out of the house when we left. Dusty had said to let him know when we were leaving, but I simply couldn't imagine talking to anyone besides Liv at the moment, so I left without saying good-bye, which made me feel guilty on top of everything else.

My phone began ringing loudly in my bag. Please, not Sam or Dusty, I prayed.

"Hey, did you give anyone my number?" I asked Liv, staring at the same unfamiliar 415 number calling me once again. Liv gave me a blank look. "Like maybe at the bar or something? Or maybe we left our card there? This San Francisco number keeps calling me but not leaving a message."

Liv shrugged. "Just answer. It's probably someone asking for money for Berkeley. Those are the only mysterious Bay Area numbers that ever call me. Get it over with so they stop calling."

"Hello?" I said questioningly.

"Emma?" said a slightly familiar voice that I couldn't quite place.

"Yes? Who's this?"

"This is Leo, from yesterday. We met at the gallery?"

"Of course. Um, how are you?" I asked, mystified as to why he would be calling.

"I'm really sorry to bother you, but you seemed like such a sweet girl, I had to call. I know it's not really my business, but then again, isn't it?"

"What isn't? Sorry, what's going on?"

"Okay, I'll get to the point. I lied to you the other day. By accident, of course, but an accidental lie is a lie nonetheless, at least that's what my Christian mama would say. But she also still insists on asking how my 'roommate' Hunter is when I call her every Sunday, so maybe we shouldn't use her as a moral guidepost." Leo laughed slightly at this.

"Is this about Hunter?"

"Yes!" Leo seemed thrilled that I guessed. "The thing is, Emma, after you left the gallery the other day I couldn't stop thinking about you. As soon as Hunter came back I told him the story of the girl with the fabulous cheekbones who stopped by the gallery looking for her father. But he was busy, so we didn't really have time to discuss it. Later that night I made a delicious osso buco. Immediately, I could tell that something wasn't right. When Hunter lies, he can't eat; that's his tell. When we sat down, he didn't touch his meal. That's when I knew he was hiding something. We thought it would be easier if I called to explain, as we met in person and had a nice little connection, I thought. Thank God you left your business card!"

"What do you mean? You called to explain what?"

"Sorry! I'm getting ahead of myself. When I said that it was impossible for Hunter to be your father . . . that wasn't technically true."

"Technically true?"

"Well, true at all, I suppose. As he finally admitted to me last night, my partner, Hunter, it turns out, actually *was* married to Caroline Moon—of course, he never told me this; it was his big deep, dark secret. I figure everybody has one, so I'm not that angry. And I know I told you that I'd been with him since before you were born, but that was a little math error on my part. It was probably just because of how young you look. I would have thought you were about twenty-five! Which makes sense. I hear Caroline is a very beautiful woman, although I'm pretty sure she's not his type." He laughed again. I was starting to realize this was how he finished his sentences, which would have been delightful had we been talking about anything else.

"Leo, does that mean he's my . . ." My heart was pounding so hard I couldn't finish the sentence, but it turned out I didn't have to.

"No, honey. Hunter was married to your mom, but—I'm sorry to say this because you seem like you would have been a lovely stepdaughter—he's not your dad." The constantly fluctuating balloon in my heart deflated wildly once again. I sat there in a stupor of shock, Liv waving frantically at me for some indication as to what was going on in the mystery call.

"But if you have time, we'd love to have you stop by. There are some things you need to know."

CHAPTER 20

"I met your mom when we were twenty-two years old," Hunter started. He had dark blue eyes and black hair and was still quite handsome. Shoots of gray around his temples gave him a kind of gravitas, but his blue button down shirt and corduroy pants were casual. So this man had been married to my mother. I couldn't get over it. Any of it. Canceling our flight at the last minute, driving to this beautiful house in the Castro, meeting Hunter . . . it all felt like a very strange dream. "At a bar in Ocean City, Maryland, called *Sea*crets. Get it?"

Yes, I thought, and I've never hated a pun more.

I silently nodded and took a sip of the tea Leo had insisted on serving once we were seated in the living room. This isn't kitchen talk, Leo had said knowingly before leading us to a gorgeous room with old-fashioned cyclists wallpaper and an ornate gold hanging chandelier.

My life had officially become surreal. There was a man sitting in front of me who had once had a relationship with my mother and seemingly held some secrets (or, sea-crets) to my past. Leo was perched next to him, way too excited about what was going on, but then again, he already knew what Hunter was about to say, so that had to be somewhat less stressful. Meanwhile, my best friend was hunched eagerly next to me, taking in every word. And Sam, who I'd spent the past four years loving and telling everything to, was nowhere in sight. Where was I? I wondered helplessly. How had I gotten here?

Oblivious to my down-the-rabbit-hole musings, Hunter continued. "Back then, Seacrets was essentially the only place to go out at night in Ocean City. It had an outdoor dance floor surrounded by huge flaming tiki torches. You know the type. It was cheesy, I suppose, but we loved it. I remember you could hear the ocean crashing from the bar. The weekend I met Caroline, I was on spring break from med school with a bunch of my classmates. It was an incredible night—"

"Wait, I thought you were an artist." I couldn't help cutting in. He looked like he was embarking on a long story, and to keep any grip on my sanity I had to keep some of the chess pieces in place. My mom vacationing in Ocean City made sense. I knew she went there growing up. But this sophisticated gay man, this Hunter Moon, artist/doctor, swaying under the cheesy tiki torches—that most certainly did not.

"I am, now. Back then I was studying to be a doctor, one of the many things I was doing to please my family. As fate would have it,

I met Caroline the last night of the trip, on the dance floor. We liked to say we fell for each other in the soul train line." He laughed, recalling a memory that no one else in the room was privy to. I closed my eyes briefly. Could my life story get any more ridiculous? "Eventually this turned into a dance-off"—apparently, it could—"which turned into talking, which turned into a long walk on the beach. She wanted to work in social policy, and I wanted to join Doctors Without Borders. We both lived in Georgetown, we both wanted to make a difference in the world, and we got along great. It worked. When we got back to D.C. we starting dating seriously almost immediately."

At this point, I started to feel a sense of foreboding. This was not a beach week romance. And, of course, given his name, this guy, this self-proclaimed nondad, was undoubtedly about to factor into my life in some major way. I had the feeling, however, that I wasn't going to like how he did.

"At the time, Caro was waitressing and saving up to go to grad school, while taking night classes for her bachelor's degree. Her family couldn't afford to help her out, so she was doing it on her own. She was the most amazing woman," Hunter reflected. "So strong and smart. She was unlike anyone I had ever met." Leo looked hurt for a moment, perhaps realizing for the first time that his partner had truly loved this woman in some way. As I knew from recent experience, no one wants anyone else to be that close to his or her partner, romantically or otherwise, no matter how ancient history it was.

"At the time, it seemed like the perfect relationship. We were both very independent; we didn't need to be around each other all the time. She was working six days a week, taking classes when she could afford them, and in the meantime reading every political book she could get her hands on in the library. I was practically living at school, trying to make it on the pediatric surgery track. An incredibly hard task made even more difficult by the fact that I had absolutely no desire to be a doctor. Looking back, it's frightening how much of my life was being lived for other people," he said sadly. It *was* sad—I felt for him—but it was difficult to focus on anything else besides the turmoil of not knowing the end of this story. I inwardly willed him to go on.

"To be fair," he said, brightening somewhat, "my life wasn't all terrible. I was dating my best friend. When we were both around, we had a great time. We had wonderful talks. We would go out dancing. She used to make what is still the most delicious homemade pasta I've ever had, tagliatelle, orecchiette, you name it." Leo looked even more flustered by this statement than he had by Hunter's earlier revelations. "We would eat her latest creation sitting on the couch with our feet propped up on the coffee table, her telling stories about her customers, me reciting the names of the bones in the hand. I would think, I can do this, I'm pretty much happy."

I couldn't picture any of it: my mom chatting for hours or dancing 'til dawn, not to mention having an entire relationship with this man. However, this was thirty years, three thousand miles, and one sexual orientation ago—I guess anything was possible.

"Did you know you were gay? Is that why you were only 'pretty much happy'?" Liv asked, speaking for the first time since she'd greeted Leo, introduced herself to Hunter, and quizzically accepted her mug of Lady Grey tea.

"Yes." He paused. "Mostly. I knew deep down, but I hadn't let myself acknowledge the truth. Like Caroline, my family was very Catholic, so it simply wasn't an option. I'd been praying so hard to get into heaven for so many years, it seemed a shame to waste it on a one-night stand with Carlos from my neurological disorders module, no matter how gorgeous he was."

Hunter paused and gave a small, rueful smile, while Leo took this as an opportunity to freshen our mugs with hot water from the teapot, fake whispering as he leaned forward, "Makes sense. He's always loved Latin men."

They both laughed appreciatively, grateful to release some of the tension, but I continued staring edgily at Hunter. I felt like I was watching a horror movie and the victim, shakily holding the steak knife she'd haphazardly grabbed, was slowly rounding the corner of every room, ready to get hosed. Just get to it already, I pleaded inwardly.

"The point is—we were pretty much happy, and very, very Catholic. Which meant no sex before marriage. This was a huge relief for me, of course. Things progressed as they were. We got closer, although we never got to—or in my case had to—test-drive the equipment, and bam, we were engaged and married six months after we met. A year later, Caro was pregnant." A sudden shock went through my body. "I'll never forget the day she told me. We were on a long weekend to Cape Cod. It was Labor Day—I remember because classes were about to start, and I was dreading going back to another year of misery in med school. We were cracking open lobsters at dinner the first night, a vacation splurge, and I poured her a beer. She glanced at it, pointed to her stomach, and shook her head. Then she dipped a claw in melted butter and kept right on eating. I knew what she was getting at—I mean, I *was* in med school. Although, thinking back on it now, she really shouldn't have been eating shellfish either. In any case, I immediately knew she was pregnant. With you," he added awkwardly.

"But then, how do you know?" I sputtered, my face turning red while I blurted out the desperate question I knew I had to ask. "How do you know I'm not . . . yours? If you were married when she got pregnant, how do you know you're not my father?" My voice trailed off quietly as I asked this and I felt everyone in the room looking at me. I felt completely transparent, as if I were wearing invisible skin. Everyone could see my heart and bones, my desires and fears, my insecurities and mostly my deep, reckless desire to find my father.

With a small, sad chuckle, Hunter shook his head and explained. "It was about nine months short of impossible. We only had sex once, on our honeymoon, a full year before, and even then I'm not sure we did it long enough for any fluids to be exchanged." He looked guiltily uncomfortable after saying this, realizing too late he was talking about sex with my mother, even if it was terrible, purely efficient sex.

"Your honeymoon?" I asked. He nodded, eager to give one of the few explanations he had to offer me.

"We went to Jamaica. We had one of those all-inclusive packages, which at the time seemed like the height of sophistication. White sand beaches, swaying palm trees, and all the frozen strawberry daiquiris we could drink. We were staying somewhere called Hedonism or something ridiculous like that. I remember Caroline joked, 'If they're gonna name it that, why don't they just call it Group Sex?'"

"You picked a hotel called Hedonism?" Leo interjected, laughing affectionately, seemingly over his momentary discomfort. "And she was surprised you were gay?"

Hunter smiled, took Leo's hand, and, still looking at me, continued. "The point is, we had some great memories, some wonderful times, and lots of laughs. No matter what, she could always make me laugh. Caro was a real funny lady." We were all silent. I wondered which Hunter thought was funnier, Caro lying about my father's identity for my entire life or the Hedonism joke.

"That makes sense because Emma's funny, too," Liv said loyally, sweetly mistaking my bitter silence for a need to be included in the compliment. Leo nodded in vehement agreement. I wanted to ask him when he'd ever heard me tell a joke.

"Anyway, it turns out it took Jamaican-strength ganja to get me to have sex with a woman, and even then I was picturing the parasailing instructor." Hunter laughed, taking a crack at the humor thing as well. I wanted to lie down on the fancy yellow brocade couch and close my eyes. It was too much. "After that week, I never tried again and Caroline didn't push it. I think she knew. Like I said, she was smart, she got me. Maybe too much."

Wonderful. My entire life story had been reduced to a lesson on casual drug usage and Catholic guilt.

"That's how, of course, I knew the baby—er, you—weren't—mine," Hunter stumbled. "I did the math. I knew, and she knew I knew. Despite that, we stayed together until you were born. I helped her get back on her feet, helped her take care of you for the first few months. Then I moved back to California and we filed for divorce. It was what was best for everyone. She could blame the whole thing on me, say I left, call me a deadbeat dad and all that. And I could finally get to be myself. I'm sorry, Emma. I know none of this has been easy on you. And honestly, I have thought of you many times over the years. Despite the complicated circumstances, I'm very happy I've been able to meet you. Again."

Hunter looked over at Leo, who squeezed his hand tight. I was completely blown away. Part of me wanted to yell at him for deserting us, for leaving me, a helpless little baby with no father. After all, I was legally his child. But you aren't, a voice reminded me, not really. The letter of the law said I was Hunter's, as his name was on my birth certificate. But the spirit of the law, the meaning and intent behind the classification of *father*, said he was not. I cursed my Legal Philosophy seminar for ingraining those concepts in me so deeply.

I had no idea what to say or what I wanted to get across. Part of me didn't want to let him off the hook. After all, he'd been party to the biggest betrayal of my life. But even while reeling from the shock, I knew it wasn't his fault. In any case, what could he possibly have done differently? I suppose he could have stayed with a wife he didn't love, raising a child who wasn't his, in a life he wouldn't have chosen. I wouldn't wish that on anyone. The anger started to dissipate, but I still wasn't happy, and I had no energy left to fake it. I couldn't be accepting and forgiving while learning that my entire life was a lie. That I came from nowhere, from no one. I had nothing left to say.

"Can I ask you a question?" Hunter asked gently.

"Sure," I said, glad for an excuse to continue the conversation. I still had no idea how I felt, and although this was where Hunter's story ended and mine kept going, I didn't want to let go of him quite yet.

"How did you find me?"

"Let's see." I dug back in my mind to come up with an accurate answer. "The one thing my mom told me about you, besides your name, was that you were from California. I picked up that you'd moved to San Francisco, after hearing her mention it to other people. Then we came here to look for you." I felt my cheeks flush at this. It was so cloak-and-dagger, so tacky. Especially since it turned out I'd been searching for someone to whom I wasn't remotely related. "We checked the library and all over the Internet for a couple days, but never ran across any of your information—"

"I told you that you need a website," Leo scolded. "He's so old-fashioned. He doesn't believe in the Internet."

"What can I say? I like to draw pictures, but I don't have any desire to tweet about them," Hunter said charmingly. I had a deep stab of wishing this endearing man was my father while I reflected on Leo's words. That explained why he'd been so impossible to locate. Why he was nowhere to be found online. The pieces were all falling into place. Unfortunately, where they fell was of little help.

"How did you find me in the end?" Hunter pressed.

"This part is pretty unbelievable. Liv picked up a postcard advertising your show at a bar one night. It was completely by chance."

"Destiny," Leo said knowingly. "It was destiny that you chose this week to look for him, the week of the show. Destiny that you saw the ad. This was meant to be." Liv nodded solemnly.

"I guess." I tried to smile.

"Why *did* you choose this week?" Hunter asked. "Why now?"

"Oh, because I'm supposed to get married on Saturday. I guess it was a last-minute effort to explore my roots. Or something."

"On Saturday? You mean, three days from now?" Leo demanded.

"Yes. This trip was supposed to be my bachelorette party, kind of. What a hoot, right?" I said, laughing derisively. "I'm sorry to have taken up so much of your time and energy. It was really nice to meet you both." I started to stand, but Liv shot up her hand to stop me from leaving.

"You forgot the most important thing," she said urgently. We all turned to look at her. "Who did Caroline have the affair with while you were married? Who's the guy? That must be Emma's dad, right?"

Hunter faltered. "I suppose it is. I'm sorry, I never knew. It didn't seem right, considering what our marriage had gone through and what a disappointing husband I turned out to be. She respected my privacy and I figured I owed her as much. I never asked, and, needless to say, Caro never said a word."

CHAPTER 21

One of the most important classes you take in law school is Evidence. It's probably the most practical course because, unlike the majority of what you learn, it actually teaches you how to practice law. The class is all about the—wait for it—*evidence* you're allowed to introduce in court. What documents you can show the jury and what your witnesses can say on the stand. You know how on *Law and Order*, the lawyer asks the witness a question, and the other side shouts, Objection! usually right as the witness is starting to get into the good stuff? Well, *Objection!* is pretty much a fancy way of saying: You can't introduce that evidence, so hush.

Lawyers object to evidence for all sorts of different reasons, but the most important objection has to be hearsay. Hearsay is a big no-no in court. The technical definition is "an out-of-court statement used for the truth of the matter asserted," which means you can't try to prove a fact by repeating something that someone else said. You can't tell a jury, "My neighbor Rhonda *told me* that she wanted to kidnap her friend's dog," or "My grandmother *said* she wanted to leave me all her money," with the implication "so it must be true." Those aren't facts, they're hearsay. Objection! sustained.

The assumption is that people lie all the time, for all sorts of reasons. Maybe (hopefully) Rhonda was joking around about the dog thing, or your nana simply didn't want to decide who got the Velázquez, so she took the easy way out and let the grandkids fight it out. Hearsay rules dictate that only in court, when the witness has taken an oath, with the pressure of cross-examination present, can what someone says really be considered evidence. Accordingly, as lawyers, we are taught not to believe hearsay, not to trust gossip. "He said, she said" doesn't count.

I don't want to brag, but I got an *A* in Evidence. It was one of the few classes I intrinsically understood. From the first day, I got the point of the class, to sift between the nonsense and make rules for how a courtroom should operate. It was one of the few law school classes that revolved around good old commonsense. I turned in my exam with a bounce in my step and wasn't surprised to find my first ever *A* the day our grades went up online. That's why it was even more shocking that when it came to the ultimate question of my life—who I was and where I came from—I hadn't applied a thing I'd learned. I'd let the hearsay in.

When Caroline told me the pack of lies about my childhood, I should have taken the lessons I learned and applied them in real life.

I should have made her swear on a Bible, deposed her, or at least questioned her bullshit, especially given how random and unspecific she was about her past, and, in turn, mine. Had I learned nothing? I felt like I should call Berkeley and have them rescind my diploma, or at least lower my GPA by a few decimals.

"What are you thinking about?" Liv finally asked, after twenty minutes of sitting side by side and silently staring at the crashing waves of Ocean Beach.

"Hearsay."

"Gotcha." Liv leaned over and ripped off a piece of bread from the baguette we'd picked up on the way there. After we left Hunter and Leo's, she ran into a corner market and soon emerged with said baguette, two different kinds of cheese, a bag of double chocolate Milanos, and a large green bottle of San Pellegrino, declaring that we were having a picnic on the beach and we would talk when we got there. I was compliant as we drove to Ocean Beach, a dark but pretty shoreline on the western coast of the city. Despite the late afternoon sun peeking through the clouds, it was mostly deserted.

"Well, we found Hunter," Liv said. I laughed despite myself.

"We certainly did. Can you believe what a liar Caro is?" I said, slicing the package open with a plastic knife and helping myself to a surprisingly good hunk of cheese, not even bothering with the bread.

"Emma, I really think you should call her."

"Why? What would be the point? Do you think she's going to tell me the truth now?"

Liv stayed silent, perhaps agreeing with me. Or else deciding I was a lost cause.

We were sitting cross-legged on the red fleece blanket I always took on flights, as I was notoriously cold on airplanes. It was the relic of an outdoor concert Sam and I attended in East L.A. two years prior. Our friend Lilly, a drummer with streaks of blue hair that flashed when she tossed her head to the side, had invited us to see her band's outdoor show. Sam and I arrived with a six-pack of domestic beer and hipster sunglasses, ready to rock out, Coachella style, only to find that what she hadn't mentioned was that it was a *marching* band—which was so retro and odd, only someone as cool as Lilly could pull it off.

The "show" was hosted by the South Pasadena County Civic Center, and you were far more likely to find battle hymns and giant turkey legs than hippies and Molly. Nevertheless, we had a blast. We shared our beers with a family up from Orange County, who in turn shared their cozy blanket. The very same blanket we accidentally stuck in our bag at the end of the night, upon which Liv and I were now perched.

"Come on, let's put our feet in," Liv said, getting up and walking jauntily toward the ocean, managing not to spill her fizzy water like only the well-coordinated can.

The sand was cold and wet, as if high tide had come and gone, and my shoulders, previously warm from the sun, were immediately covered in goose bumps. The last time Liv and I were on a proper beach was our bar trip to Greece, which we took the day after the bar exam. It was three weeks with nothing to do but island hop, lie in the sun, and try to stop our muscle memory from typing out the rule against perpetuities in our sleep. I'll never forget how I felt during those twenty days of bliss: completely free, yet also centered in a way that was rare for me. Jared and I had broken up, which felt like a giant relief, I had a job at a law firm in L.A. waiting for me, and I was with my best friend in Greece. I truly felt as if I had my whole life ahead of me.

Every day on our trip Liv and I would wake up early and head to the water, the sea rimmed with white or black sand, depending on the island. On the way we'd stop for a cappuccino and down the frothy mixture without communicating, unless it was to ask the other to borrow a euro. Then we would make our way to the edge of the water and plop down with our books, each absorbed in our own little world until midafternoon, when the sun was high in the sky and one of us would suggest a mojito. That first drink was a signal that one of us was ready to talk. To start the day, discuss the hijinks from the night before, and begin the cycle of eating, drinking, and dancing that defined each night. Once we put our books down and agreed it was time for the white rum concoction, we were connected for the rest of the day, but it was in silent agreement that we had those quiet mornings.

That's how well Liv and I could communicate, how well we could read each other. Which is why right then I didn't need to tell her that I was feeling lost, embarrassed, and angry, because she already knew.

"You know there are sharks in there," I warned Liv, as she walked out farther into the surf, recalling a frightening article I'd read about a surfer fighting off a shark attack at Ocean Beach.

"We're not swimming, Em." Liv was notoriously unafraid of sea creatures, or the water, for that matter. On our ferries between Greek islands, I'd been genuinely concerned an animal would manage to jump up on the boat and eat me, whereas Liv would spend hours in the water floating on her back, bobbing farther and farther into the blue-green surf without a care in the world, until I'd come out and shout lectures to her about the power of the rip tide.

As soon as I reached the water's edge I forgot my complaints, rolled up my jeans, and walked into the chilly spray, kicking up water with every step. The ocean wasn't as green and the sun wasn't as warm, but allowing the waves to rush under my feet while Liv hiked up her maxi dress and ventured out to where the water touched her thighs reminded me of our magical days in Santorini and Mykonos.

"What am I going to do now? Hunter, Sam, should I just give up on them all?" I said. I didn't really need a response, but I wanted to put it out there.

Even though I was standing behind her, I could see Liv looking upward, lost in thought, the way she did when she was about to say something really honest, which was often something I might not like. Right then, the waves hit my ankles hard, shooting spurts of water up my legs and dampening my jeans. I rolled my pants up another few inches and felt the whoosh of the water receding past me, back into the surf. I could have moved in a few more feet, past where the waves broke and where the calm water would gently lap at my calves, but I didn't. The hard, unexpected spray felt good. It matched how I felt inside.

"I don't think it's really fair to equate the two, Hunter and Sam that is." Liv turned around and walked back toward me, slowly trudging through the water, pausing every couple of steps as a wave rushed by and she waited for it to crash. "What Sam did is horrible, and you have to decide whether you can forgive him. But just because he fucked up, and because your mom had a big secret that she kept from you, that doesn't mean that you can't trust anyone. It doesn't make what Sam did any *more* wrong."

I considered this. My first instinct was to vehemently disagree. I wanted to say that when you discover that your fiancé cheated on you and kept it a secret for years, and in the same week you find out your mom has been lying about who your father is for almost three decades, you can't help but equate the two. It does, in fact, make it more wrong, because it hurts more. But instead I took a moment and grasped for logic. Liv was being honest with me, which couldn't be easy right now. The least I could do was not take my frustrations out on her.

"I understand what you're saying," I said slowly. "But it's easier said than done. You know what I really wish? I wish I hadn't started this search for Hunter now. I wish I had ignored his existence and gone about my business, like I did for the past twenty-nine years. If it didn't affect me for this long, why did I have to start obsessing about it now?" Liv gave me a dubious look. "Okay, I realize this isn't a coincidence. I know the decision to look for my father now has a lot to do with marrying Sam. But still, why did I have to choose this moment to start caring about the other half of my genetic material?" What I really wanted to add, but couldn't say aloud, was, Had I done this now in order to give myself some rationale for questioning my marriage in the first place, like Sam had implied on the phone?

"Emma. Can I say something? Do you promise you won't get mad?"

"Okay," I said warily.

"You keep saying how you just started caring about finding Hunter now, and how you had no interest in him before. And please don't get pissed off, but I don't think your interest in him is as new as you think. Don't you feel like part of you has *always* been looking for him?"

I stopped in my wet, sandy tracks, genuinely surprised.

"No. I really don't. I don't know what you're talking about. I've never looked for my dad or made any effort to find him. How many times have I even said his name in the last fifteen years?" I made a concerted effort to keep my voice from sounding defensive.

"Emma, I could be completely wrong when I say this, but isn't that why you moved to California in the first place?" Her voice rose a little. "Isn't that why you went to law school out here? Isn't that why you moved to L.A., because you still hadn't met him and you weren't ready to leave the state where you knew he lived?"

I was shocked. This was a theory I had honestly never considered. I'd chosen Berkeley to attend law school, same as Liv, but when it came time to pick our jobs and move to the city where we would permanently reside, the majority of my classmates, including her, headed back east. I, however, stayed firmed entrenched in California. I moved to a city where I didn't know a soul. Was it possible that I'd put the entire state of California on a pedestal not because of the Joni Mitchell song, but because of my mythical father?

All at once I realized my toes were numb. I longed for the cozy sweater I'd left lying on the red blanket. I motioned to Liv that I was going to head back, and wordlessly we clomped our way out of the fizzy surf and onto the dry sand.

"How long have you thought this?" I asked once we'd plopped down on the blanket, passing a towel back and forth in a fruitless effort to de-sand our feet.

"I think the first time I really thought about it was during our trip to Greece," Liv answered. This kind of coincidence wasn't unusual for Liv and me, one of us bringing up a topic the other had been silently musing about. Liv had taken the words out of my mouth so often that I'd long since stopped commenting on it.

"Everyone kept asking where we were from and you always said California, instead of Virginia." Liv laughed kindly at the memory. "It was cute."

"Yeah, but we'd lived there for three years, and I was staying."

"I know, I know, don't get defensive. I could tell that you *did* feel like you were from California, that you felt like you belonged here. I remember thinking to myself, why does Emma love California so much? I liked Berkeley, but you always felt more at home here than I did. You never even considered coming back east. Then I remembered one of the only times I heard you bring up your dad. It was junior year of high school, when you drank tequila for the first time and told me your dad lived in California and you wanted to find him someday. I'm not saying it was a conscious decision, but those two events, they're obviously connected."

"Maybe you're right." The sun, which had been providing spotty warmth, was now firmly planted behind a huge cumulus cloud. I scanned the horizon, noticing how gray the ocean looked.

"We missed our flight and we're stuck on a cold beach, with no idea what to do next," I mused. "And I've been looking for my birth father my whole life and didn't even know it. And it turned out that he wasn't even my dad. Things are really looking up."

"You know what's funny, Emma?" Liv said thoughtfully.

"What?"

"You're not going to believe this, but I envied your home life growing up."

I barked out a short laugh. "You're right, I don't believe that for a second. Did you want an excuse for a defiant tattoo or something?"

"I knew you and your mom didn't get along, but I always really liked her. She seemed to treat you like a real person, not like a kid. I remember I used to go over to your house and she would be heading out for the night to some fund-raiser or whatever, and she would ask what your plans were, like you were equals. It was cool."

"I guess the freedom was nice," I said, not really wanting to go into it.

"It was. And remember all those nights we would pile up sheets and blankets on the porch and talk all night?"

"Of course." Liv and I would grab dozens of snacks, magazines, and the comfiest blankets we could find, creating a crumbly nest to sleep in outside. We used to wake up feeling queasy, both from the excessive quantity of lime-flavored chips we'd consumed and from the specificity of the *Cosmo* tips on how to give a holiday-themed blow job we'd read. Still, those were some of my favorite nights of high school. If my mom cared about the noise or the damage to her bed linens, she never mentioned it.

"That *was* fun," I agreed. "I'd say the porch sleepovers make up for lying about the identity of my father, wouldn't you?"

Liv laughed a little and stood up, wiping the sand off her clothes.

Without discussion, we packed up our picnic. While she folded the blanket, I made a run for the trash can down the beach. We walked back to the car, the wind whipping our backs. The sun was officially gone.

"Plus, you had that attic room. I loved that room."

"I liked that room, too. I liked that entire house," I said. "Although living with Caro in it was pretty challenging. To be honest, I never really understood why we moved there in the first place."

"What do you mean?"

"I mean, at the time she had just started at the lobby; she was at the bottom of the totem pole. We were still pinching pennies, still eating spaghetti most nights. I know we were Italian, but still. I never really understood how we could afford that house, or why she chose to spend the little money we did have on the mortgage. After all, she hated the suburbs. We were much happier in D.C. Of course," I added diplomatically, "I wouldn't have met you if we hadn't moved, so I wouldn't change a thing."

Liv didn't seem to hear my compliment. I looked at her over the top of the rental car. She was frozen at the driver's side, keys in hand, caught in an expression of puzzlement.

"That's it," she said faintly, then with more conviction, "Emma, that's it!"

"What is?" I asked nervously.

"That's how we're going to find your dad!" She let everything in her hands go and ran over to my side of the car, dropping the blanket clean on the ground.

"What do you mean?" I said, almost scared by her level of enthusiasm. Her hands were gripping my arms so hard she was practically cutting off my circulation, and she was standing so far on her tiptoes that we were almost the same height.

"That's how Caro got the house! It has to be."

"How?" I was struggling both to keep up with her train of thought and to loosen her viselike grip on my arms.

She took a deep breath and settled back on her feet. "What if it was your dad?"

"What was?"

Liv spoke slowly. "What if it was your dad who bought the house?" She paused to allow the notion to sink in. "It makes perfect sense. You're totally right: Caro could never have afforded that house when she first got out of school and started a new job. Plus, she moved out right after you went to college. She hated it there, you're right. I'll bet you anything it was your dad, not Hunter, but your real dad, who bought it for you guys, so you could have someplace nice to live." She paused again, letting the idea fully sink in.

"And do you know what that means?"

I shook my head, starting to feel heady with excitement, realizing how much sense she was making.

"That means all we have to do is figure out whose name was on the deed at the time you lived there and that's him. That's your dad."

The answer had been in front of me the whole time, but I couldn't see it. Like I'd been searching frantically for my glasses for the last twenty minutes, and then saw them resting plainly on top of the book I'd been reading. How did Caro buy that house, and why? It was a question I'd wondered so many times. I saw it now, plain as day. My father must have bought it for us. There was no other plausible explanation. Without a doubt, I knew that Liv was right. I also knew one other thing with absolute and utter certainty. That was how I was going to find him.

CHAPTER 22

The day we moved to the house on Redwood Lane, it was Labor Day weekend, the time of year when Virginia inevitably tips from summer to fall. No matter how hot the summer, every year during the first week of September, the heavy Virginia humidity is swept away by a chilly, slightly ominous wind that settles comfortably in the sky. As the months pass, the chill digs in deeper and it gets colder and darker until winter. That day in September, however, it was perfect—cool, crisp, and gorgeous.

Caro hired the moving company Starving Student Movers. They seemed like okay guys when they got there, but I had my first clue that they might be less than reputable when I asked the one taking apart my bedroom furniture where he went to school and he looked at me blankly before hustling my scratched wooden desk chair down the stairs. Starving Students, my ass. When Caro realized at the end of the day that one large box was missing from our belongings, and started tearing through the rest of the boxes, I abandoned my job of unpacking the pots and pans.

"It's fine, Mom, it wasn't that much stuff," I said, following her around as she deftly sliced through boxes like a seasoned surgeon. "It was only the old wooden jewelry box with barely anything in it, some pictures you don't even like, and the video camera."

The fact that Caro was so upset about the theft frightened me even more than the missing box itself. It gave credence to the seriousness of the situation, made the nonstudent movers seem more like dangerous villains than the harmless stoners they probably were. I wanted the whole thing forgotten, labeled an innocent mistake. After all, I'd gotten them lunch at Wendy's. Who, except the truly evil, would steal from someone who brought them a Frosty?

"Get in the car," she said, ignoring my attempts to calm her down and grabbing the keys off the top of an unopened box. "We're getting that video camera."

The video camera in question was, at the time, my one and only prized possession. When I was younger, I spent long summer days writing, directing, and videotaping one-woman versions of various productions. At age fourteen, I still loved the camera and was randomly inspired by certain things that I thought were artistic but were mostly nauseatingly trite. Like when I set up the camera to record the day the cherry blossoms bloomed in D.C.'s Tidal Basin. I figured I'd fast-forward the footage later and it would be a kind of nature flipbook. It turned out to be the most boring eight hours of tape ever recorded, which I quit screening after approximately fourteen minutes.

As uncomfortable as the whole situation made me, I headed to the passenger seat without a word. I hugged tight to the knowledge that my mom knew how important the camera was to me.

We spent the next three hours driving from one pawnshop to the next, making efficient stops at places called Fistful of Pesos and Hock-o Bell. It was at the simply put Cash 'n Hand where we found our stolen items. By the time we got to Cash 'n Hand, I knew the drill. I headed straight to the electronics section, ignoring the muddy-complexioned teens staring longingly at the guitars and the indiscernibly aged men with streaky-gray ponytails leaning against the glass case.

"This is it!" I shouted when I found our camera in the corner, hastily propped on a tripod. I mentally congratulated myself on having dragged my book bag on the ground for several blocks the previous summer before realizing the camera was inside, giving it a distinctive metallic scratch.

My mom didn't seem to hear me, though; she was standing frozen at the jewelry counter. She pointed to the rings and the man behind the counter dug through the lowest shelf, his face locked in a grimace, before pulling out a pearl ring I'd never seen before. The man handed it to her, after shooting her an accusatory glance and rubbing his arm dramatically. My mom ignored him and slid on the ring, which appeared to fit perfectly.

I grabbed the camera and approached the counter, triumphantly announcing that I'd found it and it was definitely ours. The man, still holding his elbow as if he'd been injured at war, looked skeptical, and with an unfriendly glint in his squinty brown eyes, asked how the hell I could tell.

"Open it up," I suggested, gambling that the thieves hadn't thought to remove the evidence. "If the tape inside is me describing the life cycle of the cherry blossom, it's ours."

In the end, that was how we proved it. When the tape inside featured my pseudo-artsy voice explaining that the trees bloom *a mere week a year*, there wasn't much they could do but call the cops and let us point out our belongings.

I always thought that story was the most important thing to remember about moving day, that unexpectedly bizarre day in our lives. But what if it was something else as well? What if that was the day we moved into the house my father bought for us?

After Liv figured out that my father's name could likely be found on the deed to the house, we quickly connected the dots. We could use Westlaw, the legal search engine, to track the deed transfers over time and figure out who owned it when Caro and I lived there. The search tool was typically used to identify easements or the identities of bona fide purchasers in foreclosure cases, but it would work for our purposes as well. We would simply type in the address and search for the relevant year. First, however, we would need a law library.

Which was how we found ourselves standing in front of a heavy wooden door on the Berkeley campus, having traversed San Francisco, crossed the Bay Bridge, and weaved through the East Bay to get there.

"Are you sure this is a good idea?" I said anemically, a question we both knew was a formality. We'd come this far. We weren't about to turn back now.

"No, but it's the best one we've got," Liv answered. I couldn't believe what we were about to do, but she was right. In order to access Westlaw, and the all-powerful legal database of home listings, we'd need a user name and password. Ever since Tom Cruise showed the world how easy it was to take down corrupt lawyers in *The Firm*, law firms had become notoriously paranoid about privacy and now required their lawyers to use matter numbers, which could be billed back to specific cases and clients, to get any information off Westlaw. Although we of course had user names, neither Liv nor I was willing to get disbarred for this mission, so we couldn't use an active case number to log on. We did, however, know one person who could use his Westlaw account for anything he damn well pleased. We knew a law professor.

When STB swung open the door I was intimidated by his handsome, shit-eating grin. He looked like he was trying out for the role of sexy, disheveled professor in a cheesy network sitcom, with his blazer with the patches on the sleeves and his white collared shirt. I smugly noted the overly shiny loafers he wore, which any decent costume designer probably would have replaced with Vans so he wouldn't look like he was trying quite so hard.

I don't have anything to prove to this guy, I reminded myself. It was he who had everything to prove to me. Well, to Liv, but to me by extension. This awareness gave me the burst of confidence I needed to plunge forward with my plan and explain the situation.

"Really, we don't need much from you, besides your Westlaw log-in. I swear we're not stalking anyone or doing any illegal searches—we need to check out some relatively harmless information, which we think will lead us to my dad, but without a client to bill the matter to, we can't use our work passwords."

I wrapped up my brief explanation from the same awkward position I'd been in since we entered the office, sitting precariously close to the edge of a leather wing chair he'd offered me, while he comfortably swiveled back and forth at his desk and Liv sat with her legs tucked under her on the tan love seat in the corner. She looked far too comfortable in STB's presence for my taste. But what could I say? It was my fault we were there in the first place.

Tony agreed to my request almost at once, and I couldn't help but wonder if this was because of the ancient dirt I had on him. I searched for clues that he was still with Professor Gray, while also examining the way he communicated with Liv. It wasn't that I was worried about her getting involved with him again, but that wouldn't stop the creep from trying.

We followed Tony into a small professors-only research lab down the hall that had sleek MacBook Pros and comfortable chairs. Tony offered us a fancy coffee from the Nespresso, but I declined, ready to get started.

As soon as he logged on, he moved out of the way and let me take his place at the keyboard. As I scrolled and found the proper database, I heard him and Liv wander away, their chatting voices quickly fading away. No doubt they were headed back to his office, presumably to give me some privacy. But it wouldn't have mattered if they'd been talking directly into my ear; I wouldn't have heard them. It was as if my brain could only take so much stimulation and the task at hand was currently occupying one hundred percent of my senses.

I stared at the search screen, unsure of whether I was ready to take the final step in my journey. After this, we were officially out of ideas. Maybe I was better off not looking, and then the possibility of discovery could always be out there. Or maybe it was better not knowing at all. I hesitated.

Then, out of the blue, a memory popped into my head: the one time I told Val about my birth father. We'd been drinking Sancerre on a Sunday afternoon in my front yard and the buzz I felt gave me the freedom to share this piece of information, which I normally wouldn't have divulged. She responded by remarking that it kind of sucked not to know who he was, but wouldn't it be rad if he was some random famous guy? She went on an amusing rant about my dad as a potential rock star, whose concert we might have attended without even knowing it. She urged me to find him so we could get backstage passes for whatever awesome band he was opening for. I guess even in our fantasy hypothetical we were willing to accept that at his age, he wouldn't be headlining. I remember looking at her in disbelief and thinking how amazing it would be to *be* her, to automatically jump to the positive, unrealistic scenario in your head, before even considering any of the soul-crushing ones.

It was the memory of that afternoon, and Val's perspective on life, that made me find the right search box for house deeds and tentatively type in my home address. Val Baby did exactly what she wanted and assumed everything would turn out fabulously.

As a result, it usually did. I wanted to think like her, just for a second. I wanted to be falsely optimistic, to go for what I wanted, consequences be damned. WWVBD? There was no question in my mind that she'd run the search without hesitation. I pressed enter.

That Wednesday evening, as I stared at the computer screen and read the name of the mortgagor for the house on Redwood Lane during my years of high school, my first thought was that Dr. Majdi was right. The wave had arrived.

For a moment, I thought it was a mistake. I scanned the screen for a frenzied few seconds, looking for the name in the proper time period. When I found it, I felt the oddest sense of relief. I must have typed in the wrong address, I thought. I retyped the address, double-checked the screen, and realized with a stomach-crunching certainty that I had typed it correctly the first time. It wasn't the wrong address. It was mine all right. And it happened to be three doors down from the mortgagor's other house, also on Redwood Lane.

Mike Madigan, neighbor, father of three, defense contractor, and old movie fan, was my father.

The man who had always been so nice to me, always offered to fix things around the house, and always laughed at my jokes, even the really unfunny ones. The same man my mother had avoided like the plague.

Mike Madigan had purchased our home the month before we moved in, and he'd sold it weeks after I left for college. He was the purchaser, but he put my mother's name on the deed as well. This wasn't an investment property. He was my dad.

I left the screen up and stumbled in the general direction of STB's office. I had to ask for directions from a student I passed in the hall, as dazed and disoriented as I was. There was something else, something hugely important in the back of my brain that demanded my attention, but my survival mechanism told me to find Liv before turning to face it. The wave Dr. Majdi had warned me about was hovering above my head, gathering steam. I needed to find Liv, before I focused too hard on the implications of this discovery and determined exactly what my memory was trying to grasp.

Finally, minutes away from using the emergency phone I saw in the hall to call security and ask them to help me locate a missing person, I found the right wooden door. Without thinking, I pushed open the door, eager to find Liv and retain some sense of equilibrium. Was it true? Was Mike Madigan my father? Could there be any other explanation?

Then, at the exact moment I opened the door to Tony's office, the awful nagging thought, the one that had been jumping up and down for attention at the edge of my consciousness since the moment I'd seen Mike Madigan's name on the computer screen, took shape. The wave crashed. And I was *flattened*.

"What are you *doing*?"

Liv and Tony jumped apart as if experiencing an electric shock, probably because they assumed the person yelling at them was someone with slightly more clout than me, like his wife or the dean. I couldn't believe what I was seeing. Liv had sworn against this moment so many times, and with absolute blind faith, I'd believed her. Sexy Tony Brown, evil professor and cheating scumbag, was sitting comfortably at his desk chair, while Liv perched in his lap, talking quietly. This wasn't some split second where they were overcome by desire and he kissed her, arguably against her will. This seemed ordinary. Regular. Normal.

"What is going on?"

"Em." Liv looked at Tony for support and he sighed audibly. I realized this must be something they'd talked about dozens of times, her judgmental best friend and how she would react if she ever found out about their secret . . . what? Affair? Relationship? Both options sucked. All at once, I understood why Liv, the most desired girl I knew, absolutely never had a boyfriend. Because she always had one.

"I knew you would be upset. I knew it always made you uncomfortable. I didn't think you'd understand—"

"I do understand. I understand that there is absolutely no one in the world that I can trust. My fiancé kept a secret from me for years, my mother is a pathological liar, and my father had a goddamn secret family. You're just like all of them, Liv. I can't trust you. I don't even know you," I shouted, near tears. Liv, meanwhile, looked like she was in shock. Somewhere in the back of my mind I realized it wasn't Liv I was yelling at. It was Caro, Sam, maybe even Mike.

"Does that mean you found your dad?" Tony asked, looking genuinely interested. "You said something about a secret family. Does that mean you know who he is? Can you contact him?"

I took a short, hard breath.

"No, Tony, I can't contact him. No one can. Because he's dead."

CHAPTER 23

One of the few times Caro called me after I moved to California was two years prior, to tell me that our neighbor, the friendly but relatively inconsequential Mike Madigan, had died suddenly of an aneurysm. At the time, I was puzzled as to why this was even headline news, prompting one of her rare moments of deliberate contact. Since my mother had moved out of Arlington and back to Georgetown as soon as I escaped to college, I assumed she hadn't looked back.

"Do you still keep in contact with everyone from Redwood Lane?" I asked, trying to pay attention to my mother on the Bluetooth while simultaneously looking for parking. It was a Sunday morning and I was meeting a friend from my book club for brunch at Huckleberry on Wilshire, which happened to have the best fried-egg sandwich in

Los Angeles. I was already ten minutes late, but I knew the slightest indication of distraction would annoy my mother, so I was trying not to use my "talking on the phone in the car" voice, which Sam said made me sound like I'd had some kind of stroke.

"Who told you about his . . . accident?" I couldn't figure out how to refer to the tragedy. All I knew about brain aneurysms was that there was no way to prevent or predict them, and they killed you in about fifteen minutes. Even just talking about them felt like bad luck.

"He was only sixty-two," she said sadly, neglecting to answer my question. Caro hadn't sounded so depressed since the verdict from *Bush v. Gore*. Something else was going on, but I couldn't figure out what. I figured the call had to be context for something else. Perhaps she was coming to terms with her own mortality and decided it was time to connect with her flesh and blood. I'd never heard her express such a remorseful thought.

"That's really sad. I remember when he used to shovel our front walk in the winter. And didn't he have a bunch of kids? How's his wife doing?" I found some street parking and pulled in. I shut off the engine, but didn't get out of the car. All of a sudden, the creamy latte and blueberry cornmeal muffin I'd been looking forward to all morning didn't seem all that tempting. I felt surprisingly bereft. For someone I'd known only marginally, Mr. Madigan had seemed like a genuinely good guy who didn't deserve to be randomly kidnapped from the world. As I sat in the quiet car, my energy rapidly drained out of me. The lightness I'd been experiencing moments before at the thought of a Sunday brunch and gossip session was replaced by a tight sadness in my stomach.

I listened to my mother's blank reply as she listed where Mr. Madigan's boys went to college. As my car's interior quickly started to overheat with the air-conditioning off, frustration started to build on top of my sadness. Why was she calling me now, of all times? Was this kind of impersonal information, the births and deaths of our neighbors, really all that my mother and I had to say to each other? The last I'd heard from Caro was ten months prior, when my student loan bills were mistakenly being sent to her. Now, sitting in my black Prius, with the sun baking down on me—opening the door seemed way too hard at that moment, even though it would have solved the problem of the pool of sweat settling on the back of my neck—I started to feel more and more agitated, a common reaction to Caro popping up out of the blue.

"Is this the only reason you're calling?" I interrupted sharply. My tone instantly altered the direction of the conversation.

"What?" she responded. Slowly and in a steely voice, Caro repeated, "I called you to tell you about Mr. Madigan. The poor man woke up with a headache one day, went to his company picnic, and collapsed halfway through the pie-eating contest."

"Like, collapsed in the pie?"

"Good Lord, Emma, I was speaking figuratively. It's not funny. A man died."

"I know." I was hurt. I'd been trying to make light of the situation, perhaps morph the conversation into a real one by making her laugh. Evidently there was no chance of any real communication between us. "Listen, I'm late to meet a friend for breakfast. Is that it?"

"Yes, Emma," she responded with a sigh, her heavy annoyance

rippling through the phone lines. She was exasperated with me because . . . well, I don't know why. I'd made a joke—off-color for sure, but we were discussing a pie-eating contest, for God's sake—in the middle of a conversation about someone I didn't even really know. Nothing I ever did with her was ever right, and honestly, I was sick of trying.

"Okay, bye, then?" I said, questioningly.

"Good-bye." And that was it. That was how I found out my father died.

Slumped against the cold red brick of one of Berkeley's many eclectic structures, this one resembling a tower Rapunzel might inhabit if she decided to move to the Bay Area, I recalled this conversation in vivid detail. Suppose I had reacted differently. Suppose I hadn't made the terrible pie joke, I wondered, shuddering at the memory. Would she have told me then? Was that why she was really calling, to tell me the truth, after all those years? I closed my eyes and leaned against the wall, mentally recounting the emotional fireworks of the last hour.

After making arguably the most dramatic statement of my adult life, to Tony Brown of all people, I'd fled from his office before he or Liv had time to register what I was saying or ask for details. I definitely didn't want to talk about it, especially not with the two of them. I wanted to be worlds away from everyone who had been lying to me. The last time I glanced at Liv, her face was still flush and frozen, as if I'd slapped her across the face with my cold words.

The truth is, the second I realized what the words on the computer screen in front of me meant, something inside of me snapped. Part of me felt absolutely miserable, but the other, more self-destructive part felt strangely free. I no longer cared about anything or anyone. Learning the truth about my father and realizing that I would never know him was my Get Out of Life Free card. I didn't have to search for answers or make any of the tough decisions that had been plaguing me all week. I could give up, something that felt deliciously, wonderfully tempting.

I could do it, I realized, for real. I could start over. I could say good-bye to the lies and manipulation from Sam, my mother, even Liv, and start fresh. I considered this as I watched the Frisbee players on the lawn with their bare feet and chests, hoodies casually tied around their waists, despite the chilly September air, whizzing the Frisbee back and forth in sharp arcs. Perhaps in my next life, I'd play Frisbee.

My phone chimed. I pulled it from my pocket and opened to an e-mail with the subject line: *Wedding Cancellation*. It was an e-mail from a vintage furniture store in Santa Barbara, confirming the cancellation of a chuppah rental for Saturday.

Even though Sam and I weren't Jewish, I had always envisioned myself getting married under the antique canopy and had hunted until I found the perfect one to rent for our ceremony. The ceremony that Sam had apparently canceled. I guess he went through with it, I told myself miserably. As instructed. But that didn't matter much at this point. The pain was real no matter whose decision it was.

No more chuppah, no more wedding, no more Sam.

I felt a thick haze of despair and heartache wash over me, mixed with something like relief. It was over. I was alone. I couldn't go back on it now. I would not be marrying Sam. I had no chance to mess up our marriage down the line, because there would be no marriage. I would never lose Sam out of the blue, or the stability and comfort that he brought to my life. I didn't have to prepare for the loss or protect myself against it. Because he was already gone.

I stood up and brushed the grass off my clothes, the blood rushing to my head and making me dizzy. Unsteadily, I crossed the lawn. Where would I go and what would I do? I had the next three weeks off for my honeymoon, and not a single obligation to anyone. I also didn't have any of my stuff, other than the bag I traveled with, as my suitcase was still in the back of our rental car.

Liv would either head home, probably toss my stuff on the side of the 280, or stay in her illicit love den with Tony. Sam would move on, maybe try it again with Val. Caro wouldn't notice, and everyone else would reschedule their weekend plans. I thought about Sam's mom and her big, hard hugs. I thought about her flying in from New York the next day and arriving to hear the news that Emma was not going to become her daughter-in-law. In fact, from this point on, she would probably be a stranger. I shook the depressing thought from my head and reminded myself that it didn't matter. My life with Sam was over.

Walking down the main street running along Berkeley's campus, I blindly hailed the first cab I saw. As soon as I sat down on the plush, cracked seat, I knew where I had to go. I would leave the past that no longer mattered behind, and head toward the one person who might be part of my future. I instructed the cabbie to take me to the Marina and rattled off the address. Hours after I broke off my engagement and minutes after I ran out on my best friend, I made my third terrible decision of the day. I headed straight to Dusty's.

Once I was actually standing in front of the imposing yellow Victorian with its ridiculously steep stairs, I began to lose my nerve. I knew next to nothing about this guy, except for the fact that he had great taste in eyewear and he was fatherless. But short of hanging around Haight-Ashbury and hoping some hippies would take me in, what choice did I really have?

Despite the dearth of parental connections, before today, I'd always had Liv and Sam. Now I had no one. Dusty was it. He was the only person who wanted to see me, as well as the only person who got what I was going through. Everyone else had their own angle, their own interests at heart. Dusty had only mine. *That's because he barely knows you,* a little voice added. I politely told the little voice to shut the hell up, and texted Dusty that I was here. We had left the key behind when we "checked out" that afternoon.

Within seconds he was outside. He ushered me upstairs into the now familiar living room.

"Carrick's out, and I told him to let me know when he was on his way back," he said, when he saw me looking around.

"Didn't he ask why?"

"Nope." Dusty grinned, flashing those goddamn twinkly eyes. "Guys don't do that." His smile warmed me, and I felt slightly better for the first time all day. "I missed you when you left earlier. You must have been in a rush. Didn't make your plane, I guess?"

"Yeah, sorry," I said, remembering how I'd simply ignored his good-bye text. "Something like that."

"We don't have to talk about it. I'm just glad you're here."

"Thanks. Me, too." I paused and glanced at the couch, which looked softer and more inviting than anything possibly ever had before. "Would it be completely rude if I just lie on your couch and watch TV or read? It would be nice to get out of my own head for a while."

Without missing a beat, he handed me the remote and gestured to a full bookshelf in the corner of the room. "Feel free to help yourself to a book, but I apologize if we don't exactly have the same taste. Where's your stuff?"

"Liv has my suitcase." I didn't explain why she wasn't with me, or where she was headed, and as I suspected, Dusty didn't press it. "Can I borrow some sweatpants?"

"Of course. Are you staying the night?"

"Yes, if that's okay. I'll pay you and Carrick, of course." He refused, as I knew he would. Determining that I didn't have the mental energy to deal with the logistical problem of how I would continue this new life without any belongings, I turned back toward the books.

The bookshelf was a corner cupboard, nestled snugly into the wall, packed with dozens of classics and bestsellers alike, including some of my favorite authors. I scanned the titles, impressed by the variety. Unsurprisingly, I spotted *A Confederacy of Dunces*—or, as I thought of it, every boy in America's favorite book.

"Is this your favorite book?" I turned back to Dusty, holding it out accusatorily.

"Nope. It's good, though. Actually, I think that copy is Carrick's, so I guess we have two of them around here." He turned around, looking for something. "Do you feel like Thai food?" he asked, locating his phone. "It's the perfect 'sitting on the couch and not talking or thinking' food."

"Yes, please. That would be perfect." I briefly closed my eyes. Then, before I could brace myself or duck my head, I was hit by yet another tidal wave of pain, this time from my memory.

The previous fall, a few weeks after Sam and I were engaged, his roommates were cleaning out their house for a couple new subletters. Dante was heading to Europe, and another roommate, also in the movie business, was leaving for a shoot in Vancouver. They decided to turn cleaning into cash by having a makeshift yard sale, which they did about once a year. This inevitably consisted of them piling junk into their front yard, hours later than everyone else in the neighborhood put out their carefully tagged sales. It was the bargain bin of yard sales, which is saying a lot. I knew from experience that in a couple of hours, when it became clear that no one wanted Sam's plastic Batman communicator, Dante's half-missing Level 1 Portuguese Rosetta Stone, or the pile of black auxiliary cords they'd found behind their TV, we would bundle everything into trash bags and bring it all to Goodwill.

"Who in their right mind would want that random tangle of

black cords?" I called across the yard to the boys from my position as the cashier—also known as the front stoop, where I sat with a steaming latte on my left and a couple of ones and fives in a shoe box on my right. I wasn't concerned about having to make change for their nonexisting customer base, but I wanted the boys to think I was supportive, so I pretended to stress about it for a few minutes that morning while they hauled out their castoffs.

"Emma, people need cords," Dante explained, looking serious behind his hipster Ray-Bans, while he attempted to detangle the mess.

"For what exactly?"

"Loads of things. Stereos and stuff."

"Do people still have stereos? Don't people generally have iPhone docks now?"

Dante ignored my excellent point and dropped a box of books in front of me. "Here, nerd, sort these out." I obediently worked in silence for a few minutes, stacking books while Dante added a price tag to a broken French press.

"Wait a minute, why are you getting rid of all these amazing books?" I asked, reading off some titles. "*A Visit from the Goon Squad*? *A Fraction of the Whole*? These are some of Sam's favorites."

"Don't you have them, too?" Dante squinted at the pieces in his hand, probably contemplating if he could sell the grinder and glass carafe separately.

"Yeah, so?"

"He's getting rid of them because you're getting married. He said you don't need two copies of each and you're really psycho about clutter," Dante added, his honesty doing nothing to take away from the sweetness of the act.

Dusty called out from the kitchen and I was wrenched back to the present. He walked back into the living room with his hand over his cell phone and looked at me expectantly.

"Did you say something?" I asked, disoriented.

"Fried or steamed?"

I stared, stuck in my memory trance. "Sorry, what are you talking about?"

"The dumplings," he said slowly. "I'm ordering us Thai food." His tone was one you might use with a child, or with Brendan Fraser after he emerged from the underground bunker in *Blast from the Past*.

"Steamed," I answered automatically. I suppose I was still in wedding dress mode, worrying about calories. Then I remembered the facts. No more wedding, no more wedding dress, no more vague attempts to avoid fried food. "Actually, is it too late to change to fried?" That, my friends, is what they call a silver lining.

The rest of Wednesday evening passed in a coma of Thai noodles and bad USA movies, including *The Wedding Planner*, which neither of us acknowledged as completely appropriate or inappropriate, pausing only to comment on, and at one point attempt to measure, the enormity of J. Lo's ass. There was nothing overtly romantic in our interactions, but it was nice. There was something intimate about the casualness of the night. It was almost like we had been dating for years and were comfortable enough to joke around while we slurped wonton soup. What's more, as the night wore on, it felt increasingly similar to the images of my life with Sam, like a shadowy parallel universe unfolding in the background. It reminded me of when a movie you've seen a hundred times is on TV while you're puttering around the house. No reason to turn it off or pay close attention because you know it so well, but every once in a while one of your favorite scenes draws your attention unexpectedly.

Like when Dusty mentioned that he hated olives—the most controversial fruit, in my opinion—and I recalled a debate Sam and I once had about whether or not we could be in a relationship because we both loved olives. In all successful relationships, I argued, there is one olive hater and one olive lover. You cannot have two of the same. Sam scoffed and said I was crazy, offering a compromise that I could have first dibs on green olives for life, if he could have the black ones. For a moment, the pain that I'd been carefully ignoring about Sam sliced through my stomach—missing him, worrying about him, losing him—and almost made me double over. But somehow, I kept it at bay, in no small part due to the distraction of Dusty.

It felt like a case study of whether I could substitute my entire real life with a fake one, if I could do the exact same things over, with someone else. Maybe it would all fall into place. Maybe Dusty could easily slip into Sam's role, our dynamic instantly as natural as when I ate breakfast with Sam in Venice a few days earlier. Maybe the grumpy old theory was true, that we end up with whomever we meet when we're ready to settle down, and the rest are details you could fill in with anyone.

Still, Dusty and I never talked about it, any of it. Presumably he'd figured out that since I wasn't heading back to Los Angeles the wedding wasn't proceeding as planned. Luckily he didn't ask me about it, or about the search for my father—a reality I couldn't even begin to address at the moment. I knew he would have been more than willing to talk if I brought it up, but I didn't have an urge to open any cans of worms. One could argue that I was so deeply sunk into a pit of denial, I was caked in it. But most of the night I felt okay. I was comfortably numb. All of the bad things from the week felt very far away.

I woke up on the couch on Thursday morning to see Dusty heading out of the shower and walking back to his room in his towel. He must have been getting ready for work. I couldn't help noticing how attractive he was. His hair was dark from the shower, his long eyelashes were sprinkled with tiny droplets of water, and there was that scar, sketched haphazardly on his cheek. I idly wondered how he'd gotten it.

"Good morning," Dusty said. He stopped at his door, clearly unembarrassed by his state of undress, and said deliberately, "I've been thinking, I have to go to work today, but we could go away this weekend. I'll take Friday off. My buddy has a place in Sonoma where we could go relax, do a little wine tasting. As pals, of course," he added, somehow not awkwardly.

"That sounds really nice," I responded gingerly. "Although . . . well, I'm not sure."

"Think about it," Dusty said easily, heading to get changed.

What was holding me back? Why couldn't I agree to a free weekend in Sonoma drinking wine with this amazing man? It's time to move on, I told myself decisively, swallowing hard. I was sick of feeling unsure of myself all the time. I remembered what had happened with Sam. With Val. With Mike. I thought about the chuppah Sam had canceled. I felt the pain traveling from my fingertips, down my arms, and through my body like a poison. It was over. I walked into Dusty's room and found him in blue pants and a soft gray T-shirt, halfway ready for work, standing by his closet.

He turned and I reached up, motioning for a hug. He dropped the collared shirt he was unbuttoning and leaned down to pull me close. I closed my eyes and felt his strong arms circling my back. He was so solid. Here was physical evidence of it. Maybe he could help me forget about Sam. Maybe he could take the pain away. No, I told myself. This wasn't even about Sam. Dusty is amazing all by himself. He understands me; he gets me. He's a tall, gorgeous, completely together man. Sam has nothing to do with any of this. I was tired of feeling bad. I wanted to feel good. I tilted my head up for Dusty to kiss me and he read my cue perfectly.

Several minutes later we were interrupted by a loud knock on the door. It was a self-assured knock, an imposing one. I knew that knock.

"I'll get it," I said, as Dusty looked at me, bewildered. "I know who it is."

I straightened my clothes and shut the bedroom door behind me. Quickly, I headed to the front door and pulled it open, filled with a heavy dose of terror, but also certain that if I didn't open it immediately she'd pull a velociraptor and find a way in.

"Emma Elizabeth Moon, what in the world is going on?"

"Hi, Mom. Welcome to San Francisco."

CHAPTER 24

"Should I ask the obvious?" I ventured, after I ushered my mother into the kitchen to avoid Dusty. That was an introduction I definitely did not want to make. I inspected her. She was wearing a tailored suit and it looked like her blond hair had been recently highlighted. I wondered if it was for the wedding and was momentarily touched, until I remembered that I had called it off and the wasted time and effort would probably annoy her even more.

"What's that, Emma?" she responded warily.

"Well, there are a couple things. One, what are you doing here? Two, do you realize what time it is? And three, how in the world did you find me?"

Caro laughed crisply. "Yes, I am aware of the time. I took a five A.M. flight to get here at this hour. I've been on a plane for six hours and traveling for eight. What would you have me do? Check into a hotel for a few hours?" It had been so long since I'd seen her that even watching words come out of her mouth was a singularly fascinating activity. I'd forgotten how she spoke, how she talked with her hands far more than I guessed she realized, and her expression when she was both irritated and defensive.

"No, of course not. Okay, how did you know I was here?"

"Hunter contacted me." My mouth dropped open in surprise. I couldn't have been more stunned than if she'd said the producers of *The Voice* had called, offering her a ticket to the blind auditions.

"My fake dad called you?" I didn't mean it to sound snarky but as soon as it came out of my mouth I knew she would take it that way. That was the problem with us. There are people out there who naturally get each other, whose interactions flow easily and fluidly. My mother and I are not those people. We communicate clumsily, through stops and starts, passing the hurt and offended baton back and forth as we go.

"Yes, Emma, he did. I spoke with him and then with Olivia, who gave me the address where you were most likely staying. But before we discuss any of that, I need some coffee."

I stared at her blankly. She talked to Liv? How much did she know? Who else had she spoken to—Sam? This thought crossed my mind painfully and I willed it away, reminding myself that he wasn't in my life anymore. It didn't matter who talked to him, on my behalf or not. Wordlessly, I pulled my jacket on over Dusty's sweatpants and T-shirt, and we headed out.

"How was the flight?" I asked, after several minutes of silence. We were settled inside a cozy French café down the street from Dusty's apartment. I'd been there before, when it was bustling to the point of discomfort, but as we'd just missed the morning rush, we had the place practically to ourselves. There were a few old-timers who actually looked French examining their wrinkly, foreign-looking newspapers, and a girl in her twenties with wild hair and a short skirt at the counter trying to order a Frappuccino, much to the barista's disgust. Ah, the walk of shame. I felt a fierce stab of missing Liv, remembering our game of counting walks of shame over Sunday brunch in law school.

"The flight? Well, I didn't relish waking up at the crack of dawn to catch it, or paying hundreds of dollars to change my ticket. Not to mention telling my boss that I had to skip a congressional hearing. But I really had no choice." Caro paused for a second to take a sip of her cappuccino and allow the guilt to sink in properly. "I received a call that my child was running all over San Francisco, comparing freckles with men and living with two strange boys while her fiancé waited in purgatory. Really, Emma, were such dramatics necessary?" I felt the heat rising to my cheeks and felt myself losing it, but I gave myself a stern talking-to. This was not the time to be weak. I was not the one who should be embarrassed, I reminded myself.

"The only reason I was 'running around comparing freckles with men,' as you put it, is because for the past twenty-nine years,

I have been lied to about who my father is and where I come from." I sat back and crossed my arms pointedly.

Caro scoffed at this. "You've been watching too much reality TV, Emma. You know exactly where you come from. And as for Hunter, what difference did it make what I said his name was? He never had any impact on your life before, why should he now?" Her eyes remained focused as she said this, the picture of reason and detachment. It was the same neutral, self-assured face she made while testifying before Congress about the results of the latest tobacco study, which infuriated me further. How dare she keep her cool right now?

"What *difference* did it make? Do you hear yourself?" I tried to keep my tone firm but low, as I was pretty sure the Frenchmen wouldn't appreciate a screaming match in their pleasant patisserie.

"You're getting caught up in the semantics."

"The semantics of my *own father's name*? You're unbelievable. I can't believe you would try and twist this into my problem. You've been in Washington too long if you're going to try to spin this one. My whole life you've been doing this, dismissing me, acting like I'm this irritating, ridiculous person. Let me fill you in on something. It isn't overdramatic to care about who your father is." Caroline was silent, stirring the contents of her white porcelain cup with the tiny silver spoon they'd provided. I kept going, though. I was on a roll. "Also, you don't know the first thing about what happened between Sam and me, or what he's doing *innocently* waiting for me. It's over. And it's not because of Hunter or this trip, or anything like that. He cheated on me." My words broke on this last sentence, shattering the strength I was trying desperately to convey.

"Okay, Emma," Caro said more softly now, putting up both hands as if in surrender. "You're right. I don't know what happened with Sam. All I know is what happened with Hunter. And with Mike." She took a pause and sipped her cappuccino, appearing to need a break after saying his name. I felt a shifting in my stomach, or maybe my heart. Either way it hurt. "I'm ready and willing to tell you everything."

She sighed again and looked through her purse, pulling out several pieces of paper, folded together, reluctant to continue but determined to finish. "I know I haven't been the best mother, so I am going to take this opportunity to do something for you, something I know you need. I got you a plane ticket," she said carefully, placing the folded paper on the smooth black table. "Back to Los Angeles. This afternoon. I'm willing to offer you a compromise. If you come with me on this flight, I'll tell you everything you want to know about your father. The whole story. What happened and why it happened. What happened with Hunter, what happened with Mike, everything. Trust me, there is nothing I want to do less than talk about this, but you have a right to know." She paused. "But if you don't come with me this afternoon, there are no promises, no guarantees. I can see what you're doing in San Francisco right now, I can see the mistakes you're making, even if you can't. We may not be close, Emma, but I know you. I know you're shutting down and shutting everyone out, and it isn't right. What's more, I'm certain you'll regret it. You have to go home and face everything. Face Sam. Call off the wedding if you like, but don't do it like this.

"If you come back to Los Angeles today, I'll tell you everything you want to know. Otherwise, I will choose to maintain my privacy. But first, you have to get on the plane." She took a moment to let this sink in. She may have had a point about my ignoring reality and shutting people out—Dr. Majdi was probably nodding knowingly somewhere in Downtown L.A.—but she had been absent from my life for years. How could she really know what was best for me?

My disbelief must have showed, because she went on. "I know this is extreme, and maybe a bit silly, but I feel I have very little choice. I know I don't have any sway with you. You won't take my advice. If I say you should go back to L.A. because it's the right thing to do, you won't do it. All I have to convince you with is the truth. It's the trip for the story, no negotiations."

In one smooth motion, she picked up her cappuccino and finished it. "I'm sure you need some time to settle your affairs and hopefully to pack, so I'm going to go. I hope to see you at the airport in a few hours." Pushing the flight information toward me on the table and tapping it lightly, Caro turned and walked away, leaving me stunned into silence, still clutching my mostly foam latte.

Once, when I was about seven years old, I was at home alone, watching cartoons on a scratchy orange couch, the kind quite popular in the eighties, a decade full of uncomfortable furniture, when an advertisement for a retail mortgage lender came on and started screaming at me: *Don't lose your home because your mortgage is too high! Don't end up out on the street because of out-of-control interest*

rates! I sat glued to my seat, Lucky Charms sliding down my milky spoon, mesmerized by the television and certain that it was vital to remember every word. I tried furiously to memorize what I was seeing on the screen. It all sounded terrifyingly foreign, and I was sure that if I didn't pay very careful attention, whatever they were warning would certainly occur.

At the time, we were staying with one of Caro's friends from grad school, a very nice man named Danny, who lived in a basement apartment in Dupont Circle. Knowing what I do now about the neighborhood and cutoff jean shorts, I'm pretty sure he was gay. All I knew then was that Danny was my mom's friend, he had an extra bedroom, and he was kind. Danny didn't make me feel like he was counting down the minutes until his favor quota was up and we would get out of his apartment like so many others, and when he teased my mom or called me a chatterbox, it made me giggle. When he wasn't making us laugh or cooking amazing meals involving spices I'd never heard of, Danny was playing Simon & Garfunkel morning, noon, and night. I fell asleep at night under a blanket of safety, lulled by the smell of cumin and the melody of "Bleecker Street."

I loved living there. I loved snuggling on the wool couch on Sunday while Danny and my mom went to the market, making my trundle bed carefully every morning and watering the kitchen plants with their sprawling vines, which composed the entirety of my chores. I remember praying as hard as I could that my mom would marry Danny so we could live there forever.

On that Sunday morning, however, as I watched the threatening commercial, I didn't feel happy or safe. I felt panicked, although I wasn't even old enough to correctly identify the emotion. Was that why we lived with Danny? I wondered. Why we didn't have a house? Had we done the bad things warned of in the commercial?

I sat frozen, deep in thought, until I heard the key turn in the door. The second Caro opened it, chatting with Danny and gripping a cloth bag of vegetables, she could see the fear in my eyes.

"What's wrong, sweetie?" She quickly handed the bag to Danny and settled next to me on the couch and he headed back to the kitchen, flashing me a sweet smile on his way.

I told her what I'd seen, slightly nervous about being caught eating cereal in front of the TV, which was discouraged if not verboten, but somehow I understood this was bigger than that. "Mom, did we not pay back our mortgage?" I asked carefully, pronouncing it with the *t*. "Is that why we live here?"

"Our what? Oh, our mortgage? Where did you hear that?"

"On TV. They said if you don't pay your mor . . . mort-gage, or your in-ter-est, then you don't get to keep your house. Is that why we don't have one?" I gripped my small hands into tight balls as I said this, terribly afraid that saying it out loud would make it true. Caro gave me a long look, reaching for the remote to turn off the television with one hand, while she rubbed my back with the other.

"Emma Moon, you are a smart girl. Too smart for your own good. I don't want you to worry about those things anymore. We live here because it's fun and because Danny likes having us here. Right, Danny?" Caro called into the kitchen. He shouted something back in the affirmative, half drowned out by the drumbeats of "Cecilia."

"Now, will you please help me with the minestrone? I need an assistant and those zukes aren't gonna chop themselves." Caro gave me a kiss on the forehead and got up, leaving me sitting there with a nagging feeling in the back of my head. What she said sounded good, but even in my child's mind I understood that there was something missing from her response; there was something she wasn't saying. That she hadn't quite answered the question.

Carefully unlocking the door with the spare key I'd grabbed on the way out, I slowly opened the front door to Dusty and Carrick's apartment.

"Hey, where have you been? Are you okay?" Dusty asked, walking toward me and taking in my expression. "Who was that at the door?"

I shook my head.

"This was too fast, wasn't it? I freaked you out. I'm sorry."

"No, you don't need to apologize, it's not your fault. The thing is—" I tried to think of the best way to put it. "We don't really know each other very well. I don't even know how you got your scar," I half joked, trying to make light of the serious words I was saying.

"I know, Emma. But that's the point. We're getting to know each other. That's how it works when you start a relationship." He looked nervous as he said this, as if he knew he'd let his hand show. "And I got the scar 'sledding' on my bunk bed ladder when I was five. Yes, my twin sister and I had bunk beds, and yes, it was adorable." I laughed slightly at this. "Look, I know this weekend will be hard for you. Why not go away to Sonoma with me? It's beautiful there, and the September harvest has the best chardon-nay. Or, if you're not into that, maybe we could go camping in Big Sur."

Chardonnay? Camping? In a flash, the reality of what I was doing rushed toward me like a freight train. This guy didn't know me *at all*. I hated chardonnay with a passion, and after a harrowing trip to Joshua Tree in which we'd forgotten to bring water, Sam and I vowed never to go camping again. I felt my chest constrict and the truth wash over me. It wasn't the overly sweet wine or the fear of dehydra-tion. It wasn't even Dusty. It was Sam. I still loved Sam. Despite everything, my heart still belonged to him. But it's too late, said a small desolate voice, it's too late for you and Sam.

But it wasn't too late to make things right with Dusty, to do the right thing.

"Dusty, I can't begin a relationship with you. I'm already *in* a relationship," I said gently. He looked down, away from my glance. "At least, I was just in one. I'm ending one. But for better or for worse, it has to end properly. I'm sorry, but I have to go back to Los Angeles."

CHAPTER 25

The law of the Attempt is, in my opinion, one of the most interesting laws of them all. Attempt is a concept with which we are all vaguely familiar, but like so many things in life that make logical sense until lawyers get involved, I didn't fully understand it or its consequences until Professor Gray's first-year Criminal Law seminar.

"Attempt is the name you give to a crime when someone takes the steps to commit an illegal act and they are thwarted in some way," Professor Gray explained eight weeks into the class. "One can be charged with attempted murder, attempted arson, or attempted anything, as long as the defendant did everything in his or her power to commit said crime." As we learned, the tricky part of the concept is, you really have to have almost done "it", the illegal act, in order for the charge to stick.

You can't be charged with attempted arson for buying the kerosene and driving to your worst enemy's house with a grudge and a book of matches. You can't be charged with attempted carjacking because you stand on a street corner with a gun in your pocket. You have to actually light the match and have it blown out by an inconvenient gust of wind, or brandish the gun and instruct the driver to hand over the keys to the Jag before the victim recklessly drives away unharmed, for the law of attempt to truly be satisfied. You have to have done everything in your power to commit the crime. You were going to do it, you took the steps to make it happen, but something intervened and prevented you from getting it done.

As the plane's violent turbulence—which, surprisingly, failed to cause me even a moment of fear—smoothed out and the tattooed woman sitting next to me released her grip on the armrest, I considered my crimes. If this was a court of law, I would definitely be found guilty of Attempt to Bang Dusty. I felt undeniably awful about it. Maybe it wasn't technically cheating, since I'd called off my wedding the day before, but there had to be a relationship law somewhere on the books that I'd violated.

Because, the truth is, if Caro hadn't knocked at that particular moment, I would have gone through with it. Sitting across the aisle from her on the plane, I gave her a silent thank-you for showing up. With everything else in my life shot to hell, Caro walking up to that door felt like the one thing I could be grateful for. I may have been liable for attempt, but I sure was glad I hadn't committed the crime.

"I was in love with him, you know," Caro intoned. I turned, startled by her sudden declaration. She had been silent since we took off. "It wasn't some cheap affair. I was in love," she repeated.

"Who are you talking about?" I asked, knowing the answer full well but wanting to hear her say it.

"Mike. Your father." My guess was she'd never said the words aloud before that moment. They certainly didn't sound practiced.

"Are you going to tell me the story now? Here?" Across the aisle on a 737? I added silently. Maybe the turbulence had scared her into thinking she better tell me before we crashed and it was too late.

"That was the deal, right?" Caro said wearily.

I nodded slowly, afraid to make a sound lest I wake her out of whatever confessional coma she'd been thrown into from the choppy flight. I guess everyone within earshot of row 7 would hear the story along with me.

"We met in the oddest way," she started. "While getting our hair cut." She paused to let this sink in and I did my best to picture the bizarre scene.

"On the way back from class one day, I stopped to get a trim. I was meeting Hunter for dinner and I wanted to look nice. He hadn't shown much interest in me since we got married, and I was willing to try anything that might help." Dear God, I silently pleaded, please don't let her go into detail about the honeymoon ganja sex. Thankfully, she skimmed over the details. "Hunter was, and is, a wonderful man. I wanted things to work, even though deep down I knew I could never make him happy.

"There I was, sitting in one of those swivel chairs, and I made eye contact with the man in the chair next to me in the mirror. We were in those funny black cloaks they make you wear, wet hair, no body parts showing. We both looked ridiculous. I'll never forget it: He looked me dead in the eye in the mirror and he winked. I don't know what it was about that wink. It was intimate, strange as that may seem. I know it sounds silly, but it made me bashful. That's the only word for it. He made me smile, and what's even stranger, he made me blush, for the first time in years. I fell for him a little bit right then and there."

Caro paused as the flight attendant walked by offering us water, which she waved away. "Through the rest of the haircut, I didn't look at him again. I was embarrassed. Then we went to pay at the same time and ended up walking out together. He held the door for me and asked me how much I'd tipped the stylist. He said he never knew how much to tip at these types of things. Was it like a cab? A restaurant? I couldn't help but laugh. He asked me if I wanted to get a coffee, and just like that, I canceled dinner plans with Hunter. That should have been the first sign. We went to coffee that night for four hours. I was up for the rest of the night. From the caffeine, of course, but mostly because I couldn't stop thinking about him. Couldn't stop running through every detail of the day in my head. Why I chose to get a haircut at that time, at that place. At what point I noticed him sitting next to me. Every word he'd said at coffee. I wanted to remember it all, every minute of the day."

"I know that feeling."

Caro looked up as if she was surprised to see me sitting there. I hurriedly brought her back to the story to avoid breaking the spell. "What did Hunter say when you didn't come home? Did he notice you were acting differently?"

"Oh, I don't remember. Probably nothing. He was pathologically understanding," she said, dismissing the question with a wave of her hand. Wasn't that typically a positive attribute? She shook her head, as if recalling a litany of pet peeves, and then looked at me directly. "Emma, I want you to know this. Mike and I were honest with each other from the start about the fact that we were both married. No one was being deceptive. When we met we were both wearing rings although I suppose you couldn't see them under those silly capes. The point is, neither of us was trying to hide anything. Neither of us had any idea where everything would lead."

"If you knew he was married, and he knew you were, why did you even start anything to begin with?" I asked, softly. I wasn't trying to judge. I really wanted to understand. What happened. Where I came from. Why I existed. "Why didn't you just say good-bye and never speak to each other again?"

"That's a good question. I'm not sure. Because I loved him, I suppose. Guilt may trump happiness, but I guess love trumps guilt."

"Like rock, paper, scissors," I murmured sadly, feeling the crushing complications of life weigh heavily on my soul. Was that why Sam did what he did?

"Also, neither of us had children at the time. Both of us were unhappy in our marriages. Neither seemed permanent, at least not from what we told each other. But really, it was pure, unexplainable love. He always used to tell me that his favorite thing about me was my feet. My beautiful feet. If that's not love I don't know what is. But the real thing that got me was . . ." Caro stopped. Maybe she was worried that she'd gotten carried away and this wasn't an integral part of the story.

"What?" I urged.

"He used to tell me that he thought I was the nicest person he'd ever met." That I was not expecting. Beautiful? Yes. Smart? Of course. But nice? It wasn't the primary descriptor I would use to describe my tough-as-nails mother. "I know you're surprised. But you try growing up with Mickey Rigazi throwing you around and see how sweet you turn out. I chose tough over nice every day of the week. But Mike Madigan . . ." She sighed, as if saying his full name took a great deal out of her. "He was the first person who saw me for who I truly was, a scared twenty-two-year-old girl from Philly who was starting to realize that her husband didn't want her and she had no one in the world to rely on but herself."

This image of my vulnerable, injured mother didn't compute. I tried to make sense of it while she continued, explaining that she and Mike fell in love and were debating leaving their spouses, when she got pregnant—*completely* by accident, she stressed.

"Despite the surprise, when we found out I was pregnant, we were thrilled in a way. This was the excuse we needed to take the plunge. Mike took me out to dinner and gave me a beautiful pearl ring. He said he wanted to get me a diamond but then everyone would know it was an engagement ring. We planned to tell them both that weekend, get a quickie divorce, and remarry before anyone could do the math."

The pearl ring from the pawnshop. It was like rewatching a movie you'd already seen a thousand times, but all the other times you'd missed the first scene.

"Hunter and I were going away for Labor Day and I decided to tell him then. I called Mike from a pay phone on the side of the road for a pep talk, although honestly I wasn't even that nervous at that point. I was more excited than anything. Everything finally felt as if it was falling into place. The pregnancy felt like a sign that we should be together, and that all of our actions were worth it, that they were justified. Then, out of nowhere, right there on the call, minutes before I was going to tell Hunter I was leaving him, Mike broke it off. For the most horrifying reason possible. His wife was also pregnant. He couldn't leave her like that. I was . . . devastated. There's no other word for it. I thought I would die. The worst part was, in an incredibly sad twist, a few months later she ended up losing the baby. Of course, she had three more later, your half brothers."

I hadn't even considered that. The Madigan boys were my brothers. I decided to hold on to that piece of information until later, when I could properly digest it.

"After the phone call, after he told me they were starting a family, there was no reason to continue the relationship. I was very angry. And when she lost the baby he blamed himself. He thought God was punishing him for the affair." She shook her head at this.

"When we broke up, my heart broke in half. I could barely imagine a reality in which we wouldn't be together. But after a little time passed, things changed. I started to feel better. I loved being pregnant. Every day I woke up picturing you growing inside of me. First, a little bean, then a banana, a kiwi. Odd that a kiwi is larger than a banana." I nodded in agreement. I was well acquainted with the fetus-fruit scale, thanks to my many pregnant Facebook friends.

"I felt that because I had you, everything was going to be okay. My family wasn't that supportive, no shock there. I think they suspected something was off. But I didn't really mind. I remember thinking, I don't care what anyone else thinks. I have a daughter." I felt myself turn away slightly, embarrassed by her uncharacteristic display of emotion.

"When Hunter told me he wanted a divorce, I gave him my blessing to go, live his life, and be happy. I didn't want anything from him." She paused, laughing sadly at herself. "Although after what I did, of course, I wouldn't have been entitled to it. All I asked was that we keep his name, and that he stay until you were born. That way there would never be any question surrounding your background, or your birth." But didn't that bother my father? Didn't he care? I hesitated, but forced myself to ask.

"Didn't Mr. Madigan, I mean, Mike, you know, what did he think about that?" I asked, stumbling on what tense and designation to use to identify my neighbor/father.

"He knew he didn't have a right to an opinion," she said firmly. "I told him not to contact me, that no one could ever know the truth.

After his wife's miscarriage, he agreed we shouldn't have any more contact." She shrugged sadly. I noticed Caro didn't use Mrs. Madigan's name when she referenced her. What was it? I struggled to remember. Debbie? Donna? Were we somehow related? I didn't think so, but I'd have to make a diagram when I got home to make sure.

"He respected my wishes. He never made contact during your childhood." There was a long pause while Caro inspected her hands. "Then, thirteen years later, he did."

The story continued. Apparently, when I was thirteen years old—I shuddered to remember the mini backpack and dream catcher earrings combo I was probably rocking at the time—Mike called Caro out of the blue. He said he was sorry he'd been out of touch, although he knew that was what she wanted. Despite that, he wanted to help.

"Point-blank, he offered to buy us a house. I told him I didn't need his money. I was about to finish my degree and start working full time at the lobby. We were doing okay."

I nodded, remembering. At that time, we were renting an apartment in Woodley Park with a full bedroom and a loft. Caro let me have the bedroom and we painted it together when we first moved in, light green walls with a purple ceiling. I wanted to feel like I lived inside a flower. I loved that flower bedroom.

"But he insisted. He wanted to do something for you, and he made it clear that you never had to know about him or what he had done. But there was one condition. He wanted to buy us a house near him, in Arlington. He wanted to be able to know you on some level, to watch you grow up, even from afar." My heart instantly constricted and my throat thickened with emotion. I took a deep breath before I spoke.

"Is that why you finally agreed?" I asked when I was able to steady my voice.

"Not really. In my opinion, he lost that right when he walked away from us and chose Debbie and her kids." So it was Debbie. My almost stepmom once removed.

"But his kids weren't born yet when you broke up, right?" Caro gave me a look that said she didn't appreciate the clarification and I spoke quickly to ensure that she didn't clam up, never to speak about the topic again. "Why did you agree, then? Why did you let him buy us a house down the street from his?"

"It was a no-brainer really. I wanted you to have a home. You were growing up. You needed a place where you could close the door and get some space from me. No teenager needs her mother right in her face all the time. Little did I know that you would eventually need three thousand miles of space." Caro chuckled sadly at this and I was hit with a mixture of surprise and guilt. It was one thing to know how distant we were, and another to hear her reference it.

"I could never have afforded a place like the one he was offering, not for years, and by then, you'd be out of the house, so what would be the point. Plus, you were about to start high school. I couldn't let you attend D.C. public schools and I couldn't afford private school."

"What about Debbie?" The question popped out before I could decide if it was a good idea. "Did she know who we were?"

"She knew," Caro said simply, leaving it at that. I decided not to press my luck on that particular issue. This kind of distraction always happened when I watched a movie. I would get fixated on the side characters, worried about the guy who got left at the altar so his girlfriend could end up with the man of her dreams. Did she ever explain what happened, or did she let him find out from his goofy best friend? Afterward, did he see pictures of her and the new guy on Instagram and feel bitter every time, or did he unfollow her?

"And Mike—did you guys ever get together or . . . ?"

"Did we have another affair? No, Emma. I was in my early twenties when that happened. Don't take this story as any indication that I think cheating is okay. It isn't. And I was duly punished for it. I had to drive past their house every day, see Mike throwing the football to his sons in their front yard, watch them walk by with their goddamn picnic basket. It wasn't easy."

The picnic basket.

I could physically feel her need to end the conversation. But I had one question left.

"Did he really die?" I knew this wasn't really a question at all, but it had to be asked. After all the lies, I didn't want to leave any stone unturned.

Caro must have understood this, because she answered quickly. "Yes, he did. I'm sorry."

I felt a sudden wash of vertigo, born of pure sadness. Struggling with what to say next, I looked over and saw that no words were necessary. My mother, usually so strong, so pulled together, had started to silently weep. She loved him, I realized. He'd been the love of her life.

Ignoring the seat belt light that was still on, I got up and stepped across the aisle, putting my arms around her. I felt her shaking as I held her, but I didn't let go. As I felt vertigo overtake me, I looked out the window. Our plane was descending. I was home.

CHAPTER 26

As we silently deplaned and made our way out to the Arrivals curb, I couldn't help but remember all the times Sam and I had been there before. I thought about the year we flew back from London, where we'd met his entire extended family for the holidays, and I was sick the entire nine-hour flight home.

We'd gone out for fondue the night before and I made an ill-timed bet with his brother that I could eat more cheese than him. This led to three hours of vomiting in an airplane bathroom, with the people in the last row pretending not to hear and the flight attendant knocking at one point to ask if I was okay. Sam eventually convinced them to move me to first class, where I lay in the fully reclined chair and slept the entire way across the Atlantic. When I woke up I was miraculously cured and even enjoyed a few complimentary glasses of champagne. When we landed, Sam mistook my tipsiness for remnants of my illness and took care of me the rest of the weekend.

After grabbing a taxi to my house in Venice, and seeing me inside, Caro carefully hugged me good-bye and said she was going to check into a hotel where she had made a reservation. We may have shared more in the past two hours than we had in the past ten years, but that didn't make us different people. We both needed to take everything in, to process what she had shared with me.

After Caro left, I ignored all the little tasks I usually do when I get home from a trip. I dropped my bag on the ground and immediately took off all my clothes and got in the shower. I let the hottest water I could stand run over me. When my mind finally cleared, I was struck by one simple thought: I had known my father, and he had known me. What was more, he'd liked me, he cared about me. And I'd liked him. We had, in the smallest, most casual sense, a relationship.

Then I realized something else. That was it. There would be no chance for anything else between us, ever. That would be the extent of my communication and closeness with my father until the end of time. I would never call him Dad, he would never know that I knew who he was, and we would never connect on any deeper level. What we had those years on Redwood Lane—the friendly chats and random run-ins—was all we would ever have. Because he was gone. It was so impossibly final. The pain of this knowledge seared through me, and there, in the shower, with the water still running, I dropped to my knees and cried.

I cried for Caro, who tried so hard to give me a good life and put herself through a kind of torture in the process. I cried for Mike, who lost two babies at once, and then, so randomly, his life. And for Debbie, who had to see the product of her husband's infidelity walking to the bus stop every day, twice a day, for four years, and whose own children, now grown, were fatherless. And, finally, I cried for myself.

What felt like a lifetime later, I stood up, peeling myself off the shower floor, exhausted, yet lighter. I'd fought against feeling sad for so long, and when I finally let myself give in, I was surprised to find that I could actually handle it. I recalled a phrase of Dr. Majdi's: *Emma, you must face the abyss.* It never made any sense before. But now I got it. The dream of finding my father and having him whisk me away from my life was never going to happen. Hunter wouldn't be an escape hatch. In fact, Hunter Moon, a name to which I'd attached so much importance for so long, meant essentially nothing to me, and although I had a feeling Leo was going to Facebook friend me, we would most likely never see each other again. No whisking, no escape hatch, no Hunter. Hello, abyss. It's me, Emma. I looked down. It wasn't quite as deep as I had feared.

CHAPTER 27

I heard the telltale creak of my front gate opening, the swollen wood slightly too big for the space it occupied. The footsteps on the stone path leading to my door needed no introduction. I'd had them memorized since sophomore year of high school when we met at my locker to walk to precalc together every Tuesday and Thursday. I opened the front door before she could knock.

"Wow, you look like shit," Liv said. It was at that moment that I knew we were going to be okay. If she'd acted formal or polite, I might have been worried. I reached for my best friend and, despite the fact that she was five inches shorter than me, I managed to put my head on her shoulder and let her hug me. After a minute, she led me to the couch and I told her everything about Mike and

Caro, their history, what had happened, and the cruel twist of having known my father for years, but never knowing who he was.

"I don't know, this is going to sound weird, but . . ." I paused, looking at her, making sure we were one hundred percent okay before I went on.

"Tell me," she urged.

"I'm afraid that I was mean to him, or rude or something, and didn't even know it." I was confessing a fear I'd barely formulated in my own head.

"Em, you're not mean to anyone. Except guys in bars sometimes when they're annoying, but that's funny. I'm sure you were your amazing sweet self."

"At sixteen I was a terror," I reminded her.

"At times. I hope you didn't have too many encounters when you were on that birth control junior year that made you super crazy."

I laughed out loud, despite myself.

"It's so unfair that everyone knew but me, and I didn't even know how to act, or that when I was talking to him, I was talking to my actual dad."

Liv nodded in agreement.

"Do you remember him?" I ventured. "You must have met him, right?"

She thought for a moment. "I think I remember him from that neighborhood Fourth of July party we went to the summer after freshman year." We found the block party flyer on our fridge and decided to go, figuring we could score some good food, sparklers, and hopefully a couple beers. We'd misjudged the situation and become the de facto babysitters for the night. I had completely forgotten about it, but Liv was right. Mike was there. I struggled for some memory of an interaction, but came up blank.

"He was cool," Liv offered. "I remember him saying the deviled eggs were good and I should try them."

"I like deviled eggs, too," I said softly.

"See! Chip off the old block." We both managed a small laugh.

"Liv," I asked, in the least judgmental tone I had, "what's going on with Tony?"

"You know, if the lawyer thing doesn't work out, you really shouldn't consider a career as a spy, Em. You're not exactly subtle."

When I didn't respond, she sighed. "I don't think we should talk about it. I know it's going to upset you, and I really don't think it's worth putting our friendship in jeopardy over."

I considered her words. A phrase popped to mind that people are fond of saying when discussing legal matters. *Possession is nine-tenths of the law.* Seven combined years of law school plus practicing as an attorney, and I still have no real idea what this expression means. My best guess is that it represents how when you already own something, it's harder to take it away from you. Liv was my best friend. No matter what either of us said or did in the heat of the moment, that wasn't going to change. We had occupied this firmly entrenched position for each other for the past fifteen years and nothing short of ouster by force could change that. I made a mental note to consider the metaphor for one of the law journal articles my firm was always asking us to write.

"Olivia Lucci. Our friendship is not in jeopardy. Now tell me what's going on with STB."

"All right. Here goes nothing. But remember, you wanted to know." I nodded affirmatively. "We did break up at the end of school, as you know, but we ran into each other when I came back to San Francisco for a wedding, right after I started at my firm, and things started up again. You and I were both so busy with our new jobs, and living so far away from each other. Not to mention the fact that you said you would break both of my hands if I ever thought about texting him again. I thought I would protect you from having to know. And protect my hands. We've been seeing each other on and off ever since. Not all the time, but when Tony is in New York, or I'm in San Francisco for firm interviews. But I swear, I was just as shocked as you were to see him at that bar in the Mission."

That was one good thing. I couldn't bear the idea that Liv was lying to my face, or faking the look of surprise I'd seen when we walked over with our martinis.

"Yes, we were in contact. To be honest, we've never really not been in contact. He knew we were in the city, but I didn't invite him to come. That night, I texted him that we were in San Francisco unexpectedly and going to a Springfield Isotopes show that night—don't ask me why I got that specific, he likes *The Simpsons*. When we ran into him, he told me he had looked up the show and found us. He claimed he thought not telling me was the best way to do it, so I wouldn't have to lie to you."

Damn, he was good. No wonder the entire world hates lawyers. They're slippery little bastards.

She took a deep breath. "I've tried to break it off a million times. I'll go for weeks, even months at a time. But then something will happen to remind me of him . . . He'll be in the area, we start texting, then talking, then we meet up. Before you know it, we're right back to where we started."

As she confessed this, Liv looked distraught at the memories. But that didn't make sense. Liv *never* looked distraught, at least not over a guy.

"I'm so sorry, Liv. That sounds really hard."

"Are you mad?"

"Of course not. I wish you had told me, but mostly I'm mad at myself. I'm mad that I didn't make you feel like you could come to me, and you've been going through this alone."

"Thanks, Em. Also, if you're wondering about Professor Gray, which I am sure you are, they really are separated now. In fact, she's dating another criminal law professor at Boston College."

I nodded. I wouldn't truly believe STB was single until I saw the divorce papers, but I also knew that there was no sense in fighting about it right then.

"What about Carrick? I thought you liked him. Did I completely misread that?"

"Completely." She smiled. "I was never interested in Carrick, Em. I was just trying to distract you from Sam with Dusty, by inviting them places. Dusty clearly had a crush on you. I thought it might be good for your ego, to get your mind off the Val thing a little.

"In any case," she continued, "I ended it with Tony."

When I didn't say anything, but simply raised an eyebrow skeptically, Liv went on.

"I'm serious. I saw your reaction when you walked into his office, and I don't know, something flipped. I saw the situation through your eyes. Even if things are different from how they used to be, it's still not going anywhere. I've always told myself that maybe it is, but it's years later and we're no closer to actually being together. I don't even know how I truly feel about him anymore, it's such a habit at this point. Plus, could I ever really trust him?" Nope, I thought silently. "I ended it after you left the office yesterday, and I haven't spoken to him since. Now I really don't want to talk about it anymore. I'm sorry I didn't tell you, but I hope you can understand why I didn't."

"I do. Can I say one more thing?" I asked tentatively.

"Okay."

"I'm sorry I was so mean to you when I found out. I was reacting off the cuff." Liv's tension dissipated but she still looked sad. "I was horrible, and I didn't mean it. At all."

"I know you didn't. Thanks for saying that."

"I felt like my world didn't make sense anymore. I don't mean that as an excuse, but as an explanation."

"You are forgiven." She smiled.

While I pulled on a cozy sweater and jeans and rifled through my bathroom drawers for some magical concealer to transform my shiny cheeks from *been crying maniacally* to *fresh-faced and radiant*, Liv sat at the kitchen table, rifling through the pile of mail I'd collected on my way in.

"Have you seen this letter, Em?" Liv had three piles in front of her, which appeared to be bills, Anthropologie catalogs, and birth announcements. In her hand was a thick white envelope addressed to me with no return address. Sam, I thought immediately, my heart racing. But he didn't even know I was back. Did he?

Inside was a multiple-page letter, folded up into a fat rectangle. When I unfolded it, the handwriting looked familiar, but not immediately recognizable. It was large, looping female writing. There were carets to insert missing words and writing in the margins. It was clear that it had been through a couple rounds of edits, and that the writer had put in a lot of effort. I quickly flipped to the end to see the signature.

"It's from Val," I said in disbelief.

"Oh no." Liv groaned. I flipped back to the first page, putting up my hand to shush her, and read aloud.

Dear Emma,

I am so sorry anything ever happened between Sam and me. I don't have an excuse for why any of it happened. To say that I was not in my head when Sam and I made that mistake is not enough, although it certainly is true. I truly wish that it never happened. I think that's part of the reason I didn't tell you. I think I thought that if I never said it out loud, it would be like it didn't. I also didn't think it was my place, even though we were friends.

Liv interrupted with a scoff, but I kept going.

I thought if you found out it should be because Sam decided to tell you, not me. I stopped being your friend because I didn't think it was right to keep our relationship going. I didn't know how to handle it. I'm sorry about that, too. Finally, I need you to know one thing. It never happened again. Sam really loves you, and he's lucky to have you. I was, too. I know this is probably impossible, but I truly hope that someday we can put all of this behind us, and who knows, maybe be friends again.

Love,
Val

"Wow. Good letter," Liv offered, when she could finally speak from the shock. I nodded my agreement. "Should we call her? See if she wants to hang out?" Liv joked. I put the letter in a drawer, needing some physical space from it.

"I guess everyone has some parts of their past they aren't proud of," I said, letting out the breath I'd been holding in. I had to admit, I felt a little bit better, relieved there was some peace between Val and me, and that some good feelings remained despite it all. For now, that was enough.

CHAPTER 28

Whenever Liv came to town, we went to our favorite Mexican restaurant, Casa Sanchez. It had a mariachi band, delicious margaritas, and—the best part—free guacamole. This anomaly kept us coming back despite the fact that the location was a bit far and the wait a bit long. That was why when we got into the car and Liv took the driver's seat as usual, I was surprised when she didn't start heading east on Washington. After all, free guac is the ultimate in comfort food, and comfort food was above all what we needed.

"Did you forget the way?" I said, trying not to sound too demanding given the fact that she was driving my car.

"Nope. We're not going to Casa Sanchez and before you ask, it's a surprise."

After hopping on the freeway, she exited on La Brea and traveled

North for a while before starting down a side street in Hollywood, on a stretch of road where there aren't any restaurants or bars, only the Hollywood Forever Cemetery.

"What are we doing at the Hollywood Cemetery?" I asked. "Are we lost?"

Liv pulled the car over to the side of the road. "Nope. This is your stop."

"What are you talking about?"

"Emma, can I give you one piece of advice?" she said, ignoring my question. The car went quiet with the engine off and the radio silenced. "Give Sam another chance." I felt instantly thrown for a loop. I was doing my best to forget my ex-fiancé and canceled wedding, even though to be honest it was never more than several jumps from the center of my thoughts. Why in the world was she bringing it up?

"I know you like Sam, Liv. But it's too late. It's ruined. I mean, our rehearsal dinner was supposed to be tomorrow, and if you hadn't noticed, he's not exactly begging for one," I said pointedly, looking down at my hands and swallowing the lump in my throat.

"I wouldn't be so sure about that."

Without warning the car door on my right swung open. I jumped what felt like three feet in the air and let out an unattractive yelp. Standing on the curb, with the car door handle in one hand and a picnic basket in the other, was Sam.

Walking through the Hollywood Forever Cemetery at dusk, escorted by Sam, who was careful not to touch me or say too much, was completely surreal. For one thing, there wasn't another living soul around. Ha. I'd seen the cemetery pretty quiet before, when they had concerts or outdoor movies and shut the rest of the place down, but it was never this dead. Okay, that was enough.

"Are we having a picnic?" I asked, stretching out the words, looking for clues as to what he was thinking or feeling. He nodded but didn't elaborate. He looked incredibly nervous, wearing the long-sleeved blue collared shirt he always wore when he had a meeting with his agent. The last time he left the house in it, I remarked how cute he looked. I wondered if that was why he wore it.

We walked quietly through the wide paths, past crumbling white tombs, some at the head of narrow reflecting pools, and elaborate bronze crypts. When we finally got to the carpet of green grass in front of the Cathedral Mausoleum, the central building on the grounds, Sam put down the basket. Removing a blue-and-white-striped linen blanket and placing it in front of a weeping willow, he sat down.

"We're here," he said, motioning for me to join him. I followed instructions, sitting next to Sam against the wide tree. He opened the basket and poured us each a glass of wine from a corked bottle. Not chardonnay, I noted. It was starting to get dark and I could barely see his expression.

"Shouldn't we sit facing each other? It might make this less awkward," I said.

"Nope. There's something I want you to see." Sam pointed to the white walls of the mausoleum. Without warning, a large projection lit up the wall.

"What is this?" I exclaimed. "Are they showing a movie tonight? Where is everyone?" I had the nervous feeling you get when you wonder if maybe there was a zombie apocalypse reported on the news and you missed it.

"Watch and see." On-screen, an old-fashioned countdown to a movie reel began to play. When it hit one, it went fuzzy for a second before coming into focus. Sitting there, on the front steps of his house in the exact same spot I'd sat selling books on the day of their yard sale, was a twenty-foot Sam.

"Hi, Emma," the huge Sam on-screen said, his voice echoing through the cemetery. It was kinda spooky with the double Sams, but I liked it. "We're getting married in a couple weeks, and if you're watching this, that means you actually went through with it. First of all, thanks for that." There was some talking off-screen, as if the cinematographer was reminding him of something. I recognized Dante's low accented murmur. "Right, or I did something horrible and I'm showing this to you in a last-ditch effort to win you back. Either way, I hope you like it." He paused and added in a low, sweet voice, "I can't wait to spend the rest of my life with you." He faded out and I turned to the real Sam, who looked pained.

"The last line was meant to be a joke. I was going to show this at the rehearsal dinner, but I figured I better find a way to show it to you now, so we have a chance of actually making it there." For perhaps the first time in my entire life, I was speechless. I felt my mouth open and close a few times like a fish, but nothing came out.

"It's okay, you don't have to say anything," he said nervously.

Out of nowhere, Ray LaMontagne's "You Are the Best Thing"

286

started ringing out of speakers all around us. On-screen, the images flashed. Sam had compiled a montage of film clips from his numerous siblings, parents, and grandparents videotaped all over the world. Each different family member held a sign that displayed a different word or phrase. His brother lay next to his sign in Costa Rica while he drank a beer on the beach. His regal British grandmother perched in a hard-backed chair holding a formal, printed card. His parents sat cross-legged in their backyard in Rye, New York, one at either end of a poster board, with their dog, Smokey, running in circles around them. It went on. As the clips passed, the words started to form a sentence. The last scene was the entire family, spliced together, each member holding his or her own sign.

Together they all shouted out the words they'd been stringing together. "Welcome to the family, Emma and Caro!" Then they all cheered and danced around to the same song, which was coordinated to play in real time with the music in the video.

I was floored.

I turned to him, shaking my head in shock, tears shining in my eyes. "This is amazing. How did you pull this off?"

Sam looked at me strangely. "You do realize I'm a filmmaker, right, Em? Plus, I called in a few favors. And some blackmail." Sam looked at me and squinted his eyes, the way he did when he was very focused, or drafting his fantasy baseball team.

"Emma, I want to say something, and let me finish. I'm glad you like the video, but I don't expect you to forgive me because of that. I need you to know that I'm incredibly sorry about what happened in Charleston. I can swear to you right now that nothing like that will ever happen again. But I think you know that." He paused and looked at me, waiting for this part to sink in. "Please forgive me, and let's move on. Let's move forward, stronger than ever. Together." Again, he stopped for a minute, as if considering whether to continue. I waited patiently. "And whatever did or didn't happen in San Francisco last week with any other guy, I don't want to know. I know you were staying with some guy from Airbnb and that you went back there by yourself. Don't be mad at Liv for telling me—she was worried and talked to Caro. Then, when she found out you were still with them, she was more worried, which made me worried. Did I just say 'worried' too many times?" I started to laugh, but stopped when I saw how serious his face was. "If you were talking to some other guy, or felt comfortable staying with him or whatever, I assume it didn't compare with what we have. Correct me if I'm wrong."

Dusty. Did it compare? I knew the answer before I even finished the question.

"No, it didn't." The truth is, my feelings for Dusty had faded completely. He was an amazing person, who supported me at a time when very few could. But that was the extent of it: gratefulness and affection. I felt guilty for Dusty's sake, and hoped he didn't feel used or hurt in any way, but then I remembered how MyLocal was probably going to make him a billion dollars and how tall he was. He would be fine.

Sam took both of my hands in his and looked at me closely. "I love you, Emma. Will you please still marry me?"

I wanted to say yes immediately, to jump into his arms and shout that I couldn't wait. He was right, I did know deep down he would never do anything like that again. Some part of me knew that the past week I'd been using a mistake he'd made years before—an awful one, don't get me wrong, but an outlier for sure—to protect myself. Relationships, marriage, long-term love, it always seemed so scary, and the existence of other people in your life so temporary. But maybe I was wrong about that, I considered for maybe the first time ever. Or at least, maybe there were exceptions. After all, look at Liv and me, best friends no matter what. Look at Caro, protecting her daughter to her own detriment. Look at Sam, loving me through it all. If we got past this, we could probably get past anything.

Something was still bothering me, though. "What about the chuppah?"

"What?" Sam responded, baffled.

"The canopy. For the wedding. Why did you cancel it? I got a confirmation e-mail. I thought that meant it was really over." I trailed off, fully aware that this officially made me crazy. After all, *I'd* told him it was really over.

"Oh, that." Sam burst out laughing. "I canceled it because my cousins built us one this week when they were bored. I think they got sick of watching me cry into my beer, so they needed something to occupy their time. And they thought it might change the outcome." He tilted his head to the side, smiling to himself, perhaps thinking about how nuts I was, but loving me for it anyway.

"You really cried?"

"Emma Moon," Sam said warningly. "Are you gonna marry me or not?"

EPILOGUE

Two days later, we walked out onto the makeshift dance floor, which was really a closely clipped grass clearance, for our first dance to Van Morrison's "Sweet Thing." As I hugged Sam close and felt his warm body enfold me, I saw Liv standing on the side, flirting with Dante. I also spied Sam's brother trying to get a girl from my firm a drink as her boyfriend fumed. And Caro sat at a table, tapping on her phone, but at least stopping every few seconds to take a sip of champagne.

The weekend was perfect, full of lovely mistakes. My rehearsal dinner dress looked like it was made for me, until I spilled an entire glass of champagne down the front. That afternoon, the pastor accidentally called me Anna repeatedly when she read us our vows, which made Sam and me crack up every few minutes throughout the entire ceremony. Minutes earlier, one of our recently separated friends made a drunken speech with the closing line, "Never get a divorce, because fuck that shit." ("Never use the *D* word at a wedding," I heard Dante murmur. "Or the *FTS* word," Sam added.)

I even got a text from Dusty that said, *Have a wonderful day. You deserve it.* What an amazing guy. I could recognize this but at the same time, it didn't bring my crush back. I couldn't have fallen in love with him, anyway. It was impossible. I was already in love. Speaking of, Sam seemed pretty happy, too. He had the permanent dopey grin on his face that he always got when he'd been day drinking.

Dancing together closely and reflecting on the day, I suddenly remembered there was one more mystery left to solve.

"Sam, I almost forgot. Where are we going on our honeymoon?"

"That's a funny story, actually," Sam said with a laugh.

"What?" I said, fully ready for him to tell me he'd forgotten to buy the tickets, or he'd purchased them for the wrong year.

"We're supposed to go to Italy," Sam said reluctantly.

"Italy! Sam, that's incredible! What's wrong? Why do you sound so nervous?" When he hesitated I squeezed him. "Tell me!" I demanded, using my "I'm the bride; you have to do anything I say" voice. It had been surprisingly effective all day.

"I planned the whole thing, found little bed-and-breakfasts, and got the train schedule worked out. The plan was to travel around northern Italy, around Florence."

"That's amazing, Sam. I love that idea! And I've never been!" I exclaimed.

"I know."

"Then why are you acting so weird?"

"Well, the trip is kind of organized around the towns the Riga-zis and their relatives originally came from. That was the plan, that we could, you know . . ."

"What?"

"It's kind of anticlimactic now. But when I planned the trip I was thinking while we were there, we could do some research and . . . I don't know how to say this."

"Research? For what, a movie?"

"No, Em." He pulled me back to arm's length and looked at me, smiling sheepishly, curly hair crushed on the side I'd been pressed against, his eyes crinkled in his typical smile. "I was thinking we could try to find your family."

I put my head on his shoulder and turned it to the side. I didn't want him to see the tears in my eyes. We'd only been married an hour; I didn't want him to know what a basket case I was, at least not yet.

As I pressed my eyes tightly shut, I felt the tears of happiness, of rightness, roll down my cheeks. I hugged my husband, my partner, my love. I was wrong about him the entire time. As it turns out, he got it all along.

ACKNOWLEDGMENTS

First and foremost, thank you to Claire Anderson-Wheeler, my wonderful literary agent, who believed in me, pushed me, and taught me much more than I can list here. I could not have done it without her never-ending confidence and support, genius ideas, and the untold number of hours she put into this book. Every writer in the world should be so lucky to have someone like Claire in her corner.

I would also like to thank everyone at Berkley and Penguin Random House, especially my incredible editor, Jackie Cantor. I don't know what I did in another life to deserve having someone as amazing and accomplished as Jackie on my team, but I am sure glad I did it. Working with someone so smart, funny, and talented is truly a dream come true.

I would also like to thank my team at the Movember Foundation, especially Astrid Heward, who is the best teacher I have ever had, along with the rest of her Angels. Working at Movember makes me love coming to work every day, and I couldn't ask for a more caring and fun team of friends and colleagues.

ACKNOWLEDGMENTS

Thank you to Heather Thomason, Natalie Blazer, and Reade Harbitter, who inspired many of the ideas in this novel about friendship and family. I am so grateful for you. Also, to Zack McDermott, another friend-turned-family member who makes my life so much better just by being in it.

Thank you to Juli and Conor Welch, who listened to this idea when it was still a crazy dream and told me I had to go for it (time and time again); to my fellow creator Elizabeth Scouler for the brainstorming and for getting it; and to Steph Opitz, who I adore and admire in countless ways, and who was the first person I ever told that sometimes, in my spare time, I like to write.

Thank you to all the friends who were by my side throughout this process: my Venice family, who helped me in a million different ways, including Christine Daley, Jessica Franks, Alex Flaherty, Brian Flaherty, Jac Chapman, Mikey Wigart, Cullman Hedges, and Nora Nolan; and all of the members of our truly special one-of-a-kind "book club," including Lilly Walton, Caroline Donelan, Emily Blass, Kate Danson, Kristy Duncan, and Annie Eckhart, a group of women I couldn't live without.

Finally, thank you to Mike Knetzger. For all of the above, and for everything else.